Praise for "Chocolate Kisses" and Renee Luke's novels

"Entertaining and erotic."
—Sandra Kitt, author of *The Next Best Thing*

"The best love story I've read."
—Mary B. Morrison, author of *Somebody's Gotta Be On Top*

"A perfect ten! Once I picked it up, I couldn't put it down. I highly recommend [it] and suggest that you be on the lookout for additional novels by Renee Luke." —Romance Reviews Today

"Not only is this novel cute, it is hot . . . a wonderful tale with plenty of sex and the happy ending I so enjoy. I look forward to reading more from [Renee Luke]." —Just Erotic Romance Reviews

"Will satiate the audience's sweet tooth." —*Midwest Book Review*

"Luke expertly leads readers into an ultimate fantasy world. . . . This book is the definition of what erotica should be."
—*Romantic Times BOOKclub* (four stars)

"Emotional prose, achingly real characters, and beautifully rendered love scenes are the hallmarks of a Renee Luke romance. An amazing, not-to-be-missed experience."
—Sylvia Day, author of *Bad Boys Ahoy!* and *Ask For It*

Dipped in Chocolate

RENEE LUKE

A SIGNET ECLIPSE BOOK

SIGNET ECLIPSE
Published by New American Library, a division of
Penguin Group (USA) Inc., 375 Hudson Street,
New York, New York 10014, USA
Penguin Group (Canada), 90 Eglinton Avenue East, Suite 700, Toronto,
Ontario M4P 2Y3, Canada (a division of Pearson Penguin Canada Inc.)
Penguin Books Ltd., 80 Strand, London WC2R 0RL, England
Penguin Ireland, 25 St. Stephen's Green, Dublin 2,
Ireland (a division of Penguin Books Ltd.)
Penguin Group (Australia), 250 Camberwell Road, Camberwell, Victoria 3124,
Australia (a division of Pearson Australia Group Pty. Ltd.)
Penguin Books India Pvt. Ltd., 11 Community Centre, Panchsheel Park,
New Delhi - 110 017, India
Penguin Group (NZ), 67 Apollo Drive, Mairangi Bay,
Auckland 1310, New Zealand (a division of Pearson New Zealand Ltd.)
Penguin Books (South Africa) (Pty.) Ltd., 24 Sturdee Avenue,
Rosebank, Johannesburg 2196, South Africa

Penguin Books Ltd., Registered Offices: 80 Strand, London WC2R 0RL, England

First published by Signet Eclipse, an imprint of New American Library,
a division of Penguin Group (USA) Inc.

First Printing, February 2007
10 9 8 7 6 5 4 3 2 1

SIGNET ECLIPSE and logo are trademarks of Penguin Group (USA) Inc.

LIBRARY OF CONGRESS CATALOGING-IN-PUBLICATION DATA:
Luke, Renee.
  Dipped in chocolate / Renee Luke.
    p. cm.
  ISBN-13: 978-0-451-22031-8 (trade pbk.)
  ISBN-10: 0-451-22031-5 (trade pbk.)
  1. Love stories. 2. Erotic fiction. I. Title.
PS3612.U44D57 2007
813'.6—dc22   2006024817

Set in Sabon
Designed by Spring Hoteling

Printed in the United States of America

Almost fifteen years ago, we pledged our love and promised a lifetime. Through thick and thin, good times and bad, you've been by my side: my best friend, my strength, my rock, my lover. This book is for my darling husband. Know everything I do is for our four beautiful children, for our family, for you. Baby, I love you.

Acknowledgments

As a parent, I'm supposed to be teaching my children, but every day I feel as if they're the ones who educate me. They show me the depth of my love, the strength of my patience, and the meaning of unconditional. Their determination, work ethic, kind nature, and drive awe me on a daily basis. TLC, you inspire me.

To work with an agent means forming a partnership, and in my wonderful agent, Pamela Harty, I couldn't have asked for more. She's intelligent and market savvy, but it's her understanding and ability to communicate that remind me often how valuable she is to me. Thank you for all you've done and all that you do.

I've never seen my editor's desk, but I've got a good imagination. I see piles of paper to the ceiling, a dozen or so empty coffee cups, perhaps a high-quality cigar burning in an ashtray with a spiraling curl of smoke. There's sure to be a phone with several lines lit up, other editors shouting in through the door, numbers, offers, and terrifying rejection. In a world like this,

I am so grateful for my editor, Tina Brown, who supports and believes in me.

Aside from being a wife and mom, I spend most of my life in front of the computer screen. On the Writer's Playground, I always find the support of my girlfriends. These are bright and talented women who share my passion for writing, and all the highs and lows that go along with publishing. Together we cyber wipe tears, shout for joy, expose our hearts, split chocolate, and share hunks. I'd be lost without these friendships.

To my dear friend Sylvia Day, who spends so much time on the other end of my IM window—thank you. She's an extraordinary author, my talented webmistress, and an incredible friend. Her drive and determination inspire me to higher goals.

Dipped in Chocolate

Gimme Some Sugar

One

"A fifteen-foot bridal train," her nana said, the raspy voice echoing across the beauty salon.

Her family's absolute excitement had turned into a constant buzz of plans that tormented her like gnats around brown bananas. She'd had enough.

Alexis repressed a shiver. She slid her gaze away from Nana and Momma, tucked beneath the electric blow-dry helmets, back to where her own fingertips soaked in warm sudsy water. The gaudy wedding dress, encrusted with rhinestones and pearls, they'd picked out for her was a continual reminder of everything that was wrong with her upcoming wedding.

"Wait till you hear about the table centerpieces, Lexi, baby," her grandma shouted, clearly overcompensating with her volume to make up for the wind blowing in her ears.

Alexis forced a smile as she looked over at Nana and

Momma proudly grinning back at her. *Prewedding jitters*, she recited silently, *it's just jitters*. But repeating the phrase a thousand times wouldn't ease the gnawing feeling that she was marrying the wrong man. Not like good-looking, successful men her age were all that available.

Returning her gaze to her now-pruned skin, she stared at the solid one-karat diamond gracing her ring finger. She had a hard time believing any of this was happening. Bryan had slipped the ring on her finger, then stood before her family and announced their engagement before she'd even accepted. The problem was, she wasn't sure she loved him.

Alexis searched her heart, longing to feel the heat of passion or the small flutter of anticipation she knew she should be experiencing. Nothing. Hell, she didn't even feel pleased.

What's that saying? she questioned herself. *Stuck between a rock and a hard place.*

"You can take 'em out now, girl." Sharon, the owner of Trend, a hip salon in Coronado Village in Coronado, California, pulled Alexis' hands from the shallow bowl and wrapped them in a warm fluffy towel. "You sure must be happy, scoring big like you did."

"What do you mean?" Alexis didn't feel anything like a grand-prize winner. As an African-art importer, Bryan had made a name for himself among Hollywood's stars. But financial success didn't equate with love. It didn't increase her desire to be his wife, to spend a lifetime in his bed. Yet Sharon's brows pulled together and her dark eyes gleamed with a touch of envy.

"I mean, Bryan's got everything. A nice car, a nice crib, and if you don't mind me saying so"—Sharon fanned her face—"a nice-ass body to go along with all that money. You could do a whole lot worse, ya know."

Or I could do better. She could have a man who set her skin on fire. Who made her burn for his touch, yearn for the hard length of his body. Whose look elicited passion and lust.

Alexis chewed on her bottom lip to keep from saying the words aloud. She had no right to complain. "He's a nice guy."

Sharon didn't wait for her to elaborate. Instead she grabbed hold of the seat back and whipped the salon chair around to face the mirror.

"So, what are ya going to do with your hair? Finally letting me get rid of these braids?" Sharon dug her long, bright pink nails into the thick locks.

Alexis studied her image in the mirror. She liked the thin strands of the microbraids she'd worn all through college. Then it had been a matter of time and money, braids being the most economical of her hairstyle choices. Now it was more a matter of comfort, a decision to forgo the hot irons and picks that usual nappy-hair maintenance required.

Lifting a hand, Alexis swept several unruly strands off of her forehead. "I don't know, Sharon. I kind of like my hair as is."

"Are you talking about your hair for the wedding? Don't you want something special?" Momma asked, closing the bridal magazine that had been perched across her knees like a California buzzard with open wings. Lifting the dome hair dryer off her head, Momma rose from the chair. The multitude of pink rollers nestled on her head barely shifted as she walked toward Alexis.

Momma dropped the magazine on Alexis' lap and added her fingers to those already entrenched in her curls. "They need to be redone soon anyhow, Lexi. Besides, I thought we already agreed you'd take out these braids and let me press it

straight. I have an idea for some delicate little curls around
your face."

Before Alexis knew it, Nana was there, too. "And I have
some pearls I'd like to weave in. A little shimmer in your hair
and you'll be matching your dress."

There it was again. A mention of the dress and the knot of
dread returned as tight as ever in the pit of Alexis' stomach. Was
it the dress that was bothering her so much or was it the man?

Trying to set aside her apprehension, Alexis tuned out their
continued prattle about her hair and the glimmering adornments they planned. She smiled at her nana and momma, taking in the matching image of the pair. A likeness she'd been
told countless times closely resembled her own.

Their wide, almond-shaped eyes gleamed with excitement
and lovingly caressed her face. The small crow's-feet marring
her momma's perfect mocha complexion were a bit more defined on Nana, but nothing could dull her beauty.

Alexis' gaze roamed over their high cheekbones, down to
where their full, almost identical, lips were lifted into beguil-
ing smiles.

How can I disappoint them? They had given her and her
siblings everything they required. Even when money was
scarce, love was in abundance. It was their influence that kept
her older brother, Allen, out of trouble and encouraged him to
join the navy.

And it was their loving touch that helped her younger sister, Alicia, finish high school even when she got pregnant her
junior year.

Alexis worried the material of her skirt between her fingers. They had even supported her when she scrapped her education, after years of college, to open a flower shop instead
of becoming a doctor.

She let out a breath.

"Yes, Momma, the braids can go. You can do anything you want to my hair," Alexis agreed, the contention seeping softly from her soul.

"Oh, you'll just love it. I know you will."

"I know I will, Momma." She swallowed the lump building in her throat and pasted on her best attempt at a natural-looking artificial smile.

This wedding was bigger than some silly dress with gaudy pearls and sparkling stones and more important than a hairdo that could easily be changed. This wedding meant the world to her family, being the first formal affair they'd ever celebrated. Bryan was a nice guy and more notably, he'd make a nice husband.

Maybe just not for *her*, but that was a not-so-minor detail she was willing to overlook to give back to those she loved. She'd find a way to be content as Bryan's wife, even if she was never truly happy, even if her heart was never full, even if her body was never completely satisfied.

Sharon twisted Alexis' braided locks into a bun and secured it with a clip. "Six weeks and counting, girl. You must be so excited."

"More like nervous," Nana answered for her, pinching her right cheek. "You need some color, baby. Are you getting enough sleep or are you worrying yourself about your wedding arrangements? Your momma and I have got it covered."

Yes, they have. Part of the problem.

"I know, Nana." Alexis lightly touched the puffy dark circles beneath her eyes. "I guess I'm a bit tired is all. There's a lot to do still and time feels like it's running—"

Interrupted by the jingling bell of the salon door, Alexis turned her attention to the newcomer. Just the sight of Jackson made her skin feel hot and her nipples pucker. She was relieved to see her best friend since childhood stroll through the door, here to rescue her from discussions of wedding gowns, bridal flowers, and straightened-hair don'ts.

"Jackson."

His confident forward amble drew her attention to his long muscular form, a far cry from his scrawny teenage body. Though she'd wanted him even then. The cotton, deep blue shirt floating over his broad shoulders and sculpted arms was a perfect contrast to his coffee-with-cream skin.

Jackson Lyle was a sight to behold. Closing her eyes and drawing a deep breath, Alexis tried to calm the racing of her pulse, to tamp down the need she felt for him. This lust she felt—this wild, crazy lust—she'd had for him ever since she'd developed hormones.

She'd known him her entire life. Before she passed away, his grandmother had been dear friends with Nana. The deep connection and friendship of the families was all that kept her from expressing how she felt. Respect for Nana was all she needed to keep her feelings for him quiet, even when her thighs ached and her pussy dripped with want.

Like adding two cubes of sugar, Jackson put on the charm.

"The Payton Ladies," he said, putting a hand over his heart when he reached Nana's side. "It's nice to see you, Nana." He planted a kiss on her cheek. "You're as beautiful as always."

"You sure know how to make an old woman feel good, Jackson," Nana whispered.

"I don't see any old women in the room." Jackson turned toward Momma, depositing a kiss on her cheek as well. "If I were ten years older . . ."

Momma swatted Jackson on the arm. "Make that twenty, baby, and you got yourself a date."

Relief washed through Alexis' veins when Jackson turned his warm chocolate gaze on her. His presence always seemed to offer a measure of solace while simultaneously increasing her heart rate. Thank goodness he'd arrived. She needed something—anything—to keep her mind off the dreaded wedding looming a mere month and a half away, and looking at him was all the distraction she required.

"Hey, Lexi."

"How are you?" she asked. Looking into the rich shade of his eyes, her anxiety seemed to melt away.

Jackson moved in her direction. "Good. Now, gimme some sugar."

Alexis repressed a sigh as his full lips made contact, then lingered for a moment against her mouth.

"Mmm . . ." Jackson licked his lips. "You taste like peaches today."

Alexis laughed and she shifted the peach-flavored candy across her tongue to the other side of her mouth. They'd played this game for as long as she could remember. "One of these days I'm going to have a *non*fruit flavor, then see what you come up with for a guess."

Exaggerating, Jackson licked his lips again, making Alexis imagine that tongue of his on her skin. Turning the chair beside Alexis in her direction, he sank into the black leather. "Sweet, I'd imagine. But get real, Lexi. You always make that threat, but never deviate from choosing out of your fruit basket of flavors."

Alexis laughed again as she grabbed for her purse, just to prove him wrong. "I have peppermints." She lifted a roll of Life Savers, suspending it between them as evidence.

The small dimples in his cheeks threatened when he held back his smile. As an answer, he arched a brow. "It's not even open."

"You know, Jackson, you're going to have to quit kissing my granddaughter all the time."

Alexis' gaze snapped in Jackson's direction. The rich globes of his eyes held something dark and turbulent as he returned her stare. Feeling her nipples pull tight, she looked away, struggling to breathe. Blinking hard to ward off the sting behind her eyes.

Her mouth dry despite the peach candy, Alexis wet her lips. The question popped out of her mouth. "Why?" she asked, hoping no one else noticed how desperate she sounded.

"Just thirty and your memory's already gone," Nana teased. "You're getting married, remember?"

Alexis felt a rush of heat burn her cheeks. To keep the others from witnessing, she turned away and dropped the roll of mints back into her purse. For a short time she'd been able to put aside thoughts of marrying and simply enjoy Jackson's company.

"Jackson and I are just friends." Alexis looked back to Jackson, hoping for a confirmation, and yet a huge part of her wishing they were more. So much more.

He remained silent. The dappling of sunshine filtering in through the salon windows provided a perfect highlight, a contrast of light and shadows on his brown skin. Lush lips that were turned into a smug half smile.

Getting absolutely no help from him, she dismissed his odd look. "Bryan doesn't care," she stated firmly.

"Ain't no way *my man* would stand for it, girl." Sharon tapped her tapered fingernails against the back of the seat. "Nope, *my man* gets jealous when another man looks my direction and would lose it if a man put his lips on me."

"Bryan's not jealous." Alexis felt the rise of resentment. It wasn't like she wanted some wild beast that lost his temper or tried to control her by using jealousy as a manipulation, but there was something vaguely romantic about a man's passion escalating for love. So far, nothing she'd done had stirred his nonchalant attitude to fire.

Momma reached for the bridal magazine. She must have caught wind of Alexis' souring mood and promptly changed the subject. "I'm starved." She turned toward Jackson. "You came to take us to lunch, right?"

"Yes, ma'am. The Marina Café."

Momma touched the rows of curlers on her head. "We need at least an hour. A handsome young boy like you wouldn't want to be seen out with us until we've gussied up."

Jackson laughed. "That's right. So hurry up." He rose from the chair, then leaned forward, putting a deliberate kiss square on Alexis' mouth.

Her mouth parted slightly on a gasp of surprise as he brushed his tongue lazily across her bottom lip. Warmth spread through her blood, and it took a deliberate effort not to close her eyes, open farther, and lean into his strong embrace. His teeth nipped her flesh before he pulled away with a loud smack.

She was grinning like a fool, unable to think of anything to say, but before she could think up any sort of retort, he'd moved away. His eyes sparkled as he arrogantly winked at Nana. Making loud smacking-lip noises, he sauntered across the salon.

Alexis choked out a laugh at Nana's exasperated face, but she struggled to find her composure, arousal seeping through her blood, her body trembling inside.

"Peaches," he hummed right before he was out the door.

Jackson had no idea how that brief little kiss had affected her. And she'd rather her momma and nana not know either.

When she glanced down, the diamond on her finger glistened in the sunshine, guilt slicing through her. She was completely turned on, a dull throb aching in her pussy, just by his one kiss, yet she was marrying another man. A man who didn't leave her anywhere near as hot as Jackson did.

Forcing a smile, she put her longing aside and focused her attention on her family.

Two

Five couples loitered in the studio awaiting the arrival of the dance instructor. Alexis stood alone. She resisted the urge to look at her watch again. After ten times the numbers didn't change much. Someplace between worried and irritated, she found a small chair and sat down, pulling her cell phone from her purse.

There were no messages.

It wasn't like Bryan to be late, and he would've never stood her up. Since they'd been serious, he had never canceled a date. She glanced around the studio at the other couples. They varied in age but were all notably in love. For a moment she pondered what the others were doing here. Were they here in preparation for their weddings—like she was—or just to have fun?

Feeling agitation increase, she turned her wrist and checked the time. Seven fifteen. Bryan was fifteen minutes late, but then again so was the instructor. She'd have hated it if the class began and she was the only one without a partner. Thank goodness for small favors.

"Welcome, everyone."

Or not!

A woman in her mid-to-late forties entered the room with arms extended. She wore the most ridiculous outfit Alexis had ever seen. "My name is Helen, and I'll be your instructor for the evening." Pulled up to her waist were pink tights, a color so bright, it should've been banished to the 1980s.

Over the loud tights she wore a cow-print leotard. Bunched on the top of Helen's head, her straw yellow curls looked like a grouping of albino snakes.

Alexis bit her lip to keep from laughing.

"Please gather around. I'd like to get everyone's name before we get started."

Lexi's smile faded.

Damn him. This was all Bryan's idea. Wanting their first dance to be formal, *he'd* arranged for them to have this lesson in order to move smoothly together in front of their families. Alexis didn't mind. She loved to dance, but she would have been equally happy just holding her man to her and slow dancing for the first time as husband and wife. She didn't need fancy steps. But Bryan did.

Bryan—she gritted her teeth—who *wasn't* there.

Flipping open her phone, she lingered in the folding metal chair, away from the small gathering, as she dialed his number. Two rings and his voice mail answered.

"I'm out of here," Alexis mumbled to herself. No use taking a class designed for two when she was only one. She was on her feet when she saw Bryan across the room rushing toward her. But she felt nothing stir inside as he approached.

He kissed her cheek quickly as a greeting. "Sorry I'm late. I'll explain later." Grabbing her hand, he pulled her toward the rest of the couples, who were in a circle getting to know one another.

When the introductions reached them, Bryan spoke before she could, telling the class both of their names. Smiling outwardly, Alexis wondered why he hadn't allowed her to introduce herself. It was such a little thing, done most likely with the best intentions, but so telling of his personality. A tad too controlling, a little too in charge.

The sound of the instructor's voice shook Lexi from her thoughts. "Normally, I don't dress like this, but for ballroom dancing it's important for you all to be able to see my legs and feet. I want you to be able to follow along."

When the group murmured their understanding, Helen smiled and moved to the stereo. "Okay, then. Let's get started." She gave a short list of instructions on how to hold their partners, then hit the play button.

"I Give My Heart," a waltz, hummed across the speakers. *I give my heart*, she silently repeated, her nerves on edge. To whom? Not Bryan. But she was determined to have a nice marriage for the sake of her family.

Forcing away the burn at the back of her eyes, she focused on the lesson. Helen lifted her voice to be heard over the instrumental. "For now"—she swished to the music as she moved between couples checking their holds—"I just want you to sway. Get a feel for one another. I'll teach you the steps soon."

Bryan's hand rested on Alexis' hip, and in his other hand

he held hers, but his touch was light and conveyed no emotion. His body was taut, and he moved awkwardly against her, twice stepping on her foot. Alexis tried to move with him, but when she adjusted her step, her thigh slammed into his.

Closing her eyes, she took a few deep breaths, trying to relax, to be pliant in his arms and allow him to lead. She swayed with the rhythm of the music, allowing the notes to move through her body, but even that didn't help. Bryan's rapid jerking movements tugged her quickly out of her want-to-be musical trance.

"Like this." Helen readjusted Bryan's hold, then moved on to the next couple.

Alexis exhaled, trying to rid herself of frustration and allow the feelings she wanted. The feelings Jackson evoked. The crazy, dizzying need to be close. To touch. To make love. Desperate now to feel something from the man she was going to marry, she kissed Bryan's neck when they began to move again. He didn't smile or respond.

This wasn't working. Bryan's obvious distraction made him oblivious to her and the rhythm of the music. It was pretty clear that this was the last place he wanted to be. She whispered in his ear. "We could go back to my place and order in."

Bryan shook his head. "I just need to loosen up. It's been a long day."

Her stomach tightened, as she knew something wasn't right. She had the distinct feeling he was lying, although she couldn't be sure. Alarms sounded, acid rising in her throat. She shivered. Bryan was a nice guy, a good catch. She cared for him, but it wasn't *love*. Yet in five weeks' time she'd be his wife, despite the fact that she felt she didn't know him that well.

A bolt of pain shot up her leg as Bryan's weight crushed

her toes and jolted her back into the present. They were moving again, each step causing their bodies to slam together. It couldn't be called dancing and it sure as hell didn't feel good.

In the six months they'd dated, they'd never been dancing. Before, Alexis wondered why, but as they shifted and clashed, she knew. They didn't fit well together; their bodies just wouldn't meld comfortably. Forcing it wasn't going to work.

Taking a shuddering breath, she was about to tell him to forget the dancing, but was saved by the ringing of his phone. She stepped back as he fumbled through his pocket, looked at the incoming number, then answered.

I called and got only his voice mail.

He took a step away from her and closed his eyes, his jaw tense as he listened.

"Right," he said, his voice strained. "Right."

The song was nearly over by the time he hung up the phone and turned back to her. "Listen, I'm real sorry. But I have to go."

"I'll come with you." Alexis took a step toward him to follow.

He put up his hand. "It's all right, Alexis. You stay here. I already paid."

"But—"

"You can show me later." Bryan turned and walked out of the studio, leaving her with no explanation and completely humiliated. The more sympathetic glances were tossed her way from the others, the tighter Alexis balled her fists, an attempt to keep the anger from showing. To keep from charging after him.

On the outskirts of the dancing couples, Alexis gathered her things, her hips swaying to the rise of tempo. Helen's voice

lifted over the new tune as she gave instructions on hand place-
ment. Alexis looked back. The couples twirling around the
room were smiling and having a good time. This was the sort
of class she could really enjoy if she had a partner who didn't
cause bodily damage. Or abandon her.

Biting her bottom lip, she realized she wanted to stay, so
she shuffled through her purse for her phone. She'd call Jackson. She needed a partner and he didn't live far.

She reached him by the third ring. She'd only said, "I need
you" when he replied with an "I'll be there." Ten minutes later
he was strolling sexy-as-can-be through the door.

Dark eyes on her, with a grin that deepened his dimples,
and a body she wanted naked—and hard—he moved directly
across the room and to her side.

"Hi, sugar." He took her into his strong arms and spun her
onto the floor, spinning until tears of laughter streamed down
her face and she was dizzy. From circles and lust. From being in
his arms, where everything felt so right.

The yard work be damned, Jackson thought, feeling Lexi's
soft body press against his own. She was wearing an oversized
T-shirt that did nothing to show off her curves, but he could
feel every lush one of them.

"What happened to Bryan?"

Alexis shrugged.

Fine, she didn't want to talk about it. He didn't either. He'd
much rather spend the time having her sweet-scented body
flush against him, the beat of the music humming through his
pulse like a wild rhythmic drum.

Despite the fact that the big-band sway of ballroom tunes
wasn't what he'd have chosen, there was something appealing
about sharing the experience with Lexi. Placing his hand upon

her hip so the slope of her ass was caressed by his fingertips, Jackson pulled her closer.

She came willing, moving more fully into his embrace, wiggling her sassy hips against him. Blood stirred in his dick. Closing his eyes, Jackson sucked in a breath and tried to repress the rise of his erection. This was Lexi, his childhood friend.

An engaged woman.

They'd hugged and danced plenty of times, but his arousal didn't lie. She was having a physical effect on him. *Cold water, cold water, cold water,* he silently chanted, willing to do anything to get rid of the blood pumping to his groin.

Swallowing down the dryness in his throat, he knew his hard-on only confirmed the twinge of emotion he'd felt last week in the salon. Jealousy that'd caused him to kiss her a little more deeply than their regular sugar-kissing game.

Her delicate fingers fisted in his shirt and she moved against him, eliciting a low groan, and causing his rocked-up cock to throb. He knew she felt lust pound against her, because she glanced up at him with a knowing smile glowing in her eyes. Her fingers crept around his neck; her other palm rested on his chest, where he knew she'd feel the thump of his heartbeat.

She was soft and warm and in his embrace, her breasts so close, he could feel her beaded nipples through their clothing. But as alluring as Lexi's body was, it was the smile she was giving him that had him turned the fuck on. Breathing hard.

Jackson fought the need to shake his head to clear the confusion. His Lexi? His entire body ached to sex his best friend.

It wasn't easy keeping her on the dance floor. He'd much

rather have spun into a dark hallway and had his way with her. But she wanted to dance and he meant to show her a good time. He guided them into the step, leading in synchronized movements easily picked up by watching the others' feet.

Bending, he pressed his lips against her temple, breathing in the feminine scent of her skin and the subtle hint of watermelon. "Did he kiss you?" he asked softly.

Her brows pulled together for a moment. Then understanding passed in her exotic almond-shaped brown eyes, and she shook her head. "On the cheek."

He winked at her. "I like watermelon too much not to." Any excuse—hell, any damned excuse—to get his mouth on hers again, though what he wanted from their kisses was much different from the innocence of their game. They swayed easily, moving with the rhythm around the room, the few simple steps falling into place without thought.

Laughing, he spun her out of his arms, catching her by the fingertips, then brought her back to his chest. When she had her arms around him, he bent his head and captured her smiling mouth with his.

The touch was light at first, a mere absorption of watermelon-scented heat. After he lingered for a second longer than he should've, there was no going back. Jackson completed the contact, deepening the kiss as their bodies moved in unison with the beat.

She didn't protest or falter when he slipped his tongue past her lips, into the wet heat of her mouth, then touched the fruit candy, grinning when it clinked on her teeth. "Mmm . . . you don't eat watermelon often." He kissed her again, nibbling her bottom lip with his teeth. "I like it."

Alexis giggled and buried her face in the material of his

sweatshirt. "You would know," she murmured through the cloth.

He laughed. "Blueberries are good, too." Again his mouth was on her, unable to get enough. But he kept it quick and playful. With his hand on her hip, he moved in step with the other twirling couples, watching Lexi's gaze, enjoying the lyrical sound of her laughter, the lighthearted feeling of just being with her.

Trying to ignore the way blood rushed to his cock, Jackson spun her, then arched her back over his arm to dip her low. When she was upright again, he tugged her firmly to his chest and added a little groove to their steps. Tucked close, he kissed her cheek, her throat, the sensitive skin below her ear.

"What's up with Miss Eighties Chick?" he asked with a tilt of his head toward the instructor.

"I. Don't. Know," she replied, laughter tainting the firmness of the words.

"At least she's not trying to teach us to do the Running Man."

"Or the MC Hammer dance."

He chuckled as he slapped her ass, then added a growl when he nipped at the fleshy globe of her ear. "Hey, Hammer was cool."

There was a pause in the music. The motion around them stopped, but Lexi clung to him, her lids half-closed, a relaxed smile on her been-kissed plump lips. They stood for a moment, her warm breath washing across his skin. Her nearness making his breathing difficult.

But Lexi was playing vixen, rocking her hips forward as if the music were still playing—inciting the throb of blood in his hardened cock. Tilting her face, she looked up at him, passion burning in her chocolate eyes.

Hell, Jackson was in trouble. *Deep freakin' trouble.* Only the return of the music, the five other couples, and the instructor—with the ridiculous pink outfit—kept him from falling to his knees and dragging Alexis down with him for a good fucking.

Hell, what was it about tonight that had him wanting Lexi as a woman rather than what she'd always been—a friend?

Fighting to breathe, Jackson turned them in a circle once again, picking up the rhythm with ease, desperate for distraction. He twirled her and she responded with laughter. He spun her again, adding a little jig to the routine steps until the room whirled around them.

"You're making me dizzy." She didn't try to slow their steps, but joined him, coming together with him again as the music slowed, then ended. They were both breathing heavy as their hands fell to their sides.

You make me dizzy with lust. Dizzy from the shock of the realization.

His gaze moved across Lexi's glowing skin, damp now with a shimmering of sweat. The dark disks of her nipples were visible through her thin shirt. He swallowed. Desire had him wondering how long it'd take to get them back to his bed.

"You dance well together." Helen touched him on the arm, ending the sexual nature of his thoughts. "You've danced a long time together?"

Lexi answered first, her voice broken as she tried to catch her breath. "We've been friends for a long time."

"I can tell. You really know how to anticipate each other. You move in harmony perfectly."

"It's a rhythm thing." Jackson winked at Helen. The

woman didn't even seem to notice that Bryan had come and gone and Jackson had taken his place.

Helen smiled in understanding. "Your registration said you were getting married. You're wonderful together."

Jackson's heart seized up; his smile was forced. "Nah—"

"Thank you," Lexi interrupted him, taking his hand and twining their fingers.

His gaze falling from her face to their joined hands, he wondered what the hell was up with Lexi tonight. What had gotten into her? Him? But hell, it didn't really matter. Whatever it was felt good. Natural.

Alexis wasn't sure why she didn't want to acknowledge that it wasn't Jackson she was marrying. But the reason didn't matter. All that mattered was Jackson's reaction to her touch, the way his cock had throbbed against her, the way he'd deepened their sugary playful kisses into something sexual.

She didn't want to think of Bryan's absence. She wanted to explore Jackson's physical response—and never let him regret it. This could be her one and only opportunity. A pang of longing tightened in her gut and sent her pulse racing.

Around them the other couples were gathering their things. The dance studio was slowly emptying out.

Helen waved good-bye to several people, then turned back to them. "When's the wedding?"

"A few more weeks." She forced a smile, but her stomach twisted into knots.

"Wow, that's soon." Helen glanced at her watch. "I'll tell you what. I've got to go, but you're welcome to stay and work on the steps. The lights are on a timer and the door will lock automatically when you leave." She touched Jackson on the arm, grinning at the two of them. "Give you two a little more practice time."

More time in Jackson's arms? Yeah, baby. "That sounds great. Thank you, Helen."

"Sure thing." She wiggled her fingers good-bye as she followed the rest of the class attendees out the door with a final resounding click.

When they were alone in the middle of the dance floor, Alexis turned toward Jackson. He stood with his feet planted shoulder width apart, his muscular arms hanging by his sides, and an intense look chiseled into his face. God, he was beautiful, an example of a perfect male.

Feeling her knees go weak and her panties wet, she turned toward the shelf holding the stereo and a stack of CDs. Flicking through the clear cases revealed them all to be ballroom-dancing-type music, nothing even remotely jazzy. Since the radio would have to do, she turned to a channel playing the latest R & B and hip-hop. Music with enough funk to get her sway on.

Tuned in midsong, the lyrics were on point and the rhythm was pounding. Alexis turned toward Jackson, her breath catching when she found him in the exact same spot, standing the same way, watching her every movement.

She went to him, wiggling her body as she moved, reaching for his chest, brushing her hands over firm pecs, feeling his heat. Absorbing it.

She inhaled his scent, her lids drifting closed as she thought about all the times she'd imagined this moment. Imagined being able to touch Jackson in any way but friendly. And she wouldn't have been so bold now, so daring, had she not felt his hard dick against her abdomen, had desire not shimmered in his dark eyes so brightly.

Allowing her breath to ease from her lips, she looked up at him, words lingering but left unsaid. She wanted to beg him for just this once—just this once to love him as she longed to.

Before she was married. Tears burned behind her eyes, but she shoved them away. This wasn't about Bryan—about being unfaithful. This was about being faithful to her heart.

She needed this—needed Jackson before it was too late. She was marrying another man. The ball was rolling now, unable to be stopped without disappointing her family. But she was going to need this memory to keep her warm in a freezing marriage.

The heat of him washed through her senses. The beat of the music was strong now, forcing her into motion. She touched his neck with her fingertips, his pulse drumming. Dragging her nails lower, she scraped them over his flat nipple, biting her lip to keep from laughing when it puckered and his breath hitched. She shimmied lower down his body, swaying her hips in rhythm.

"Dance with me?" She moved around him, keeping one hand lightly on his body, caressing him as she danced for him. She stood behind him, reached up, and touched his shoulder blade, outlined the contour of his spine, skimmed over his firm ass. "Dance with me, Jackson."

She hugged him close, brushing the tips of her nipples against his muscular back. Her arms went around him, her face pressed into his T-shirt. It held the subtle saltiness of sweat.

Rolling her hips, she laughed—partly in relief—when he moved with her, joining the beat of the pounding bass. She flicked a nail across the button of his jeans, in a manner that caused him to groan.

"You going to dance with me?" He was already moving with her, but Alexis didn't wait for a reply. She wrapped her fingers around his hard cock, the length swathed in denim.

Blood pulsed against her palm as she stroked him up, slowly. Down.

"Lexi, what are we doing here?" The uncertainty in his tone was clear.

Through his jeans, she fondled his solid flesh, then increased the tempo of her strokes, unwilling to allow doubt to interfere with his obvious desire. "Dancing."

His hand closed firmly around hers, his fingers curving a half circle over hers. Air hissed between his teeth as he guided her hand down—all the way to his base—then up again.

His dick jerked against her palm, and a shiver moved through his body. "Just dancing?" he asked, angling so he filled her hand more fully.

Alexis bit her bottom lip, a smile tugging at her mouth. She could feel how his body changed—when his decision to continue had been made. "You want more than a dance?" The way he was throbbing now, she knew he did.

"Depends, Lexi." Their hips were rolling in rhythm with the movements of their hands over his rocked-up dick. "You going to give me some sugar?"

She giggled, but tightened her hand around him until he bucked and her aroused clit tingled. "I've got grape, I think."

"Grape is good."

"It's over there in my purse." Across the room.

"Screw the candy." He growled, his other hand reaching back to smooth across her hip. "I don't need candy. I just need your lips."

The song on the radio changed to something slower, but more sensual. A woman's voice sang of making love, and the sway of their hips slowed, the grind harder. Up and down, she moved, Jackson's warm fingers above her hand, the cloth-covered erection beneath her palm.

Her breathing sharpened. "Just my lips, baby?" An ache started in her thighs, desire coiling inside her soaking pussy. She moved her other hand to his fly and popped the buttons one by one, lust driving her.

Against her cheek she could feel the rumble of his groan as she tucked her hands inside his boxer shorts and shoved the material down and out of the way. Though she'd dreamed about it, she wasn't prepared for the length of hard cock that sprang forward and filled both hands.

She shuddered, her nipples beading up and pressing against the lace of her bra. Wrapping her fingers around him, she wasn't surprised when her fingertips didn't meet her thumb. She slid from the base of his cock, moving over rock-hard flesh and smooth satin skin, to the swollen plum-shaped head.

The rhythm of his hips faltered as a tremble went through his body. His breathing short and choppy.

Alexis closed her eyes, absorbing the feel of him, her heart pumping in time with the pulse beating down the length of his erection. Leaning her forehead against his back, she struggled to go slow, to keep her hands from working him fast and hard, in a tempo she longed to fuck in.

He felt incredible, but she wanted to see him naked.

The lights clicked off.

"The timer," Jackson said.

Alexis swayed with the music. Dropping one hand from his flesh, she moved around him, keeping her other hand draped over his heat. She was grinning as she danced. She didn't need the lights. The moon was close to full and through floor-to-ceiling windows bathed the studio in a milky silver glow.

In front of him again, she closed both hands around him, stroking upward from the base and drawing out a pearly ball of pre-cum. Her mouth watered. "Just my lips?" she repeated.

He touched her lightly beneath her chin, slanting her face upward to his. "Yeah, sugar, your lips are sweet enough for me."

He brushed his mouth across hers in a kiss that was so intimate, tears gathered in her eyes. She didn't allow them to fall; instead she welcomed every bit of feeling he gave. The second pass of his mouth was firmer, with a warm swipe of his tongue.

Her knees shook; her aching inner thighs made it hard to stand. If she stood there for his kisses, if she opened her mouth and allowed his tongue inside, she'd be lost to him. Lost in his touch and unable to touch him the way she longed to.

To lick him. To taste him. To kiss every inch.

With a whimper, she ended the kiss before it deepened, then lowered to her knees before he had a chance to stop her.

She swiped her tongue across his head, lapping up the bead of moisture. His body shook. Hard.

"Lexi." The word was strained, followed by a breath of air that hissed through clenched teeth. She heard him swallow.

"Sugar." His hands were on her shoulders, on her head, grabbing on to her hair. "Shouldn't we talk about this?"

She grinned. "About this?" She swirled her tongue along the ridge of his head, then followed the vein downward. "This?" She cupped a hand around his balls.

"Damn, girl." His hips bucked, and his fingers tightened in her braids. "No. No, about what's . . . going on."

"I don't want to talk." She caressed his sac with one hand. The other tightened around him and smoothed over the damp trail where her mouth had been. "I want to dance for you."

He growled.

"And I want you to remember how this feels." Running

the tip of her tongue over his velvet head, she lapped at the tiny slit, tasting his lubricant. With him wet now, she rubbed him across her lips, then opened and took him inside.

"Oh, shit." His body pumped into her even though Alexis could tell he fought for control.

The fact that he was losing the battle had her smiling as she tightened her fingers around his cock and stroked in beat with the hip-hop rhythm pulsing from the speakers. Up, up. Down, down. In and out, she sucked in her cheeks and took him deeper so that he was pressing against the back of her throat.

The music took over, the drums pulsing through her body. She swayed with it, her hips dipping forward so her clit pressed against her panties. Her breasts jiggled, her lacy bra stimulating her nipples.

She worked him, driving deeper—harder—tightening the suction. Spurred by Jackson's broken and jagged breaths, by the sexy wet slurping sounds, by the salty bitterness of his pre-cum, by the way his cock swelled against her tongue, by her own need. She increased the speed. Up. In. Down. Out.

Her pussy was dripping now, her panties soaked as the tingle of climax started deep inside. The sensation grew as his cock throbbed beneath her lips. And she could feel it against her palm, his wad of cum building at the base of his dick.

Dropping her hand from his sac, she slid her fingers into her panties and touched her clit. She circled twice, pressed with her thumb to finish herself off. Her body began to shake.

"Lexi." His body shook, then went rigid, and she knew he was letting go. The ball of cum shot past her hand. "Sug—" He pulsed hot and sticky into her mouth.

One press of her thumb and she joined him in climax, her body clamping down, then shuddering in rhythm with the cum that filled her cheeks and slid down her throat. Closing her eyes as orgasm rocked her body, Alexis kept her fingers tight around him until he'd pumped the last drop and he slid semihard from between her lips.

He was still breathing hard when he helped her to her feet and folded her into his embrace. He held her, his arms banded around her back, his pants dropping around his knees, and started to dance to the slow jam on the radio.

Alexis was grinning as he hummed the lyrics; then she pressed a kiss to his chest as the music ended and commercials began. There was a giggle bubbling up as she stepped away and saw him standing there, with the same stance and intense look on his face, but with his pants half off. The desire appeased.

She chewed her bottom lip to keep from laughing. "Want to go get a milk shake?"

Jackson reached for his jeans and dragged them over his hips, taking a second to compose himself, to think over her comment. Lexi, his closest friend, had just sucked him off—the best blow job he'd ever had—and now was asking for a milk shake? This shit didn't even make sense. A week ago, he'd never have guessed there was anything between them but the lifelong friendship they'd always known. He'd made the mistake of kissing her a little too long. A little too deeply.

Then all of sudden she'd been in his arms, and everything about the moment had felt unbelievably right. As if his body had known before his head, he'd hardened. They'd danced. Then—

Sucking in a gasping breath, Jackson reached for her hand, twining their fingers. "Lexi, sugar, we've got to talk."

He could see the small tremble that moved across her body, feel the slight shake of her hand. He could see the combination of joy and a hint of anxiety in the chocolate hues of her gaze. Liquid pooled on her lower lashes, but she slanted her face away before he saw a single tear fall.

Her voice was low and soft. "Please just don't say this was wrong. A mistake."

What was it, then? He tightened his hand around her fingers and pulled her a step in his direction. She lifted her face and looked at him—fury coiling in his gut when he saw the tears on her cheeks, the look of shame.

Framing her face with his free hand, he used his thumb to swipe the moisture from her skin. "Hey, not a mistake, sugar. We just got a little carried away."

She nodded, then sniffled. "I'm not married yet." Her voice dropped to a whisper. "We were dancing. Just dancing—you felt good, Jackson. It felt right." A slight smile touched her plump lips.

She licked away a tear and he became hard instantly. But this erection was going to get ignored. Hoping she wouldn't notice, he stepped back, putting a little distance between them. "Yeah, it felt right. The music—" He cleared his throat. "The moonlight."

"The moonlight?" Laughing, she rolled her eyes at him. "Don't try to romance me, Jackson." She shrugged, her gaze moving slowly from his face down to his erection, which he hoped was hidden by his jeans and the shadows. "We've known each other a long time. I just had to know. Before I—"

"So now you know," he cut her off, not wanting to hear about her marriage, the jealousy resurfacing.

She hadn't lifted her stare from his crotch and he felt his body throb in response. "Now I know." There was so much longing in her voice, he felt it all the way down to his core. Finally she looked into his eyes. "We're okay?"

If he gave the answer she wanted, it'd be a lie. He wasn't all right at all. He was standing in the dark in a dance studio so she could practice for her wedding to another man. And he'd just cum down her throat. And worse yet, he wasn't sure how he felt, whether he was bothered more because he was rocked up again and wanted to sink into her—to fuck her hard and fast, and sweet and slow—or because she was supposed to marry someone else.

Trying to relax the coiling tension winding through his body, he gave the only answer he could. "All but one thing. You promised me some sugar. Grape."

Lexi smiled, then with a laugh moved away from him toward her purse.

Three

She'd been thinking about it. Thinking about the kissing, the dancing, the way his skin had tasted. Thinking about Jackson, and little else.

Trying to forget the guilt, desperate to be in the present, Alexis strolled across the ballroom, appreciating the beauty of the vast parquet floors and the ornate velvet window valances. The rich material was perched atop a row of French doors lining the entire western wall. Grasping the scooped neck of her blouse, she pulled the ivory silk away from her skin, feeling like she couldn't draw a full breath.

"Are you all right?" Bryan called from behind her.

Without looking back, Alexis managed, "I'm fine."

Within seconds she heard his voice murmur on, giving directions to the hotel representative on just what he expected for the reception. Between Nana's and Momma's abundant plans and Bryan's strict demands, Alexis was given very little say in the preparations of what was supposed to be *her* day.

The click of her sandals on the hard floor vanquished the carrying rumble of Bryan's words. Trying to focus on the one area in which she'd been given *almost* free rein—the flowers—Alexis' mind whirled through her choices. But even thoughts of beautiful bouquets were now tainted with Bryan's stipulation they be white.

"To match your dress," he'd said.

Now every time she tried to decide how to set up the bridal flowers, all she could imagine was large chunky rhinestones and dull fake pearls. Her mind revolted, refusing to come up with a viable idea for the arrangements, even though time was running out.

Alexis at last reached the French doors leading outside, twisted a knob, and pulled them open. Relieved by the zephyr of air rushing in, she sucked in a deep breath of the sun-warmed ocean air. The scent of salt mingled with fish and seaweed filled her lungs, and for the first time since Bryan had picked her up at her shop, she felt like she could breathe.

Thanks to a cancellation, they'd managed to book the Hotel del Coronado, a place sought after and reserved years in advance for weddings and other celebrations. But being here now, with the weeks ticking by, felt all too real and way too soon, and once again the fear of Bryan not being *the one* threatened to suffocate her.

She crossed the freshly stained balcony, resisting the urge to run. For miles in every direction the beach spread out before her, the mineral mica sparkling in the late-afternoon light. Locals called the fine bleached sand "sugar sand." It beckoned to her, like Jackson did, the term reminding her of how he asked for his kisses. Though the way they'd kissed at the studio hadn't been sweet, but full of passion, and had warmed her pussy like honey, just as he'd melted in her mouth.

Closing her eyes, she smoothed her tongue across her lips, savoring the memory of his skin, the hardness of his dick, and the urgency of his climax. She took a deep breath, opened her eyes, and tried to assure herself that she and Jackson were fine, like he'd said. That the way they'd tested the boundaries wouldn't affect their closeness.

He'd said they'd merely gotten carried away—but she'd known what she was doing. Would do it again, given the chance. She'd loved Jackson forever. Longed for him. During the nights that'd followed, she'd replayed their *dancing* over and over. Hadn't stopped thinking about him.

But she wondered, too, if he was also thinking about her. If only she'd expressed her desire for him before Bryan had come into the picture. Squeezing her lids closed for a moment, Alexis pushed back the tears, knowing it was far too late for *if only*s.

Alexis hiked her skirt up to her knees, slipped off her sandals, and buried her toes in the sugar sand's warmth, trying to steady her breaths. To slow her heart rate.

With the magnificent Pacific Ocean as a backdrop, this was where she would have chosen to get married, with her feet bare and her braids intact, and a simple wedding dress, the man of her dreams waiting at the end of the aisle. But Bryan had insisted on a church wedding.

"A formal wedding," he had called it. Nana and Momma had taken the idea and run with it, spiraling the entire event out of Alexis' control.

Sighing, she struggled to hold back a frustrated sob. *I bet when Jackson gets married he'll allow his bride the wedding of her dreams*, she mused, closing her eyes against a fresh sting of tears and tilting her face toward the flawless azure sky.

Large hands settled on her shoulders, jolting her out of her reflections. Startled, Alexis spun around to see who had touched her, only to realize it was Bryan.

He wrapped his arms around her and pulled her to his chest.

"You startled me," she said, still trying to catch her breath.

He kissed the top of her head as he began to move his palm in slow circles across her back. "I didn't mean to. You all right?"

Alexis nodded.

"What are you doing out here?"

She tried to relax into his embrace, resting her head in the cove created beneath his chin. The musky scent of his cologne seeped into her senses. "Just breathing the ocean air," she replied in a whisper. She hugged him, holding him close and trying desperately to deepen the connection between them. To find some warmth.

"I thought you'd want to be inside listening to the plans."

Listening! He didn't say *helping* or *contributing*, but *listening*. That's because, like she'd known from the start, she had no input or opinion, at least not one that seemed to matter.

Hoping he didn't hear the sarcasm in her tone, she said, "You have it covered." She didn't want to hold it against him—after all, he took control with the best of intentions, thinking it'd ease her strain.

"Yeah, Alexis, I do."

Alexis. He still called her Alexis so formally. Her friends and family called her Lexi. Jackson called her Lexi. But for some reason the man who would be her husband in a matter

of four weeks refused to call her a nickname or any endear-
ments at all. Always Alexis. It bothered her. Or perhaps her
reaction was overly harsh to cover up her growing frustra-
tions.

Bryan is a great guy, she reminded herself. *You're lucky
to have him*. But in many ways her soon-to-be husband was a
stranger to her. Though she'd known him casually in college,
sharing a few of the same classes, it wasn't until six months
ago that they'd begun to date.

Though she had fun with Bryan, their relationship
seemed to always be missing something. Heat. Desire. Passion. All the things she felt when she was with Jackson. She
swallowed the lump in her throat. Maybe her reaction had
been because her body was starved for physical attention.
In the months of dating and engagement, she hadn't even
been to bed with him. She missed that sort of touch and
pleasure.

Attempting to create some excitement with Bryan,
Alexis rose onto her tiptoes and touched the smooth skin below his ear with her lips, a light combo of kissing and whis-
pering. "Are you going to tell me where we're going on our
honeymoon?" Shifting her berry candy to her cheek, she
teased his skin with her tongue, drifting across the fleshy
lobe of his ear.

When his only response was a noncommittal mumble and
a tightening of his hold around her body, she nipped the flesh
between her teeth and dropped her hands to the fullness of his
ass. She gave a firm squeeze. "Tell me!"

"Not a chance." Bryan used the palm of his hand to
smooth a few stray braids out of her face, then dropped his
fingers beneath her chin and tilted back. "You won't convince me."

"I can try."

"Not a chance," he repeated as he covered her lips with his. His half-opened mouth was warm against her skin, the kiss light and undemanding.

It didn't even leave her mildly warm, let alone hot. Didn't leave her aching for more.

He pulled away, his brows furrowed together. "Spit the candy out, Alexis."

"I like the fruity flavors."

"It's such a childish habit."

She gaped at him, unable to say a word. No sparks to his kisses and he didn't even appreciate the sweetness of her candy lips?

Bryan kissed her cheek as he lifted his head. "Now that the arrangements here are all set up, I have to get back."

That's it? He insulted her, then wanted to walk away? Alexis didn't want affection; she wanted lust. She didn't want half-open mouths. She wanted deep kisses with lots of tongue. Sparks. Fire. She wanted her body to melt from desiring it so badly.

When his arms dropped from around her back, Alexis realized she wasn't going to get any of that unless she took a stand. Gave it another try. Before he could move away, she grabbed his sleeve and pulled him back. Moving her fingertips up his shoulders, she banded her arms around his neck and pulled his face down to greet her upward lift.

She touched her tongue to his firm, unyielding lips. When his mouth opened to mumble something, she took advantage and swept inside. He seemed to give in. Their tongues met and swirled. Slanting her head, she deepened the kiss, searching for the elusive excitement of awakening desire.

She pressed closer, until her breasts were flattened between them and they were thigh to thigh. She wanted to absorb his scent, to taste his need, to feel his arousal. Her body craved the stimulation.

But the intensity behind the kiss was dull rather than thrilling and she didn't feel so much as a trace of arousal from his body. Giving up, she broke off the kiss and rested her forehead against his chin. Though she hated to compare the two men, the two kisses, that's exactly what she did. Bryan made her feel nothing. Jackson made her feel everything. Tears burned behind her eyes.

"We could get married sooner," Bryan suggested, rubbing a hand down her arm.

Alexis almost whimpered. All that kissing and he hadn't even needed to catch his breath. But hell, that tepid kiss hadn't come close to fire, and she had to admit she wasn't anywhere near being turned on either. "Four weeks is soon."

"We could go to Vegas and do it tonight."

Alarm shot through her body. She gulped in a breath of his cologne as her mind raced for stall tactics. Nothing about this felt right. She couldn't let him press the issue. "Didn't you have to get back?"

Flipping through the pages of a floral catalog, Jackson sat on the stool behind the counter of Lexi's elite flower shop in Coronado Village, the Flower Basket. Even though he'd only stopped by to drop off a package of scented candles his mother had made for the bride-to-be, he'd ended up watching the shop as a favor to Lexi's helper, Sue. Her daughter had gotten sick at school and needed to be picked up.

Folded corners on several of the pages caught his eye.

White flowers don't properly fit Lexi's personality, he thought when he realized what the dog-eared pages indicated. White was too simple, too ordinary, too uptight.

Feeling annoyed that Bryan didn't recognize it, Jackson shut the catalog and tossed it on the counter. "How much longer?" he mumbled to himself, narrowing his eyes and knowing his irritation didn't stem simply from white flowers.

No, it was our encounter—and the fact he wanted her again.

Jackson tried to swallow past the vise grip in his throat. When Nana mentioned he'd have to stop kissing Lexi, his gut had clenched so fiercely, he'd struggled to hide the pain. Struggled to breathe again. So he'd kissed her fully to prove a point.

But it'd been an entirely different physical reaction when he'd held her supple body against his in the dance studio. Blood had rushed to his cock so quickly, he'd almost felt dizzy from it. The heat from her lush lips wrapped around his cock as he came had lingered with him over the last week.

Hadn't stopped aching for more since.

More of her.

A movement outside the front window drew his attention. Lexi and Bryan approached the shop, but stopped short of coming in the door. Though he couldn't put his finger on what it was, every time he saw them together, he disagreed more with her choice of men.

Is it jealousy talking? Jackson rubbed the bunching muscles on the back of his neck. The longer the couple stood on the sidewalk talking, the tighter his shoulders tensed up.

It wasn't Bryan, Jackson decided. He was a decent guy, but it was the two of them as a pair. They just didn't seem natural, like they'd been made for each other. The closer the wedding date crept, the more they didn't sit right.

Hell, the truth was, at this point he seriously doubted seeing her with any man—other than him—would be okay.

He *was* jealous. Damned near insane with it. He'd taken for granted his relationship with Lexi for years, but never examined his feelings about something stronger. During the last two weeks, he realized he'd be losing her to marriage, and the rage that infused him with made him understand that there was something deeper.

The possibility scared the shit out of him. As much as he wanted to see her happy, he also wanted her for himself.

If Lexi was bubbling with joy and excitement, he'd know his gut was wrong and he'd keep his newly discovered feelings bottled up no matter how much pain it caused. But she didn't seem happy to him. She seemed rushed.

Jackson rose to his feet and rolled his shoulders, working out the tight muscles plucking havoc like an instrument.

"What should I do?" he murmured. A friend would offer support, but a true friend wouldn't stand by and allow her to make a mistake.

But what would a friend do if he wanted to be her man?

He couldn't do nothing and allow her to "I do" her way into a life of unhappiness just because he wasn't sure of the guy, and because after a lifetime of friendship, he wanted a chance at romance. After years of playing at kissing, always quick but never deep, he wanted a shot to find out if there could be more between them.

Hell, judging by the passion of their last encounter, he knew there could be.

He loved Lexi. Always had, always would, but the erection

mere thoughts of her caused set off warning bells. The ring-a-ding-ding that the kind of love he'd thought he had for her was truly something more.

And a whole lot more serious.

Sucking in breaths and ignoring the way his blood pulsed at his temples, Jackson swiped a hand over the beads of sweat gathering on his brow. He started to turn away from the window when Bryan bent to kiss Lexi, causing a wild streak of possessiveness to curl his fingers into fists. The quick peck to her lips hardly lasted long, but that didn't calm him down. He wanted to be the only man to touch her lips.

The only one to taste her candy kisses.

Feet planted to the ground, he made himself stand there, sucking in jagged breaths. A second later Bryan was walking toward his car, parked farther down the street, and Lexi stood alone.

"What an ass." Jackson shook his head, thinking of the sort of kiss he would lay on a woman he loved when saying good-bye.

I'd kiss her deeper, show her a little something-something. He liked the idea. He'd *show* her how a man should kiss, how a man should make a woman feel, he thought, but it was more than kissing he wanted. His cock bucked, lust drawing up his sac just from him imagining sinking into Lexi.

Lust pumping hard, Jackson held his breath as he waited for her to turn around. His chest burned. His body throbbing with desire, he reached over and plucked a violet daylily from a nearby bucket and waited for her to come through the door.

The air whooshed from his lungs when she strolled inside, her eyes widening when she saw him. Her smooth brown skin flushed in the twilight. The setting sun seeped through the glass front windows and illuminated the profile of her lush lips and brightened the tips of her braids to a shimmering gold.

"For you, Lexi." He presented her with the stem when she walked toward him, her sweet scent making his cock push against the confines of his jeans.

"Jackson. *For me?* Really?" she teased, accepting *her* flower from *her* shop. "You shouldn't have."

"No trouble." He winked. He wanted to reach for her, to capture her lips, to fit himself into her pussy.

"What are you doing here? Where's Sue?"

"She had to leave when I got here." He slanted his head to the counter. "Brought you some candles from my mom. I told Sue I'd wait around till you got back."

She licked her lips, her dark gaze dropping slowly to his mouth. "I'm glad you're here," her words just above a whisper.

That's all Jackson needed. While having milk shakes after their *dancing*, they'd agreed it'd be a onetime thing. That didn't matter now. He wanted her. Needed her. Needed to show his feelings for her were genuine, if to no one but himself.

He lifted a hand and touched her cheek, the softness of her skin pouring desire into his rocked-up hard body.

"Come here, sugar." He framed her face with his other hand, smoothing fingers into her hair, down her neck where her pulse beat rapidly, then slid his thumb across her quivering lower lip.

With the slightest pressure, he pulled her toward him and she came willingly, her eyelids fluttering, her gaze locked on his. Lazily her lashes lowered to rest against her cheeks and a sigh—fruit scented and warm as a summer breeze—a sigh of contentment spilled out.

He kissed her.

He'd show her *contentment*, the kind she'd feel after she came. The first brush of his tongue and he was rewarded with the taste of strawberry candy and the sweetness of her lips.

Alexis gasped, surprised by the rush of need one stroke of his tongue created. Need that had her aching and soaking wet. She'd yearned for this for years, for his tongue, his heat, his texture. Longed to have him kissing her like a lover and not a friend.

Not giving a damn about the *Why now?* she was not going to let him step away. She needed this kiss, needed him. Slanting her head back and lifting on tiptoes, she attempted to bring him closer, but with a hand to her hip he kept her mere inches away. She touched his chest, running her fingers to his shoulder, then curling an arm around his neck to drag him down.

He chuckled, nibbling her bottom lip and gently sucking it into his mouth. The tender caresses caused her nipples to pucker. Made breathing difficult.

Alexis leaned into him, touching her aching breasts to his chest. Her movement spurred him into action; he parted her lips with the tip of his tongue, slid past her teeth, swept inside.

Finally. Oh, yes, finally.

She moaned as she shifted the strawberry candy across her mouth to tuck into her other cheek. "Mmm," he murmured against her lips, touching the hard candy with his tongue, then maneuvering it back into his mouth.

She didn't lament the loss, too distracted by the building heat. His tongue was inside her, thrusting in a tempo that made her pussy wet, arousal seeping down her thighs. Desire made her grip his T-shirt in both fists to anchor her trembling body.

She'd been kissing him for years, but this was the exact kiss she'd been yearning for.

She heard his groan when her tongue mingled with his, increasing the tingling to her inner thighs, the tips of her breasts. Making her light-headed.

Putting his hands on her hips, Jackson lifted her onto the counter and stepped into the V of her legs, the hard length of his cock brushing along her clit. Alexis slanted her hips, attempting to prolong the contact, to feel his erection against her again. She wrapped her legs around the backs of his thighs, holding him there.

Releasing his shirt, she roamed over the contours of his body, feeling the muscles flex beneath her fingertips. His hands left her hips, sliding upward over ribs; then covering her breasts, he took the weight in his palms.

"We're not dancing," he said against her mouth.

Damn, she wasn't going to mention it. "No, we're not."

He left one hand cupped over her, his thumb and forefinger rolling her beaded nipple through her silk shirt and the lace of her bra. "You still okay with this?"

"Jackson, pleeease." Arching her back, she whimpered into his mouth, wanting her clothing out of the way.

Wanted him skin to skin.

While he worked her nipple, his other hand slid downward between their bodies and he added his fingers to where his dick thrust against her. She could feel his heat even through pants and panties. Could feel the pulse of his cock, the seductive rhythm of his fingers against her clit.

Holding her breath and keeping her lids clamped, she allowed sensation to increase, forgetting everything but the tightening of her body, the crazy tingling, the spasms of release. And that it was Jackson—*finally*—making her feel this way.

"Oh, God," she cried out as her body clamped down, then shook violently. She grabbed at his shirt again, vaguely aware that she clawed more skin than material with her nails, faintly hearing his groan as she struggled to breathe. She tasted the strawberry of her candy as he laughed against her lips, tenderly kissing her through her climax, stroking his tongue in time with the pulsing of his dick, each of his movements prolonging her orgasm.

Jackson was grinning at her when she sucked in a breath and opened her eyes. An arrogant look of satisfaction marred his perfect smile. His dimples deepened.

"Mmm . . . strawberry."

She shook her head and gulped in puffs of air as she tried to make sense of what happened. "You made me feel so good."

His grin widened. "Feel right?"

She stared at him, wondering if he'd been asking a question or making a statement. "I was going to lock up," she whispered, feeling heat sting her cheeks. Jackson had made her cum and that's all she could say? She swallowed. "I'd invite you to dinner, but I'm meeting Nana and Momma for some girl talk."

Jackson watched Lexi's eyes, saw the uncertainty along with confusion, and felt the need to reassure her by tucking her into his arms. But embrace her now and he might forget where he was. The only thing that kept his cock in his pants was the plate glass window of her storefront. He took a deep breath, his teeth clicking on the strawberry candy.

"That's all right. I have to go." He took a step back, cool

air sliding over his body. He damned well had to find a way to settle down and get his lust in check. He was a stroke or two away from blowing a nut in his boxer shorts. "Jackson, you kissed me."

He grinned. "I always kiss you, Lexi."

"But not like that."

Leaning toward Lexi, he captured her mouth and pressed a quick kiss to her luscious lips. "Mmm . . . strawberry," he repeated, then arched a brow. "Better?"

Her mouth fell open, her dark eyes searching his. He laughed when she nodded. Then he stepped toward the door.

"Wait."

"Yeah?"

"Don't you think we should talk about this?" She slid a hand down her body, indicating her puckered-up nipples and the damp apex of her thighs.

His palm itched to touch her the same way, to run across her flesh. He shook his head. "What is there to talk about, Lexi? People change. Circumstances change."

"What does that mean? You've changed? You want me to change my wedding plans? We can't just keep fooling around. My family's planning the wed—"

"Lexi, I'll stand up for you as your 'man of honor' if that's what you really want." He scrubbed a hand over his face, bile rising from his gut, but knew it was true. "We came up together, Lexi. Been friends forever. You know there's nothing I wouldn't do for you."

Her warm eyes held his, a slow sigh seeping from her full lips. "What do you want me to do? Call it off? Disappoint everyone?"

Hell, yes, call the damned thing off. Swallowing down the

words, he looked into her eyes. He wasn't sure confessing his feelings right now was the thing to do. And the wedding—that was a decision she'd have to make on her own. He shrugged.

"Only you know what feels right to you. What *is* right for you."

He gazed at her for a moment longer, then went out the door, knowing if she called him back, he'd go running. She didn't. He walked away.

Four

I'm pathetic. Absolutely pathetic!

Alexis stared through blurry eyes into her open car trunk. Frothy white tissue paper sprang from a multitude of wedding-gift bags littering the entire space. Sadly, not a single present was really for her. She didn't want lacy white bras with matching thong panties or massage oil that tasted like cotton candy, or a Tantric book on how newlyweds should make love.

Not when they were meant to be used with Bryan when the only man she truly wanted was Jackson.

Hit by a wave of dizziness, Alexis gripped the side of the car with one hand and closed her eyes. All her friends had roared with laughter when she opened the tiny bag from Nana that contained nothing but crotchless panties, designed for when a couple just couldn't wait. Too bad the wrong man had her ready for some prenuptial sex.

Struggling for balance on the three-inch heels Alicia had chosen to go along with the white bridal-shower dress, Alexis wished she hadn't indulged in the last few margaritas. She should have just left when everyone else had instead of lingering at the bar. The cool crushed ice had numbed her mind while the tequila took care of the rest of her body.

Opening her eyes, she glared down at the oversized ribbon bouquet made from the adornments of the gifts she'd received. She was supposed to carry it down the aisle during her wedding rehearsal, but the silly thing was hideous. She tossed the jumbled ribbons into her trunk and slammed it tight.

In no condition to drive, Alexis turned and leaned her ass against her car. Jackson would help her. He always helped when she needed it. She'd sure as hell needed to cum and he'd helped her do that—*he'd help her.*

Pushing off her trunk, she started walking in the direction of his house. They hadn't talked about what had happened in the flower shop, but she couldn't stop remembering the heat, even with a few too many drinks. He wouldn't care if she showed up close to midnight, drunk off her ass, and in need of a ride home after a good fucking.

The damn stilettos kept getting caught in the littlest of sidewalk cracks. "I hope I break one of the stupid things," she growled as she tripped again. "Or better yet, I could break my ankle and call this whole thing off." Like she should've done herself if she had more backbone. Nana and Momma would probably put her in the gaudy dress, with the fifteen-foot train, and push her down the aisle in a wheelchair.

Luckily the Mexican restaurant where her bridal shower had been held wasn't far from Jackson's house. Coronado was a tiny island and the fresh sea air was already working wonders on the fuzz of alcohol buzzing in her blood. Still, her feet ached by the time she reached his place at the end of the next block.

It didn't take more than a few light taps for the door to be pulled open. Pale lamp radiance seeped out and Jackson's silhouette filled the frame. In the faded streetlight, the brown skin on his bare muscular chest looked taut and smooth. Naked broad shoulders tapered to a narrow waist, where his abs were chiseled, and gray cotton shorts hung low on his hips.

He looks yummy. Her gaze traveled down the dark curls descending from his lower abdomen. Lower to the length of cock beneath his shorts, which was filling with blood as she stared. She licked her lips.

"Lexi?"

A rush of heat shimmied across her skin, his rich timbre conjuring up all sorts of temptations. Had she been wearing panties, they'd have been soaked. Her inner thighs were. Halting her train of thought before she acted on it and made a fool of herself, she snapped her eyes back to his face. The sudden movement spurred a wave of dizziness.

"I need your help."

Jackson stepped forward. Wrapping an arm around her, he steadied her just when the ground began to spin. "You walked here?"

Alexis burped, then laughed. "I couldn't drive."

"You've been drinking."

"You can tell?" She straightened her spine.

He nodded and she frowned. "And you walked?"

"I walked." *I'm slurring my words?*

His gaze dropped to her feet. "In those?"

A shiver danced across her skin. "Hooker shoes," she finished for him. She much preferred flat sandals, but these were a gift from her sister and she didn't have the heart to refuse.

"Wasn't your shower tonight?" Jackson assisted her inside his house and shut the door behind them.

Needing his warmth and comfort, Alexis leaned into him and was welcomed by his immediate embrace.

She smoothed her cheek across his chiseled pecs, brushed a light kiss or two to his skin, and felt his dick swell. She grinned. "Mmmhmm. Don't remind me." With her cheek pressed against his naked skin, Alexis inhaled his exotic scent. *He smells so good.*

"Your momma left you there like this?" Jackson ran his palm down her back.

She burped again, the sour taste of tequila filling her mouth. "I wasn't like this when they left."

"You stayed behind?"

She trailed her fingertips up his bicep, then draped her arm around his neck. Closing her eyes again, she used his strong body for support as she fought against the ebb and flow of vertigo, instead focusing on the throb of his erection pressed to the apex of her thighs. "Um-hum."

"Why?"

Alexis tried to hold it back, but the genuine concern in his rich voice broke the well free. She wanted to feel sexy—wanted him to want her—instead she ended up weeping like a baby. Big, fat tears seeped from her eyes and dripped from her lashes. She choked on the words. "Because I'm pathetic."

"Lexi, you're crying."

"I warned you I was pathetic."

His body on fire, Jackson held back a growl. Without offering a verbal response, he scooped her into his arms and carried her to the couch. He tried to put her down, but she clung to him, her body shaking as the sobs continued to grow. Instead, he sat down and settled her on his lap, knowing damned well that she could feel his hard dick press into her flesh. Not like he could help it, not when he opened the door in the middle of the night to the woman who'd been in his dreams.

"Tell me what happened, Lexi." He gently wiped tears from her cheeks, but it did little good. Fresh ones quickly replaced them. "Did Bryan do something?" Jackson almost hoped he did. Then at least he'd have a solid reason to dislike the guy other than just Bryan's marrying the woman he wanted.

"No." She hiccuped. "I did."

"Did you add some pink flowers to your wedding bouquet?" He wanted to stop the tears, protect her from all her ails.

"I kissed him."

Something tightened in Jackson's gut. *I don't want to hear this*. Running his hands up and down her back, he hoped to offer comfort, but distract her from continuing on about the kiss. His irritation rose just at the thought of Bryan's mouth touching lips he'd always considered his.

"I kissed him, Jackson."

"You're marrying him." The words stung his throat, his heart.

Alexis wiggled until she was sitting up, straddling his lap, and facing him, causing her skirt to bunch around her waist and giving him a shadowed glimpse of short dark curls. He closed his eyes for a moment while he dragged in a few breaths to ward off the ball of cum her ass against his dick was building. The sight of her naked flesh, the sweet scent.

"No, you don't understand. I kissed him and nothing happened. No sparks. No flames. No heat. No passion." Her gaze dropped from his, a fresh sob reverberating through her body.

Shit! Jackson ached, wanting so badly to help her—to free his cock from his shorts and get inside her and make her forget about every man but him. But she rushed onward with her confessions before he could think of the right thing to say. Before he was stupid enough to take advantage of her intoxication.

"There's something wrong with me. Don't you see it? I can't be turned on except *by* you. I can't feel desire except *for* you. I don't even know how to kiss a man to bring him to arousal. I'm pathetic."

"You're wrong, Lexi." Oh, God, did she have no idea what she was doing to him? He was throbbing now, remembering how she'd cum with a few strokes of his fingers. He swallowed. She was drunk, didn't know what she was saying.

"No. You don't get it." She cupped each of his cheeks in her hands and stared directly into his eyes. "I kissed the man I am going to marry and felt nothing but blah. Do you hear me? *Blah!*"

Her hands drooped from his face, resting on his shoulders. Her body went limp, the apparent fight dissipating. "There's something wrong with me. It's only our candy kisses that make me feel anything."

"Maybe because the candy kisses are with the right man." *Me.* He wanted to thump his chest.

She shook her head. "No. I don't know." She whimpered. "I think it's me," she whispered with a raw voice.

"You're wrong." Jackson gripped her chin with his thumb and forefinger and tilted upward. Wrapping his other hand around the nape of her neck, he gave a slight tug. She leaned forward. "It's not you, Lexi. It's the man you kiss and I can prove it."

Their mouths crushed together. He touched his tongue to her plump lips, tasting the faint hint of lime and tequila. He pressed past her teeth, stroked into her mouth, groaning when she swirled her tongue against his.

He hadn't meant to kiss her again, not when he hadn't recovered from the last time. Not when he had a hard-on pumping with blood in his shorts and it'd be so easy to get caught up in lust. Not when he could taste the booze and knew her mind had to be fogged with it. Knew fucking her now—like he wanted—would be taking advantage.

Her lush lips were damp and pliable, open and willing as he thrust into her with his tongue. Arousal, stronger than the tequila Alexis had been drinking, spread like wildfire through his body. His dick bucked and his sac pulled up to his body as Lexi wiggled on his lap while she tentatively brushed her tongue across his lower lip.

She's got to feel my cock pulse between her thighs.

Damned right, she did, whimpering as she rolled her hips along the ridge and melting into the kiss, opening her mouth and slanting to get a better angle. Jackson closed his eyes, struggling for control as she deepened the kiss, then overwhelmed his senses, exploring his mouth with the sweetest touch.

This was no fruit-candy kiss, even if she did taste of lime. She'd taken his tongue between her teeth, scraping over it, then soothed him with caressing lips. Then she added suction, sucking his tongue in a rhythm she'd sucked his dick—what his dick begged for now, keeping beat with the rolling of her hips.

His hands closed around her waist, fisting into the bunched material of her skirt. It'd be so easy to slide his fingers downward, to touch her arousal-soaked curls. So easy to spread her lips with his thumb and forefinger, to sink inside of her tight pussy. So easy to free his cock from his shorts.

Too easy to forget she was drunk and he was supposed to be her friend.

Shaken, Jackson attempted to slow the kiss, to regain sanity. He was breathing hard, his knuckles white from gripping the hem of her clothing. A bead of pre-cum seeped from the slit on his swollen head.

"Please," she whispered against his lips. "Please. You're the only one, Jackson." She ran her hands over his chest, flicking her nails over the flat disks of his nipples. "Please, Jackson. You're the only one who makes me feel. Make me feel, baby, please."

She rolled her hips against his and what little shards remained of his restraint snapped like a brittle twig. He reversed their positions, moving her beneath him against the velvety couch cushions.

Her legs wrapped around his back. Her hands roamed freely across his burning skin, further inciting his lust. Through his shorts he could feel her damp heat, smell the fragrance of her need.

Make her feel? Hell, yeah, he'd do that. He'd make her feel how right this was. He'd make her feel so good she'd cum on his hands, on his tongue. Caressing her body, he skimmed across full breasts, nipples puckered up tight beneath her dress, down a narrow waist, over hips that rose from the cushions into his fingertips.

Curving his hands around her naked flesh, he kneaded her

ass, slid downward across luscious legs, smoothed forward to
find her inner thighs already slick.

Bending his head, he closed his mouth over a nipple, to hell
with the dress. He suckled the puckered flesh into his mouth,
twirled his tongue around it until Lexi's back was arching off
the couch. Until her breathing went uneven.

Leaving a large, round spot wet on her dress where his lips
had been, Jackson scooted lower, drawn downward with a
desperate need for a taste of her wet pussy. He kissed a hip—
skin so smooth and soft and holding the fragrance of her floral
shop—slid his tongue over the manicured curls above the hood
covering her clit.

"Do you *feel* this, Lexi?" he said against her, pushing back
the flesh. He licked her clit, closed his eyes, tasting the rush of
the sweetness of her juices. "Do you feel *me*?"

"Yes, Jackson." Her hands curled over his shoulders, her
nails biting. "That's what I want . . . the feeling I want."

Groaning, he sucked the little bead of flesh, working his
tongue in circles. He slid a hand up her thigh, opening her
wider, then touched the wet slit with his fingertips, parting
her lips gently before thrusting inside.

She was drenched, arousal sleek and shimmering. His fingers were covered in it—his chin—as he plunged in and out of
her tight flesh, making her writhe and moan. He licked lower,
touching his tongue to her petal-soft skin, lapping at the flow-
ing arousal.

Pushing his throbbing dick into the pillows of the couch,
Jackson struggled to keep his cool, to keep from blowing his
wad in his shorts while he licked her pussy, twirled his thumb
against her clit. Restraint beaded sweat on his brow. Tension
hummed through his blood.

Curling his fingers forward in a tempo that matched his raging pulse, he flicked the tip of his tongue over her flesh, tasting and teasing as he worked from her soaked lips to her swollen clit.

Pre-cum had his shorts damp, his own orgasm building along with Lexi's. Breathing hard, he thrust inside her just as the first shudders of climax began. Not over the edge yet, her body trembled. Her nails tightened into the skin on his shoulders as her body moved against him.

Alexis was close, the tingle, the flutter, increasing with each stroke of his fingers, each caress of his tongue.

Dusted in sweat, her silk dress clung to her skin as she rolled her body, bringing her hips up to his face. Holding him tight, she moved to his rhythm, danced her pussy across his face as if they were fucking.

This was the craze of lust, the excitement of passion, the burning of desire. This need, this absorbing yearning, was what she'd been missing. Everything she'd been after.

With her palms on his shoulders, she reveled in the smoothness of his naked flesh, the power in his flexing muscles, the masculine scent of his skin.

"You taste good," he murmured against her, his tongue pausing only briefly, picking up the beat he'd been stroking in.

The vibration caused by the rumble of his words was all she needed. "Jackson," she cried out, her back coming off the couch, her body shaking. Inside she tightened down, orgasm pulsing hard. The incredible feeling of climax shimmied through her inner thighs, across her skin.

Overcome by sensation, Alexis' chest burned for air as she gulped in jagged breaths. But even as the quivering of orgasm began to subside, she continued to tremble. No matter how she tried, the burning of tears at the back of her eyes couldn't be cooled. Fat drops dripped from her eyes.

She swiped them away with the back of her hand. "Jackson." He was sitting now, pulling her into his embrace, tucking her into his strong arms. Sniffling, she tried to get her emotions in check. She'd wanted Jackson all her life; being with him now felt so right. Every bit as good as she'd imagined. "Jackson," she whispered, turning her face and kissing his naked chest, trying to ignore the nagging guilt and her ties to another man.

"I'm here, sugar."

She reached for the waistband of his shorts, needing him to feel what she did. Yearning for him inside her.

Jackson immediately ended the attempt, covering her hands with his larger ones, and removing them from his shorts. When she reached for him again, he curved his hand into hers, linking their fingers, his dark gaze intent on hers.

Alexis shivered, the buzz of alcohol faded, yet replaced by something equally as drugging. Jackson. She watched his face, then licked her bottom lip. "I want to spend the night." His dark chocolate eyes shimmered with the same hunger she felt.

He was breathing hard, his toned body heaving. "I have to take you home."

"I want to stay."

"I have to take you home," he repeated. He stood, keeping their hands clasped, and pulled her to her feet, then held her steady when she wobbled.

"You made my knees feel weak." Alexis dropped her gaze to her legs. Jackson, her best friend, made her knees feel weak the way a fiancé should. She closed her eyes, marrying-the-wrong-man dread threatening to choke her.

She loved Jackson. The guy who kissed her to taste her fruity candy. The guy who always asked Momma to marry him. The guy who called Nana beautiful every time he saw her. The guy who'd been her confidant and best friend.

Her eyes opened and her gaze descended to his shorts, where the length of his thick cock was evident. She swallowed past the dryness in her throat.

And he was a man.

She wanted him. In her life. In her bed. Between her legs. When she returned her gaze to his, she could see the battle he waged with restraint. She knew when the honorable thing won out. He was stronger than her, for she'd have given in.

He cleared his throat. "I have to take you home."

Who's he trying to convince? she wondered. Alexis shuddered, a touch of reason emerging from the fog in her brain. She was engaged, soon to marry a different man. She couldn't spend the night fucking Jackson, despite how her body ached to.

Air whooshed from Jackson's lungs as he let go of her hands. "I'm taking you home, Lexi." He took a step back. "Have a seat while I get dressed, and hell, take off those ridiculous shoes before you kill yourself."

As he walked out of the room, she followed him with her eyes, then slid back down on the sofa. He'd be back soon. She stared at the ceiling, determined to will away her pert nipples and avoid any more crying. She wanted Jackson, and all that he offered her, but another man would be becoming her husband.

The pain tightened in her gut, orgasm a fading memory. Alexis took a deep breath. Her family expected this wedding to go down, and she couldn't disappoint them. Not for her own selfish cravings.

Oh, man. Jackson was right. She did need to get out of here, before she did something they both would probably enjoy immensely, but sorely regret.

She closed her eyes and waited for his return, determined to keep her hands to herself during the drive back to her place.

Five

Pressing her fingers to her temple, Alexis tried to forget the pounding headache causing her eyes to hurt. She tried to forget the feel of Jackson's presence beside her and the knowledge his eyes were fixed upon her. She could feel it. The bakery was no place to think about last night's kisses and climaxes.

"Shouldn't we have chocolate cake? Most people like chocolate better, don't they?" Alicia asked before filling her mouth with another bite from the display of samplings.

Momma pushed the chocolate samples to the far end of the table. "Wedding cakes aren't chocolate. They're white." She turned in her chair to face Alexis. "Which one do you like, Lexi? We need to make the final decision today."

"I want chocolate, too, Gramma," Tiana's seven-year-old voice piped in. "Can't we have chocolate under white frosting?"

Alexis looked at her niece, silently praising her for speaking her mind, a trait she was personally struggling with.

"We're going to have to decide about that, baby." Momma took a bite of white cake with a smooth sugar frosting. "I think this is my favorite."

"Lexi likes chocolate . . . ," Alicia began.

"Lexi can't tell when she's got that candy in her mouth," Nana commented.

Momma shook her head. "The wedding may be for Lexi, but the cake is for the guests."

The cake might be for the guests, but the wedding wasn't for her. It was for *them*, Alexis realized as her weary gaze roved over the faces of her loving family—avoiding Jackson.

Resisting the urge to walk out of the tiny elite bakery, which was decorated in shades of pastels and heavily scented with sweet fresh pastries, she turned her attention to the cakes spread out before her. An unsteady breath remained trapped in her lungs.

They didn't really need her here, since the decision wasn't actually up to her. She'd have had a much more productive day if she'd never gotten out of bed.

Jackson glanced at his watch. "We can't stay here all day, ladies. The final dress fitting is in a half hour."

Alexis glared at the watch adorning Jackson's wrist, the gold a brilliant contrast against the richness of his creamed-coffee skin. The muscles of his forearm bunched beneath her appraisal.

Cheeks flushed, she turned away, hating to think about losing her cozy gray sweatpants and plain T-shirt to don *the gown*.

Jackson shifted in his seat, then grinned at her in a way

that had his dimples deepening, and conjured up memories of their kisses. The skillful way he'd used his lips.

"What should we order?" Momma asked, garnering her attention.

Alexis shrugged, viciously narrowing her eyes at the slivers of wedding cakes adorning a dozen tiny porcelain plates. Thanks to her solitary drinking binge last night, not even over-the-counter painkillers could put an end to her throbbing temples.

"I can't tell them apart anymore." The queasy rolling in her gut wouldn't allow another single bite. No amount of Tums could soothe her hangover-sour stomach, the lingering hint of lime and tequila tainting every taste. "You decide, Nana."

Nana was silent for a moment as she dipped her finger into the frothy peaks of whipped cream. "I say we go with the white chocolate with raspberries in the middle."

At the mention of raspberries, Alexis' gaze snapped in Jackson's direction only to find him smugly staring at her lips. Aware of his nearness in a way she'd never been before, she'd been thinking of their kiss when Nana had spoken.

Raspberry candy was what she was sucking on when Jackson picked her up today for the afternoon session of cake tasting and the final fitting of her gown.

Like last night had never happened, he'd said, "Gimme some sugar," and kissed her full on the mouth, giving her just a tempting slide of tongue. Then he'd smacked those lips—which had given so much pleasure—and commented on the raspberry flavor of her kiss.

Lost in the warmth of his eyes now, she said nothing as she sucked the hard candy in her mouth, but Jackson ended the exchange, glancing at Nana. "I like *raspberries* and white chocolate."

Nana slid the small yellow order form in her own direction and fished in her purse for a pen. "Thank goodness that's decided, Lexi, baby. I couldn't have eaten much more of this." She smiled as she filled in the form with the cake identification.

Each box was clearly marked: four tiers, white cake, white chocolate frosting in a basket weave design, raspberry filling, and most important, an African-American figurine couple as the crowning jewel of the masterpiece.

Rising from her chair, Alexis made her way to the door. "Thank God that's over." She placed her palm over the sloshing in her stomach as she headed toward the door.

A warm hand settled on the small of her back and an arm reached around her to open the front glass door, allowing her escape. Jackson. The heat of his touch caused a shiver to run the length of her spine. His distinct exotic cologne flashed memories of his naked skin.

By the time they cleared the building, she was breathing heavily, sucking in gulps of the ocean breeze doused in sunshine. The expansive blue sky was marred only by a dusting of high clouds.

"You all right? You looked a bit green in there."

"I ate too much cake, is all."

"It's not about last night?"

The boyish uncertainty in the tone of his voice caught her off guard. Unlike Jackson's usual abundance of confidence, the slight hitch made her realize how deep his concern was.

Turning fully to face him, she took in the sight of her best friend. A hometown boy, he wore a Chargers jersey, baggy jeans, and tan Timberland boots—looked handsome even if a little thuggish. His muscular body towered above her. She chanced a quick glance at his crotch, wondering if he was as hard and chiseled there as he was everywhere else she'd seen.

Looking up, she realized she'd been caught, warmth melting his rich chocolate eyes. She heard him suck a breath of air between his teeth.

She drew closer. Draping her fingers across his arm, she ignored the rise of awareness of the heat that seeped through his body when she touched him. Leaning toward him, she rose on tiptoes to whisper in his ear, "It *is* about last night."

Alexis stepped back as she heard her family approaching, and watched Jackson's body react. Stared into his eyes. Felt the same arousal she saw there. Reaching into her pocket, she pulled out a candy, unwrapped the cellophane, and popped it in her mouth.

Raspberry—again. "Mmm." She sucked, her mouth filling with fruity sweetness. "Mmmmmmmm . . ." She closed her eyes, purposely trying to incite Jackson.

And he reacted. "Gimme some sugar, girl."

Alexis laughed as he swooped in and banded his arms around her, spinning them as his mouth covered hers and his tongue slipped between her lips to stroke against the candy.

"Jackson!" Nana said as they neared.

Alexis was giggling hard as he stepped away from her sheepishly. "Sorry, I've got a thing for raspberries." Jackson winked at her, then turned and took Nana's hand.

Places like this weren't designed for men, Jackson decided as he sprawled onto a dainty chair. All the frilly lace, silky ribbons, and undernetting were more torture than any man should ever have to endure, but since he was man of honor, it was his duty to sit here, despite how his heart ached and gut churned.

He didn't want to see her prepping to marry another man. Had he figured out this shit sooner, he could've been the man in her life.

Repressing a groan of pain, he stretched out his legs in front of him, folded his arms across his chest, and tuned out the continued chatter of the Payton Ladies. He felt like a fool, not having examined his love for Lexi before it was too late. Though she hadn't said she felt the same about him, her body spoke for her. She melted, climaxing with caresses of fingertips through clothing. Cuming against his tongue.

Jackson swallowed hard, trying to cool the effect on his body, trying to get rid of the hard-on hidden in his loose jeans.

Watching the small platform, surrounded on three sides with mirrors, he awaited the appearance of Lexi, knowing, too, that she wouldn't be here if she didn't want to be. She was a smart woman, and knew her own mind. Even if her body spoke loud and clear, it was her words he had to respect, adhere to. And Lexi was getting married. If she'd wanted it different, she'd have said so. A jagged breath eased past his lips as he got a handle on himself and got square with where he stood.

The man of honor. Waiting to see the bride in her dress. Oh, God, why did his chest feel so damned tight?

She emerged moments later and stepped up onto the pedestal. The microbraids were pulled into a ponytail atop her head and flopped in all directions. Her wide, dark eyes shone with stunned disbelief. A rose flush stole across her milk chocolate skin. Straight white teeth worried her lush lower lip.

She wasn't smiling.

If he'd thought he was possessive before, Jackson's blood heated to a boil and he had to ball his hands into fists to keep them from shaking. He stared at her, his throat burning, his breath stolen. Filled with jealous appreciation, his gaze roamed over her, moving from her shimmering eyes to where her pulse throbbed against the hollow of her throat, to the full swells of her luscious breasts.

Her graceful arms were crossed over her chest, shielding many of the glimmering rhinestones and tiny pearls from sight. Her hands shook as tight knuckles gripped the edge of the low bodice.

Something was wrong, but Nana asked before he could. "What's the matter, Lexi, baby?"

She lifted the bodice, hugging it to her breasts, and angled her body so they could see the open back. The pure white dress looked unappealing compared with the smoothness and richness of her skin. The row of pea-sized buttons gaped open, affording him a vast view of her naked figure. From the glimpse he was granted, he could tell she wore nothing but plain pink panties, the material caressing the swell of her generous backside. The erection he'd been fighting rocked up hard.

"I ate too much cake." She faced them again, liquid gathering in her eyes. "It won't button."

"You can lose five pounds in a couple weeks," the assistant said, fluffing the skirts and extending the expansive train.

Alicia laughed. "Is it that time, girl? Maybe you're retaining water."

Lexi shuddered, then shook her head. "Maybe I should just choose another." Her gaze traveled to the far dress-lined wall.

"Nonsense." Momma left her chair and went to Alexis, putting her hand on her daughter's shoulder. "Let me see how tight."

Let her choose another, Jackson thought, anything to make his girl happy. What she wore mattered little, so long as she loved it and was comfortable in it. No dress could hide the gorgeous lines of her perfect curves.

Watching her closely, he saw her gaze travel several times to the rows of simple gowns, longing in her expressive eyes. Couldn't her family see this wasn't the dress his Lexi wanted?

His Lexi? When had he begun to think of her as his? About the same time he'd decided that her sweet kisses should only be sampled by him. That every curve, every lush slope, every inch of her, should be touched only by his hands. Unable to stop the memories, he thought of the night before and how she'd confessed to kissing her fiancé and feeling nothing. Yet that lucky bastard would be the one getting the benefit of her fruit basket of candy kisses, while he'd be forbidden?

A cell phone rang.

With the sting of emptiness in his gut, he absentmindedly searched his pocket for the offending phone, feeling like the best thing that'd ever stepped into his life was about to step out.

"It's mine," said Lexi, pulling him from his thoughts. She slanted her head toward her purse. "Momma, could you get it for me?"

"Sure." Momma fumbled through the purse, extracting the chirping phone, and fiddled with the buttons. "I don't know how these things work. Here, Jackson, can you answer?" She handed him the phone.

"Lexi's phone."

"Where's Alexis?" a deep male voice asked from across the line.

"Here." Jackson walked to her side extending the phone, but quickly realized that her hands were busy keeping the wedding dress from falling into a puddle around her feet. He moved closer, the wide skirts rustling, and held the phone to her ear. She looked up at him, and he swore in the depths of her watery gaze he saw a silent plea, but hell, he had no clue on how to go about fixing things. What she was asking from him.

"Hi, Bryan," she whispered. Her eyes strayed away.

Jackson was close enough to hear every one of Bryan's pressuring words. The voices around them faded, all focus on the woman standing before him. Alexis' groom was begging for a quick trip to Vegas just so she wouldn't call off the wedding.

"I'm not going to do that."

Bryan's voice rumbled on, telling her how much he wanted this wedding, how important it was to him, and how worried he was that she was having second thoughts.

Second thoughts? He'd give her third, fourth, fifth . . . anything so he wouldn't lose her to this wedding.

Jackson stepped closer, shoving the material out of the way with his boot, close enough that their bodies touched. So close he knew she could feel the length of his dick wedged between them, his wide shoulders shielding her reaction. Her gaze came back to his and held.

With a whimper, she licked her lips. The sensual caress sent a faint hint of the sweetness of whipped cream and raspberries on her breath.

Tension cruised though his body; his cock bucked.

Height had its advantages, Jackson thought, able to see right down her bodice. The shadowed cleavage. Dark brown nipples that puckered under his appraisal, little beads his mouth watered for. Holding the phone to her cheek with two fingers, he used his thumb to stroke along her jawline, her mouth. She kissed the pad with those tempting plump lips, then, with a teasing smile, allowed the bodice to fall farther away from her body.

She wanted him to see. Wanted him to see that she needed him as badly. Her nipples were all perky, just begging for some attention. Her breathing was choppy, and mixed with the scent of raspberry, he caught the sweetness of her desire. Oh, hell, what would Nana say now if he kissed Lexi the way he wanted to?

He closed his eyes and ground his teeth to keep from doing it. In the silence came Bryan's voice through the phone line. He damned near forgot about him, Jackson realized.

In a few short weeks she'd be a married woman. The things he counted on in their relationship would be coming to an end. He needed her laughter and smiles like he needed to breathe. He needed her wisdom and understanding, her affection and sincerity, as bad as he needed the sugar of her candy kisses.

What an idiot he was to know only now why he rarely dated. Because no woman had ever been able to compare. No woman had ever measured up. Alexis Payton was the woman he wanted, but he'd taken for granted her being there, never thought about the day she'd be gone.

That all changed with Nana's warning in the salon.

His chest ached. His throat burned.

Confused, Jackson fixed his eyes on the delicate curve of her ear and focused there. He knew what he wanted. Her. But if Lexi wanted it, too, would she be engaged? Would she be standing here in a wedding dress? He'd told her in her flower shop that the decision had to be hers. Apparently the decision had been made. He swallowed, a victim of his own game—the fruit kisses had been fun, but he was going to pay the ultimate price.

His broken heart.

Alexis was an engaged woman, and no matter what he wanted, one truth remained the same. While Lexi had just said good-bye to Bryan, it hadn't been forever and it never would be.

Bryan was between them.

Jackson felt the tension recoil in his spine. He was the other man. Bryan's place was secure because she was marrying him. Completely numb, Jackson hardly noticed when Lexi went to the dressing room to change, and couldn't wait for the day to draw to an end. He needed the fuck out of here.

Six

Holding a glass of iced tea in each hand, Jackson guided Nana across the lawn to a grouping of chairs set up in the cool shade of an aged cotton tree and away from the noisier events of the cookout. It wasn't that Nana needed the assistance—Lord knew, she had more energy than Jackson did half the time—but her hand resting on his forearm was much more about the years of established innocent flirting.

"Can I get you anything else, beautiful?" Jackson waited until she was settled in a chair before he handed her the glass of tea.

"Just your company."

He smiled as he adjusted his frame into the chair beside hers, and took a long sip before replying. "With pleasure." Lounging back, he rested his arm on the back of Nana's chair.

"I hope next Saturday is as lovely as today has been. There isn't a single cloud in the sky." Nana sighed as she slanted her head back and looked up at the heavens.

Wishing to avoid thoughts about the following Saturday and Alexis' pending nuptials, Jackson studied Nana's stunning profile. As the matriarch of the family, her bloodlines were strong, dominating her daughter's and grandchildren's features. Other than the faint laugh lines about her mouth and eyes, the brown complexion of her skin was smooth and supple. The tone was beautifully even.

Although Lexi had managed to keep her braids for a few more days, and Nana's head was covered with a sprinkling of salt in her pepper shade of freshly washed and pressed hair, in profile and facial structure they closely resembled each other.

"As man of honor, are you going to be throwing Lexi a bachelorette party?" Nana tapped Jackson on the knee as she spoke, laughter tinting her tone.

"Yeah, I have a little something planned." A frown tugged at his lips and he had to work against it. The coiling tension in his gut and chest tightened. The party he wanted to have included two people. Alexis, him, and a tangle of bedsheets.

Suppressing a groan, his mind went back to the dance studio, where it'd been fixated. Even after he'd blown his wad down her throat, things hadn't changed. Lexi hadn't said a word about ending the engagement, but moved forward with her plans, greeting out-of-town family as they arrived. And the fool that he was, he kept his mouth shut because above all else, he wanted her happy. Even if he died inside.

Jackson shook his head to clear the thoughts. Lexi was a strong, intelligent woman. If she didn't want to marry Bryan, she wouldn't have agreed. And if she wanted to call it off, she would have, no matter the time or money that had gone into the planning.

There was this little nagging feeling that Lexi couldn't have sexed him so passionately if she felt nothing for him at all. But even all that good sexing hadn't convinced her that there was something powerful between them. More than merely a sexual distraction until she entered her husband's bed.

Rage pulsed hot and ugly through his blood. He was jealous. Damned jealous. He shook inside, but attempted to remain still, breathing out his nose and counting backward from ten.

Clearing his throat, he glanced over at Nana, who had her eyes fixed on him as she sipped her tea. He forced a light smile, and though his body ached just saying it, he made himself ask, "Are you excited about the wedding?"

"You know, Jackson, I always thought it would be you."

Silence spilled around them. *I want it to be me.*

A minute skulked by.

"What would?" He knew what she meant already.

"I thought you and Lexi would marry. Your grandma thought so, too. Her momma and I have been talking about it for years, wondering when you two kids were going to realize you were in love."

Again there was silence and Jackson wondered if the trembling in his soul could be seen or heard by Nana.

"You are in love with her, aren't you, Jackson." It wasn't a question.

His heart thumped against his ribs. Unable to take the intensity of her tone and penetrating ebony eyes, he glanced away, over to the gathering of people enjoying the cookout. The yard was filled with familiar faces of loved ones, family and friends alike.

Did Nana's years of life garner her a wisdom of his heart, or was he really that transparent?

He loved Alexis. He had for years. They were friends, but there was more. Something deeper, stronger, explosive. *Something that'll break my heart.*

"You've been such a large part of her life and you're family to us. I always thought you and Lexi were right for each other." There was sadness in her voice so deep and profound that Jackson couldn't bear to look at her without revealing his soul. Instead he kept his gaze roving over those who had come to celebrate Alexis' day.

"Bryan just arrived," Nana said softly.

Jackson nodded but didn't look. He couldn't. Seeing them together stirred pain.

Nana cleared her throat and kept her voice low when she continued. "I want Lexi happy. That's it. I'm excited about the wedding because it's a celebration unlike any our family has ever had. We've come from the bottom, Jackson." She patted his leg. "You know our past."

Jackson nodded, knowing their family history well and understanding Nana's pride in getting her grandchildren educated and successful in their lives. Alexis' brother, Allen, could have ended up in jail or worse—dead. Alicia could have dropped out of high school when she'd gotten pregnant, and lived off welfare. But because of the tight weave of love in the Payton household, neither of them did.

Nana had every right to be proud.

"Look at Alexis. She's a business owner. An entrepreneur."

Jackson couldn't keep his eyes from searching through all the faces until his gaze landed upon Lexi, wearing black cotton capris and a pink halter top that showed off her lush figure. He wanted her. His body's response was immediate and overwhelming.

She was in the center of a group of women, her head bent close to that of Toni Ray, the woman who owned the photography studio next to Lexi's shop, and had agreed to shoot the wedding. They were laughing about something, but in Jackson's opinion Lexi's happiness didn't reach her dazzling dark eyes.

"Yes," said Nana. "I'm excited about the wedding because I want her to be happy. I've put my heart into this wedding. Planned everything just as right as I can get it. But the whole affair could be tossed out with last week's garbage if I caught wind it wasn't bringing her joy."

Nana's gentle touch on Jackson's shoulder brought his gaze back to her face, though with a slight reluctance to look away from Lexi. Nana's eyes brimmed with unshed tears and caused his chest to clench up tight. She asked, "Does she look happy to you?"

For a third time silence drifted over them as they looked at Alexis across the large yard. Bryan was making his way toward her, barely greeting his other soon-to-be family members.

Nana stood. "So much tea has got this old lady running for the pot." She put her glass on a nearby table. "You'll do the right thing, won't you, Jackson?"

"Yes, Nana." His voice cracked slightly but he didn't think she noticed, or if she had, she ignored it. He'd do the right thing—he just had no idea what in the hell that was.

"You're such a good boy." She patted his shoulder and smiled as she moved away.

Jackson sat motionless for a while, contemplating every-thing Nana had said. He wished he had a better understand-ing of what she was alluding to. Was she putting down a stern warning to keep his newly recognized feelings quiet, or offer-ing him up an opportunity to go after Lexi?

With the wedding one week away, there wasn't much time to think about it. If he was going to act, it needed to be soon. Looking back toward Lexi, he saw that Bryan had made his way to her side and was hovering around her like a bee at a honeycomb.

But her groom-to-be just didn't fit by her side the way Jack-son thought a man should. *The way I do.* Alexis and Bryan didn't belong together and the more he saw them, the more convinced he was of it.

Alexis should be by his side, in his bed.

Needing a distraction, he left his seat and found Allen at a domino table. After giving him a hug and a clap on the back, Jackson joined the game.

Alexis tried to keep from looking over to the pair of chairs tucked beneath the cotton tree where Jackson and Nana had been involved in what appeared to be a serious discussion. Her ears had burned like crazy.

She'd been about to casually join them by approaching with an offer of food, when Bryan had arrived and completely monopolized her time. She was barely able to move without him underfoot, and he'd checked his watch a thousand times, clearly wondering how long he'd have to stick around. It'd been so obvious that he didn't want to be at the cookout, she wondered why he'd come. He'd been bothersome, nothing but agitated and oddly distracted.

By the time she was able to break free from her fiancé,

both chairs were long empty. Disappointed, she went to them anyhow and sat down alone, settling a half-eaten plate of food in her lap.

"What's the matter, baby?" Momma sat down beside her.

"I just have a lot of work to do. I should be at the shop getting all the flowers ready. Do you have any idea how many stems it takes to make a bouquet?"

"Don't fret about it. Sue's at the shop and can handle it for the afternoon." Momma picked a handful of chips off Lexi's plate. "Is there something else? The wedding?"

For a moment, Alexis thought about telling her momma everything bothering her, starting at the beginning—that she'd never even accepted Bryan's marriage proposal—and finishing up with the most devastating. She was in love with another man. Jackson. She licked her lips, the memory of his taste still so strong.

But the worry in Momma's eyes kept her from spilling. All the hours of love her family had put into preparing the perfect wedding couldn't be selfishly tossed aside just because she'd been a coward and kept her love to herself. They shouldn't have to pay for her mistakes. Guilt sluiced through her.

A single hot tear slid down her cheek. Instead of swiping it with the back of her hand and drawing attention, she turned her head away so Momma wouldn't see. The burning at the back of her eyes continued, but she sucked in a few breaths and tried to calm herself. When she glanced down, the blueberry pie on her plate had her thinking back to a comment of Jackson's about blueberry candy. Her cheeks heated as her gaze traveled to Jackson. He sat playing dominoes with her brother and several of her male cousins.

Allen smacked the table hard and the ivory bones jumped. Laughter erupted from the table as his points were marked down onto the tab of paper where they were keeping score. She smiled.

"Alexis?"

She brought her attention back to the conversation she'd been having. "Yeah, Momma?"

"Is there something else?"

"No." This wedding was as much for them as for her. *All of them*, she thought, glancing around at the large extended family who'd trekked from all over the state and country to be a part of her wedding celebration. This was bigger than her. This was a Payton wedding, and no matter what her future held, she wouldn't rob them of enjoying the day.

But mostly this wedding, with the big fluffy snowy dress with the rhinestones and pearl-encrusted bodice and fifteen-foot train, the white chocolate cake with raspberry filling, the white flowers, the pressed unbraided hair . . . it was all for her momma and nana, who would have given her the world no matter what sacrifice it cost them.

And in return she gave up love. But she was determined to be happy—at least satisfied—with Bryan. He was successful, good-looking, and fit. He treated her well, was respectful. Caring. Her feelings weren't his fault. Her sacrifice was minor in comparison with what Nana and Momma had given to her.

All Alexis gave up was Jackson.

And passion. And fire. And tender kisses that curled her toes and dampened her panties. And laughter.

Yeah, laughter. Only Jackson could give her those things.

Fighting another tear, Alexis' gaze found Bryan. Bryan offered her a way to repay her family's love.

"A penny for your thoughts," Jackson said, unexpectedly at her side. "A million for your decision."

Looking at his handsome face, the hint of dimples chiseled

into his cheeks, she was hit with an overwhelming rush of desire that puckered her nipples and soaked the lace between her legs. The full impact of what she sacrificed halted breathing. Her throat went dry. She swallowed back the tears.

Shaking her head, she tried to imagine Bryan and all the reasons she was marrying him. They were valid, but that didn't stop the pain of losing the man whose game of fruit-candy kisses made her long for things to be different. And only she controlled that decision.

Seven

I can't go through with it.

Alexis sat on the edge of her bed, her gaze fixed on the wedding gown hanging in front of her mirrored closet. She'd picked it up two nights ago, but hadn't had the desire to look at it. Now, feeling the mounting anxiety of the mere forty-eight hours remaining before she was due at the church, she wanted one more peek at the monstrosity she was supposed to wear.

After removing the clear plastic covering, protecting the fine cloth and adornments from gathering dust, she'd fluffed the skirt and extended the abundant train to its full length.

She'd wanted an ivory gown, something plain and simple that flowed around her body. Alexis could do without the miles of netting that kept the skirt all puffy, scratched her legs, and made her look ten pounds heavier, even though she'd lost seven to get into it.

She glared at the bodice and at each chunky rhinestone and oversized pearl. A frustrated smirk made its way past her lips. This dress had never been her pick—just as Bryan hadn't. But she was picking now.

She didn't want to be Bryan's wife. She didn't want to settle. But she'd kept her mouth shut for too long. Closing her eyes, she thought of the past weekend, when her family had gathered for a barbecue.

They'd come together to see her join her life with the man of her choosing. They'd come to see her happy—but after countless hours of thinking of her loved ones, she had to believe that if they knew she wasn't, they'd understand her decision.

Taking a deep breath, she thought about Jackson and the passion he'd made her feel. And more important, the history they shared. He was the one who'd told her she had a choice. Until today she hadn't believed it, feeling so trapped in wanting the happiness of those she cared about, she risked her own.

Jackson wanted her—that was clear—but even if he wasn't in love with her, didn't feel as deeply as she did, she still couldn't bind her life to a man who made her feel nothing but cold.

Opening her eyes, she just wished that guilt hadn't kept her bottled up so long. She wished she hadn't waited to share how she felt. She could have saved herself and her family a lot of time and trouble—had she only followed her heart.

Nana had hand made every single wedding invitation, using calligraphy she'd learned at a San Diego Parks and Recreation class. Momma had helped make the bridesmaid dresses, and so the man of honor would match, she'd even hand sewn a silk tie and vest for Jackson.

"Oh, Jackson." Alexis heaved a sigh and tossed herself back on the bed to stare at the ceiling. Why hadn't he kissed her six months ago like he did in the flower shop? Why hadn't she kissed him? They kissed all the time—candy kisses she could have easily deepened.

She giggled. It didn't matter anymore why things had happened in the order they did. All that mattered now was seeing Jackson and telling him the decisions she'd made.

Couldn't wait to give him a candy kiss.

Rolling to her side, Alexis caught sight of the wicker basket filled with cellophane-wrapped fruit candies she kept on her dresser. She got to her feet, grabbed the basket, and took the first candy in her hand, wanting to remember the tenderness of their game.

She opened the candy and plopped it in her mouth. *Coconut.* Sugary sweetness flooded her mouth and she smacked her lips. Sucking on the candy, she moved to her dress and held it up to her body. "Oh, brother," she said, giggling at the thought of getting out of wearing the hideous dress. The coconut candy dropped from her lips onto the dress, followed by sugary drool.

"Perfect." She rolled her eyes, grabbing a tissue in an attempt to mop up the fruity stain. Those little beads Nana loved so much were now sticky and splashed with the scent of summer and fruit.

At least with the coconut candy stain, the dress was uniquely her own. She was laughing as she fluffed the gown and checked out the spots of drying candy when the doorbell rang.

While Jackson walked up the sidewalk to Lexi's home, Nana's words continued to haunt him as they had the last few days. He still wasn't sure what she'd been trying to tell him, but one thing was for certain: He needed to talk to Lexi. Needed to tell her how he felt about her. Needed to know what was in her heart.

It'd been foolish of him to wait.

With just two days left before she married another, he figured his chance had come and gone. He drew a deep breath. For his sanity, he wanted to tell her. Wanted to watch her eyes while she learned the truth. Prayed to God she'd want to continue their friendship after.

Holding his breath, his chest aching, he jammed his finger against the bell. He didn't have to wait long for Lexi to answer. She stood in the doorway wearing blue jersey shorts and a Chargers T-shirt. A girl after his heart, he silently noted, his gaze moving over breasts that perfectly filled out the numbers. Blood filled his cock; he wanted her instantly.

"Jackson."

Her voice sounded light. Airy.

"Hey, you."

Her cheeks were lit with an inner glow he hadn't seen on her for a while. Her dark eyes shimmered and a sensual smile curved her full lips—damn, he wanted to kiss them. Wanted to back her against the wall and fuck her nice and slow until she admitted she loved him.

He settled for a candy kiss. Pressing his mouth to hers, he kept the kiss short because the last thing he wanted was to forget why he was there. Her lips opened slightly and her tongue touched his, but he pulled back, smacking. "Coconut? A new flavor?" He licked his lips and arched an eyebrow.

She winked at him but changed the subject. "Come in. There's something I want to show you. Something I *have* to tell you."

Jackson stepped into the house and closed the door behind him. "Your hairdo? It's been years since you've had the braids out. I like it."

"I don't. The braids are going back in as soon as I get the chance." She touched a hand to her straight hair and smoothed down a flyaway strand. "Come in here." She curled her finger and Jackson followed into her bedroom. Glancing at the bed, he wondered what she'd do if he tossed her on it and stripped off her clothing.

Alexis grabbed his hand and pulled him down onto the bed beside her, facing the draped-out wedding gown.

"Do you like it?" Her voice was husky and held the hint of laughter.

He slanted a look at her. "Do you like it?"

She laughed, the rich sound filling him with desire. "No." She freed her fingers and rested her hand on his shoulder, then leaned into him. "No. It's ugly and gaudy and loud. Everything I didn't want."

Her voice was filled with laughter. Her lush bottom lip was tucked between her teeth, but the corners of her mouth tipped upward and her eyes shone with amusement.

"Then why are you happy?"

"Because I stained it."

"I don't see anything."

"It's almost dry, but the beads are sticky. I'll never have to wea . . ." Her voice trailed off, her smile faded slightly, as she stared at his face. "Jackson—" She broke off and turned toward him, touching his cheek with her fingertips, curling her hand behind his head, and dragging him downward. "What's wrong?" she whispered, licking her lips.

Jackson focused. If he kissed her now, he'd forget

how badly he needed to talk to her. Putting his hand on her shoulder, he eased away. "Lexi, I need to tell you something."

"Yeah, baby, tell me anything."

He took a gulping breath, his gaze on her face. He touched her face, ran his thumb across her lush lips, smoothed down the slope of her neck. "Sugar, this is serious. I l—"

The phone chattered loudly from the table beside the bed, and Lexi's gaze swung toward it. Putting up a single finger to tell him to hold on, she kissed him quick on the lips, then leaned back and answered the ringing phone.

"Hello?" Her brows furrowed together; then her lids slid closed. He saw a slight tremor move through her body. She was nodding her head, but saying nothing.

"What is it?" he asked, softly enough for her to hear but not the person on the other end of the line.

She didn't respond to him, but spoke into the phone. "Yeah, I know where it is. Not far from my shop. Fine, I'll meet you there in a half hour." She hung up.

Her gaze found his and melded. Jackson tried to read her, but didn't understand what he was seeing. Her hand curled into his, and she squeezed tenderly. "We'll talk later."

Later? Later would be too late.

"I have to go," Lexi said, letting go of his hand and slipping her feet into a pair of flip-flop sandals. "Can you lock up for me?" She didn't wait for a response before she'd grabbed her purse and was out of sight.

Alexis sat at a table by the window of her favorite coffee shop. She sipped from a bottle of water, her nerves too wound for her to even think about coffee. She glanced at her cell phone, noting thirty-five minutes since the call, and wondered if the woman would show or stand her up.

As her gaze lifted, she saw a young Hispanic woman come through the door, her long dark hair free around her shoulders. The woman caught her eye and moved toward her.

Alexis studied the woman, seeing the scared look within the lady's brown eyes and how her hand trembled as she lightly touched her stomach. *A rounded belly that was at least eight months pregnant.*

Alarm shot through Alexis, but she remained still and pretended to be unaffected as the woman slid into a chair across from her. "You're Alexis Payton, right?" she asked, a hint of Spanish accenting her voice.

"Yes."

"I'm Maria Chavez. Bryan's ex-girlfriend. Has he ever mentioned me?" Maria's hand stroked protectively across her extended womb.

Alexis shook her head, but couldn't find her voice, could hardly think at all over her heartbeat. A shimmer of tears sprang to Maria's eyes, but she remained poised and confident. She cleared her throat and proceeded.

"I didn't think he'd go through with the weddin'. I mean, I thought Bryan did it just to make me jealous so I'd change my mind about kickin' him out, but I guess I was wrong. He is going to marry you."

Alexis nodded, too stunned to say anything, though denying it lingered on her tongue.

"You're a rebound." The meaning was harsh, but Maria's tone indicated she meant no malice. The woman rushed on. "I'm eight months pregnant. Bryan's baby. I was tired of livin' with him with no commitment, so I told him to marry me or leave."

"He left?"

Maria nodded, her tanned skin flushed. "Then I told him I was pregnant. I thought he'd propose for sure. The next thing I heard, he was marryin' you. He wanted me to come crawlin' back to him. I didn't. And I won't."

"He didn't come back when you told him you were having his baby?" Alexis' mind whirled through her hasty relationship with Bryan, her body filling with relief rather than anger—at least he couldn't be too angry when she told him the wedding was off and they were over. What kind of man left his girlfriend and child? It just didn't seem like the Bryan she knew. Then again, she didn't know him all that well.

"Have you slept with him?" Maria asked.

Alexis shook her head. She could see the visible sigh of relief shudder through Maria's heavy body. Her hand lightly caressed her extended stomach.

Maria took a deep breath, then let it out slowly before she went on. "I think he still loves me. I mean"—she drew another deep breath, her voice cracking—"I'm sure you're nice enough, but we're supposed to be a family. He brings me things for the baby and took me to the hospital a few weeks ago when I was havin' some pains."

"Why are you here?" Alexis knew why Maria was there. She wanted Bryan back. She wanted her baby to have a daddy. And Alexis knew why she herself kept sitting there. She wanted Maria to have him. She'd grown up without her father and though she'd had a nice life, no child deserved it.

Just as she didn't want to settle for second best, she didn't want to ever be second either, and that's exactly what she'd be getting. Maria was right. She was a rebound for Bryan, and Bryan was an excuse for her to keep from facing her real emotions. She closed her eyes for a moment, drawing in the coffee aroma in a deep breath.

"I want my man back," Maria said softly, a single tear making its way past her lashes.

"You'll have him." *And I'll have mine.*

Eight

Closing her eyes, Alexis leaned her head back against the car seat. Flashing images of Maria's swelled stomach and sad eyes renewed her sense of urgency. That, and the fact that the day after tomorrow she was supposed to walk down the aisle robbing an unborn child of its father and Maria of the man she loved.

Her heart ached, but it wasn't sadness that caused it to pound rapidly or her lungs to feel as if they'd caught fire. It wasn't regret. *It was elation.* Alexis finally felt free—free to admit her feelings to Jackson and hope that the heat they shared was based on emotion.

Withdrawing her cell from her purse, she dialed Bryan's number. Her fingers shook with an overabundance of caffeine, the effect of three cups of coffee she'd indulged in after abandoning her water while listening to Maria explain her situation. One mug in the afternoon was too many and with the multiple refills, Alexis knew she'd be paying the price with a sleepless night.

The phone rang. It rang again, but no one answered. It rang a third time. Lexi was about to hang up, not wanting to leave a message on his voice mail, when Bryan finally answered. "Bryan here." His voice was gruff, as if he'd been sleeping.

Alexis glanced at her watch. It was early evening, not even dinnertime yet, and his tone surprised her. "Hey, Bryan. It's me, Lexi."

"Alexis? What's the matter?"

Not a damned thing, she thought with a smile. *We're not getting married.* "We need to talk." She paused for a moment, thinking over the best location for them to meet, wanting it to be on mutual territory so they'd both be on equal footing. "Do you think you could meet me at the marina? It's important."

There was a slight pause, but Alexis didn't miss the heavy sigh that whistled through the earpiece of her phone.

"Yeah, sure. I need about an hour to wrap up some things here. I have some mail that needs to get out before we leave for our honeymoon."

There'll be no honeymoon. Repressing the shiver running down her spine, Alexis agreed to meet Bryan in an hour at the Seafood Shack, the locals' favorite place to get fish-and-chips and a soda.

Arriving before Bryan, Alexis purchased a bottle of water, then waited. The time slipped away quickly and before long Bryan approached, his thick brows pulled together and worry lines marring his forehead. "Hello, Alexis."

"Hi, Bryan." Alexis stood to greet him. He squeezed her

shoulder, leaning toward her for a kiss, but she slanted her face away.

"What's the matter?"

Alexis almost smiled. He was pinning her with a stare that conveyed he was expecting—even wanting—bad news. But it wasn't. Not for either of them.

"I thought we should talk." Alexis took a step and Bryan moved with her down the uneven boards of the docks, away from shore. On either side of them, boats gently rested upon the forgiving water between Coronado Island and the mainland of San Diego.

The loud clatter of seagulls and the waves caressing the white sand beaches filled the gaping silence, though above the heavy beat of her heart, Alexis barely heard. It was time to face the truth. They'd never been anything more than friends. Pretending otherwise had gotten them engaged and nearly down the aisle.

For both their sakes—for Jackson's—it was time to set things straight

"Bryan," Alexis began slowly, a large lump lodged in her throat. Her heart was racing, and only the seriousness of this kept her from smiling as she did what she should've done long ago. "Bryan, we can't get married."

His strides faltered, but he didn't stop moving down the docks. His nonreaction had her wondering if he'd heard her. Only the continuous bobbing of his Adam's apple gave him away. She heard him take a shaky breath before he spoke. "What are you talking about, Alexis? The wedding's in two days."

"Today at the coffee shop, I met a woman. She was pregnant." There was quiet again, interrupted only by wind against the water. She swallowed, then swiped her damp palms against her shorts. "Your baby, Bryan."

He stopped walking, and turned away from her. For a moment Alexis worried he'd walk away without offering an explanation. Before she had a chance to confirm the end of their engagement.

Staring at his back, she watched as his shoulders slumped and a shiver passed through him. His hands balled at his sides, as he gathered up courage, she guessed.

Bryan turned and faced her, his eyes filled with regret. "I didn't mean to hurt you."

"You're not."

He pursed his lips. "I'm not?"

"No."

A muscle on his neck bunched and twitched. "I should have told you about it."

"Tell me now. Tell me now, Bryan, all of it." She'd heard one side of the story already, and his side didn't matter all that much. What did matter was making him see where he belonged. Not with her. Not by her side, but by Maria's.

He nodded. "I'm going to be a father. My ex—my ex is pregnant."

"And you were going to marry me and never say a word?" Though she had plenty of justification, she couldn't muster anger. Not when she was filled with so much relief.

"No. Yeah. I guess. Hell, Alexis, I don't know." Bryan's confusion poured out of his mouth, and she just listened. "I love her. I've always loved her, but she kicked me out and pushed me away. Gave me an ultimatum. Marry her or leave."

"And you left?"

"It's not like I wanted to, but she forced me. She was pressuring me, wanting to go to the courthouse. To get married before the baby was born."

"You should have."

"But—"

"You were willing to marry me. Same commitment, except you love *her*. You're having a baby with her."

"Are you suggesting I go back to Maria? Marry her?" Bryan stepped back, stumbling over a board, then caught himself before he fell.

Biting down on the inside of her cheek, Alexis tried to keep from laughing. This charade was almost over, and breathing seemed easier. "Yes, Bryan, I guess I am."

"You're not mad?"

She couldn't help the laughter as she shook her head. "No. I'm furious. You're a selfish asshole who almost stole my happiness by forcing me into a loveless marriage. Did you ever once consider me?"

His chin dropped slightly as he shook his head.

She smirked. "It doesn't matter anyway, Bryan. I was ending the engagement today. I'm not in love with you."

His brows came together, wounded pride darkening his face. "Why did you accept my proposal?"

"I never did, but once you put that ring on my finger, I felt roped into expectations. And I was afraid to go after the man I really wanted."

"Jackson."

"Yes." Alexis turned the rock on her finger and worked the band free. She was grinning as she handed it back to him. "I don't need this, but Maria needs you. Your baby needs you."

Nodding, he accepted the ring and dropped it into his pocket. "I guess I'll start calling my family and letting them know it's off for Saturday."

This time it was Alexis who nodded. She closed her eyes, breathing a sigh of relief, her mind going over how to tell her family the wedding was canceled.

How to tell Jackson she loved him.

Bryan smiled, the first genuine one she thought she'd ever seen. "Come on, I'll walk you back to your car."

"You know, I think I'll stay here for a while. I could use the fresh air and need some time to think."

"You're sure you're not upset?"

She shook her head. "I'd be kicking your ass if I wasn't so relieved."

Before she knew it Bryan was gone and she was alone with the fading sun, the golden glow of the orange-cast sky, and a host of clucking hungry seagulls.

Turning back, she retraced the way they'd walked down the docks until the deep water shallowed and the beach extended for miles in each direction. Slipping off her sandals, Alexis jumped to the sugary sand, sinking her toes into the sun-warmed grains, then strolled along the water's edge so the coolness of the waves could lick against her ankles.

There was one man on her mind. One man who needed to hear her. Hear "I love you." She just had to figure out the right way to say it to the one man who mattered most to her.

Jackson Lyle.

Jackson Lyle with an incredible smile and sweet lingering kisses. The boy she'd once shared a playpen with, learned how to jump rope from, and chased relentlessly in games of tag was now a man.

A man who showed her she had passion and a woman's

desires. A man who made her feel alive and reduced her to laughter with ease. A man who was mindful of her thoughts, respectful of her opinions, and considerate and caring.

The boy of her childhood was now the man of her dreams.

The only man she'd ever loved.

But did he love her?

Does he want to be with me?

Alexis nearly stumbled. Glancing at the darkened sky, she was surprised to see how quickly the sun had sunk beyond the horizon to let free the twinkling of twilight's first offering of stars. The cool ocean winds danced across her face, around her bare legs.

Banding her arms around her middle to ward off the chill, she turned her thoughts to how to tell him. Tell him the wedding was off. Tell him that he was the man she wanted touching her, caressing her, sexing her, loving her.

Reaching into her pocket, she took out a candy and put it in her mouth. The kisses—these sugar kisses—they were only for Jackson.

Nine

Jackson lay on his back, staring at the ceiling. The pale milky light of dawn crept in through the half-open blinds, the cool ocean breeze fluttering the light drapery. It'd been hours since he'd awakened, aching for Lexi. Since then, sleep had eluded him.

He'd be the man of honor tomorrow when her brother, Allen, walked down the aisle and gave her away. And for Lexi, he'd keep his mouth shut though every fiber of his being wanted to shout, to scream, to fall upon his knees and beg for her not to go through with it. And he'd tried to tell her how he felt, but she hadn't heard him out.

Feeling like his heart was being torn from his chest, he groaned and tossed his forearm over his eyes, trying to block out the lasting image of her smiling face as she giggled about the candy stain on her dress.

Instinctively, he licked his lips. There, lingering in his mouth, was the hint of coconut, reminding him of the sweetness of her fruity kisses. But tonight, lonely and aching, the flavor felt like a dagger to his gut.

For Alexis Payton he'd sacrifice his happiness to ensure hers. He'd hold his tongue about his feeling that Bryan was wrong for her, even though it was killing him inside. Even though it meant living a lifetime without the woman he loved.

Kicking the covers from his feet, Jackson rose from the bed and moved to the bathroom sink to toss cold water over his face. He tried to think back to when he'd first recognized how much he loved Lexi, and realized there had never been a time when he hadn't. It'd taken losing her to recognize it.

She was an intricate part of who he was, vital to his existence.

As the water cooled the burning pain behind his eyes, Jackson's mind turned to the phone call she'd received and the way she'd rushed out of her house. But a light tap at his front door interrupted his thoughts about who had called Lexi.

He quickly moved to the door and tugged it open. There, illuminated by the mild glow of the streetlight, as if conjured up by a dream, was Lexi. Opaque ocean mist whirled around her feet.

"You, again," he said, laughter tainting his tone as he stepped back to drink in the sight of her. The damp sea air curled the hair around her face, which her momma had spent hours blowing straight. She wore the same blue jersey shorts and Chargers T-shirt she'd worn when he'd seen her last. With the exception of her sandals. Instead of adorning her pedicured feet, they hung limply from one hand. "Have you been drinking?" he teased.

"Not this time."

"Crying?"

"No," she laughed. "I haven't been crying. But I have been out all night and I'm freezing." She stepped into the house without further invitation.

Jackson stepped back and allowed her entry. He shut the door and leaned against it to keep from chasing after her, pulling her into his arms, ridding her of her clothes, and making love to her until not a single inch of skin was cold. Blood rushed to his cock and he bit back a groan.

"I'm sorry to wake you, again." She tossed a glance back at him as she moved toward his sofa.

"Don't be. I couldn't sleep."

Lexi sat down, sighing as she sank into the pillows. The wistful breath made his dick throb, the memory of her breath on his skin. Her mouth.

"Sit with me." She patted the pillow beside her.

There was no way to hide the erection in his shorts, no way to ease off the need coursing through his body. Balling his hands, he stood there breathing heavy. Even across the room he could smell the saltiness of the ocean, the sweetness of her skin.

She patted the spot next to her again, and like an obedient puppy he went to her. He touched her shoulder, ran his palm down her arm, and took her hand.

She smiled, twining their fingers. "Jackson, I have to tell you something."

"Anything. You can talk to me." He cleared his throat, trying to swallow down the dryness, the tightness in his chest, the burning in his gut.

Her delicate fingers stroked softly across his hand. The serene look on Lexi's face mirrored her softly spoken words. "Jackson, I'm in love with you."

He wasn't sure he heard her correctly. Was it his imagination? His heart chose a rapid cadence, drumming loudly behind his ears. Beads of sweat gathered on his brow, the effort to keep from touching her draining.

She touched his knee, her caress light and seductive. His reaction was immediate; his cock bucked hard, drawing her gaze. She smiled and touched him through his shorts, tightening his sac. She teased him with her fingertips, stroking along the ridge, down and up again. "Did you hear me? I love you, Jackson."

He cleared his throat, but his voice shook anyway. "You're getting married tomorrow," he managed, the words biting.

She smiled at him, with all the brilliance of the sun. "No. I'm not."

No wedding? "What happened?" His heart thumped; a tremor moved through his body.

Alexis tried to keep her fingers from shaking as she smoothed them across his rocked-up dick. Tried to keep from trembling. With want. With need. With fear. She'd confessed her love for him. He said nothing, though his pulse beat rapidly beneath his smooth brown skin she wanted to taste with her tongue.

Her gaze trailed over him, his smooth naked chest, his chiseled abdomen, the line of hair that dipped beneath the waistband of shorts hanging low on his hips. The thick length of hard flesh she ached to have inside her.

She wanted to touch him, to fill her senses with his texture and heat, to open her legs and allow him to end the emptiness inside her.

Her breath held in her lungs as she waited for him to

reply. She glanced at his face, staring into dark captivating eyes.

He reached for her, cupping her jaw in his hand, his thumb lightly tracing the line of her lips. "What happened?" he repeated, his breathing slow and shallow.

She kissed the pad of his thumb, touching the tip of her tongue to his skin. He groaned in response, moving toward her slightly.

"You owe me a million dollars." She couldn't repress a smile. "I called off the wedding."

"Why?" he whispered, his lips hovering scant inches over hers. His heat warming her skin.

Bryan and Maria weren't relevant. Though Maria acted as a catalyst to end the engagement, the truth was, Lexi would have found a way out, would've never walked down the aisle to say "I do" with Bryan. *She'd never loved anyone but Jackson.*

"There's no room in my heart for him, when the only man I've ever wanted is *you*." She closed her eyes, absorbing his nearness, refusing the burning tears behind her eyes. Fear had no place here. These words had to be said. Whether they were emotions Jackson shared or not, she simply couldn't keep them bottled up any longer.

"I'm glad." He brushed his lips over hers, a caress that caused her to shiver. "I'm glad. It would've killed me to let you go through with it." He kissed her again, but the tender touch of his lips didn't linger. Just a quick glide of tongue.

She leaned into him, wanting him to deepen the kiss, to end the torment of his teasing lips. She curled around his dick, feeling the same pulse of arousal beat in her clit. She pressed her mouth to his skin, felt his heartbeat against her lips, licked across his nipple until it puckered and his cock jumped.

"I still have to tell all my family the wedding is off." Each word was separated by her feathering of kisses across his chest. He touched her shoulder, smoothed his hand down her spine, curved around her ass.

Jackson's lips touched her temple, and the rumble of his words vibrated through her body. "Why? Why call off the wedding?" His other hand slid between them, covering a breast and tweaking the nipple.

Alexis sighed, lolling her head to the side, and arched her back to give him room to work the sensitive flesh, every movement of his hand wetting her panties. She was panting. "I have no groom."

His mouth touched her neck. His tongue slid down to the base of her throat. "I could stand in."

Banding her arms around his strong back, she ended his kisses before she was lost in them. Tucking her forehead beneath his chin, she smothered a laugh against his skin. *Her hero* to the rescue, always ready and willing to save her from the worst quandaries. "You silly. You can't stand in as groom and not stand in as husband." Leaning back, she reached up and kissed him soundly on the lips, knowing her breath lingered with cherries.

He tried to deepen her kiss, touching his tongue to her lips. "Gimme some sugar, and I'll be a stand-in husband, too."

She laughed and licked his mouth with a quick swipe of tongue that had him grumbling. "Jackson, you can't stand in to protect me from admitting the truth to my family. I was an idiot to have let things progress as far as they have. They'll be disappointed"—Lexi sighed—"but it's my responsibility. I'm tired of pretending."

Jackson shook his head. He'd done this all wrong. He'd been taken so off guard by her declaration, he'd forgotten to tell her what he'd wanted for so long to be able to say, that as in-nocent as their kissing game had started, it'd sealed his fate long ago. "Why disappoint them, Lexi? Why does it have to be pretend?"

Easing out of her embrace, he slid to the floor on his knees before her and took each of her hands in his. Brushing his thumb over her knuckles, he intended to remove the slip of gold Bryan had placed around her finger, but found it already absent. He grinned.

"I loved the look of determination in your eyes when Allen said you couldn't ride a bike without training wheels," Jackson reminisced.

"I was five."

He shrugged, then continued. "I loved the way you outran the boys on the track team—"

"You."

Jackson smiled. "Yeah, me, but you never teased about it. And remember the time you put rubbing alcohol on my mos-quito bites? It burned like hell. You should have used calamine lotion."

"I was trying to help."

"I know, and I loved you for it."

Lexi sighed. When she spoke, Jackson could hear the hitch in her voice, feel her racing pulse along her wrists. "We were kids then. We've been friends a long time."

Releasing her hands, he reached for her, brushing the curls from her cheeks, and framed her face in his palms. "What I'm trying to tell you, Alexis Payton, is that I've loved you since we were children. I love you even more today, as a man."

Lexi closed her eyes, but he wanted to see into the depths of her inner beauty. "Look at me, Lexi." He waited until she turned her attention back upon his face. "I wouldn't be pretending to stand in as your groom or pretending to stand in as your husband. I'd be honored, if you'd have me."

"What are you saying, Jackson?" she whispered, liquid welling up in her warm brown eyes.

"I'm telling you I want to marry you. That I want you to show up at the church tomorrow, just like your family is expecting, but take *me* as your husband. To be my friend. My lover. To be my wife tomorrow."

Alexis shook her head, and fat droplets spilled from her lashes. She'd been desperate to hear his feelings for her, but his words were more than she'd expected. "Jackson . . ."

"It'll be our secret, but we'll give them all the wedding."

Taking a deep breath, she tried to calm the speeding rhythm of her heart. Her body hummed with need; arousal seeped from her body; her clit tingled—every nerve ending aware of his close proximity, the heat coming off his skin, the pulsing of his hard-on, the sweetness of his words.

Leaning forward, Alexis kissed his lips, stroking her tongue along his teeth, then sweeping into his mouth, pressing her tongue to his. She nipped at his lower lip, touched his cheek with her hand, smoothing over his dimple.

He drew back a fraction of an inch, and spoke against her lips. "You were eating candy. Your sugar belongs to me."

Alexis giggled as the power of his kiss pressed her back against the couch.

"Jackson . . ." A moan escaped her parted lips, her thighs aching to wrap around his back. "Jackson, we've been friends since we were little. Tomorrow I'll be your wife. Can we start with the *lovers* thing now? Tonight?"

With a hoot of victory, Jackson was on his feet, and Alexis

yelped as he scooped her off her feet and cradled her in his arms. "Damn, sugar, that's one tempting offer." He kissed her, hard and quick. "Promise me you'll be at the church on time, and I'll give you anything you want."

"I'll be there." She wrapped her arms around his neck, wiggling her ass against his hard dick. "Now love me."

His blanket had already been kicked to the floor, his sheets already rumpled. With her in his arms, he knelt on the bed, her hands smoothing across his shoulders, down his back. As soon as her legs touched the mattress, she was turning in his embrace, sliding her hands beneath the hem of his shorts and drawing the material down as he pressed her to the bed with his massive body.

He groaned as she touched his muscular torso, chiseled pecs, carved abs, but he kept his caresses slow, his touch tender. When his fingers crept beneath her shirt rather than removing it, Alexis arched her back and pulled the Chargers jersey over her head and tossed it.

His laughter vibrated across her skin, made her pussy wet. "In a hurry?" His tongue slid across one extended nipple, leaving it damp and cold as he moved to the other and suckled it into his mouth through her lacy bra.

"Yes. Hurry," she said, wiggling her body to get rid of her shorts and panties. When she had the cloth pushed over her hips, he helped her out, his big hand shoving it down her legs so she could kick it away.

Pushing a hand between them, she closed her fingers around his cock, smoothed her thumb across his silken head to spread the pearl of pre-cum. She didn't need his lubricant. She was soaking, aching, desperate. Pulling back her knees, she arched her back off the bed and attempted to guide his dick to her opening.

A firm hand settled on her hip, stalling her movements.
He chuckled, his mouth everywhere on her. "Slow down," he
said against her lips, moving to her neck, her ears, her eyelids,
sucking beaded nipples into the heated depth of his mouth.
His tongue soothed and tormented. "We have a lifetime."

Curling her legs around the backs of his thighs, she
pushed against his hand. "I've waited a lifetime." She rolled
her hips, thrusting him several inches inside her. Her head fell
back, her eyes closed to absorb the feeling.

Above her, Jackson's massive body shuddered, restraint
gone. One hand curved around her thigh and dragged it up to
drape high over his hip, leaving her open as he rose up
slightly, then filled her completely with one deep plunge. Her
breath catching as she cried out.

Oh, shit, this wasn't going to last long, Jackson realized, her
tight pussy hugging his throbbing flesh, so hot and so wet.
Resting his weight on his forearms, he captured her mouth,
sucking her tongue, tasting the lingering cherry. Every muscle
in his back strained as he pumped into her, one long hard
stroke in, a smooth glide out.

And again he took her, filling her as she rose to meet his
thrusts. Her little throaty whimpers into his mouth were driving him insane. But it was the fluttering of her flesh, the building of climax, that had cum balling up thick at the base of his
cock.

Wanting her orgasm as badly as his own, he moved a hand
between them and brushed his thumb against her clit. One
touch and her body shook.

"Jackson," she cried out, her voice raspy.

"I'm here, sugar." And he let go, the tightening of her
pussy coaxing him easily into climax. One last thrust and he

roared, his husky voice mingling with her cries as he came hard, pouring into her.

His skin shimmered with sweat, the sheets damp around them. Jackson closed his eyes and rolled to the side, bringing Lexi with him. Drained, he gathered her close, smoothing his hands down her back.

"You didn't want slow," he whispered against her temple.

He felt her laughter. "We can do slow later. We have a lifetime."

Ten

Alone at last, in the bride room of the church, Alexis sighed with relief. Toni Ray had come with her camera, all the bridal pictures were taken, the guests had arrived, and the flowers from her shop were in place. Everything was ready. In less than an hour she'd be Jackson's wife.

Biting her bottom lip, she resisted the urge to adjust the formfitting bodice, which she'd had to lose seven pounds to get into. Alexis smiled as she thought of her morning of preparations, when she'd decided to forgo shaving her legs and use Nair to be extra smooth as she wrapped around Jackson's body later. She'd polished off with a dusting of powder to protect her skin from the irritant of the many layers of netting.

Batting at the wide skirt, she tried to push down the fluffy pure white material piled into a ball around her and was greeted by the wafting scent of coconut.

I'm a coconut snow cone.

She smiled as she caught a glimpse of herself in the mirror leaning against the far wall. The stain had completely disappeared, but the beads were still sticky. They glistened in the late-afternoon sun that streamed in through the open windows.

The gaudy rhinestones weren't ugly at all, she realized, mesmerized by the shimmer. The hideous dress she'd once resented wearing now held special meaning. She donned the wedding dress with pride.

Touching her fingertips to her pressed hair, Alexis adjusted a tiny pearl clip that held blooms of baby's breath in place. Braids were her past. She'd begin a new life with a new hairdo, she decided, actually enjoying the feel of each smooth strand.

The draft of salted sea air cooled her skin and offered a measure of rejuvenation after a long night spent in Jackson's bed. The tingling between her thighs reminded her of how well he'd loved her.

"Lexi, baby," Nana said, entering the room carrying a gift bag in one hand.

"Hi, Nana."

"You look so beautiful. Stand up, baby, so I can get a good look at you."

When Lexi complied, Nana fanned her face as she stood back appraising the gown draped over Lexi's body. "I just knew this dress was the right one for you."

"You were right. I love it." Alexis held her hands to the side, smiling as she spun in a circle, showing off all angles of the gown.

"I brought something for you." Nana extended the gift bag toward her.

"Oh, Nana, you shouldn't have."

Nana shook her head. "Jackson told me to give this to you. Said it was a gift from your groom."

The laughter lodged in Lexi's throat. "Oh." She accepted the gift bag, but resisted looking inside until she was alone. Considering last night, who knew what her groom would be giving her?

"It's almost time." Tears welled in Nana's eyes as her gaze drifted over her. "It's your wedding day, baby."

Lexi smiled. "It's a happy day, Nana." She kissed Nana's cheek. "It's a happy day."

After a moment's embrace, Nana swiped the tears from her eyes and moved to the door, wishing her love and luck. As soon as the door was closed behind her, Lexi turned her attention to the gift bag, overflowing with white tissue paper.

Withdrawing a small card, Alexis read the words aloud. *"Easier to dance for me in. Fitting of your beauty."* She moved on to the gift; her fingers wrapped around cool, smooth material, and she pulled the garment from the bag. Her eyes widened as she saw the simple sundress emerge.

It was made of fine pure silk, and the creamy color looked like butter in her hands. The tranquil lines and shape of the knee-length summer dress would be perfect near the beach.

Alexis turned her attention to her momma as she came in the door.

She twirled twice. "What do you think?"

"I think I came to soothe your nerves, but you don't need me one bit."

Alexis laughed, joy bubbling up from her chest. Leaning into her mother, she kissed her. "I need you, Momma, but not to help with my nerves."

"Not you, huh? You're not nervous?"

"Nope."

"It's going to be a whole new life."

"Yes, Momma. But I'm marrying the right man." Lexi thought of Jackson's handsome face, of his warm, understanding touch, his passionate kisses, the way he stroked her to climax.

"Well, Lexi, if you're certain, I'll go find my seat."

Alexis nodded. Her gaze followed Momma as she exited the bridal room. Her brother, Allen, stood in the open doorway, his arms crossed over his chest and a big smirk slanting his lips.

"It's not nice to lie to Momma, Lexi," Allen said once Momma was out of earshot.

Lexi's gaze snapped to his. Heat covered her cheeks. "How long have you been standing there?"

"Long enough to hear you fibbing."

The layers of fluff puffed around her as she sat down on the bench, attempting to ignore her brother's teasing. "I didn't lie to Momma."

Laughing, Allen came into the room and placed his hand reassuringly upon Alexis' shoulder. "Sure you did, little sis. Jackson told me."

"Jackson told you what?" She bit her bottom lip and waited.

Allen leaned forward and whispered in her ear, the amusement clear in his tone, "That he's your groom."

"Why'd he do that?"

Through a chuckle, Allen answered, "Probably so I wouldn't knock the snot out of him when he came forward at the end of the aisle to claim you instead of Bryan."

"You would have hit him?"

He lifted an eyebrow at her, to further escalate the tease. "No. I'm happy you came to your senses. Jackson's family and the two of you hooking up is cool. It's the way it should be." He took her hand. "You ready to be his wife?"

"Just a second," she said, moving to her bags. Unwrapping a candy, she popped it in her mouth, smiling as flavor flooded across her tongue. She'd show Jackson that life as her husband wouldn't be as predictable as he thought.

She took her brother's arm. Guided by Allen, Alexis entered the church, her eyes sweeping over the pews where her loving family waited. Alicia and Tiana stood in matching flower-girl dresses by the altar. Sitting in the front row were Momma and Nana. A rainbow of light spilled across the vaulted ceilings from stained-glass windows backlit by the brilliant glow of the setting sun.

Lexi heard the din of the oohs and aahs from the crowd when they saw her for the first time, her snowy coconut gown glistening and fifteen feet of satin and lace trailing behind.

Her gaze moved to the front of the church, settling on her man.

Jackson could hardly breathe; she was so stunning. The people faded away; there was nothing but Alexis, his bride.

There before him, Allen presented Alexis. Squaring his shoulders and tilting his chin, Jackson stepped forward, shaking Allen's hand, then accepting Lexi to his side. The gesture was greeted by an uproar of hoots and hollers, laughter, and applause from all those in attendance.

Slowly the cheers died down as vows were read off and repeated. Lexi's sweet voice vibrated through his body as she bonded her life with his, just as their sugar kisses had done years ago.

She whispered, "I love you," and he moved in for a kiss, just before they were pronounced man and wife. Her lips were soft beneath his, her tongue sweet and exploring. But something was seriously off. Ending the kiss, Jackson laughed as he lifted her into his arms and smacked her ass. The little vixen. His wife tasted like *cinnamon*.

One

I'm gunna kill 'em.

Thinking of her friends and how they'd talked her into this ridiculous event, Toni Ray struggled to stay seated. And appear interested.

Surrounded by hushed murmurs and excited whispers, couples faced off at the scattering of tables, here for the hookup they'd failed to get on their own. The dimly lit lounge pulsed with the sexual tension known only to those who were desperate.

And Toni.

So what, she hadn't had a boyfriend in two years? So what, she hadn't been laid in nine months, three days, and seventeen hours? She could find a man on her own, *if* there wasn't a deficiency in available good guys. How those now ex-friends had convinced her that speed dating was the *it* thing to snare a man was beyond her.

It was more like a freak show than a display of quality eligible men. Complete with a parade of dweebs, geeks, and assholes, the succession had been endless and tedious.

Biting her bottom lip to keep from grinding her teeth, she waited for the bell to ding. Waited for the dork across from her, with his overgelled hair and dull, annoying voice, to have his three-minute turn be over.

One more. I can deal with one more, Toni thought, glancing at her watch and willing the too-damned-slow second hand to kick it up a notch. With any luck, the final man to move to her table for his three-minute chance to impress the pants off of her wouldn't notice her hurry to blow this joint. By now the Kings-Lakers game would be at halftime. If she hurried, she'd be able to watch the second half.

Ding.

"Nice meeting you," the dork said, shuffling to his feet and sticking out a hand toward her. "I'll be here for the cocktail party if you'd like to have a drink."

Toni stared at his hand, reluctant to reach for it. No telling where it'd been, but from the looks of him, it'd been holding a video game controller and not his joystick.

In the moment of indecision, he lowered his hand and moved away quickly. Feeling slightly bad for him, Toni dropped her chin and squeezed her lids closed. But not bad enough that she wasn't glad to see him go, she realized, breathing a sigh of relief.

Over time, she'd become accustomed to the attention and admiration of men, always taking a look from afar, but the good ones keeping their distance. In her younger years, she'd used it to her advantage, teased and flirted shamelessly, but now she longed for something more. *Something serious.* She always ended up with the jerks who thought they could handle her, never the ones worth settling down with.

With a renewed sting of regret, Toni steadied her breath, attempting to calm the pang of heartache. The pain of feeling like she was missing out on something special.

The sound of wooden chairs scraping against the floor mixed with rising voices as the men rotated tables for the final cycle of the speed-date circuit.

She felt completely humiliated; her face flamed and her stomach churned. Who was the bigger moron: the dork for thinking she'd be thrilled to know he was sticking around and interested, or her for her state of manlessness?

The chair across from her shifted on the floor, echoing painfully in her throbbing temples. At least this jerk smelled good, the subtle hint of cologne settling around her.

Ding.

Their date had started. Maybe if she just kept her eyes closed, he wouldn't say anything. They could sit in silence and just let the three minutes tick off the clock.

He chuckled.

Drawn into the richness of his laughter, Toni opened her eyes and lifted her gaze to the man sitting across the table, her breath catching in her throat. Damn, she'd wasted at least fifteen seconds she could've been looking at him.

Oh, yeah, baby, he was the kind of man she'd been hoping to meet tonight.

He sprawled casually in the chair, broad shoulders draped in the fine twill of a charcoal Armani suit. Short, dark hair was trimmed to neatly fade at his neckline, and accentuated his strong jaw. His smile spoke of confidence, but it was the arrogance in his alarming gray-blue eyes that soaked her with arousal, as if he knew the exact effect he had on women.

Like she'd had a shot of wormed tequila, her body heated. Her nipples puckered.

The effect he was having on her.

His gaze lowered to her chest—briefly—long enough for her nipples to harden further. They pressed against her thin cashmere sweater, no doubt giving him the evidence he'd been looking for. His eyes moved back to hers, the connection unwavering.

"Hi," she whispered.

His smile widened.

Deliciously dark and clean-cut, he didn't belong to the can't-hook-a-chick crowd. Pressing her thighs together to ward off the rush of wetness, Toni wondered if the rest of the room would notice if she ripped off her clothes and jumped him. Gave him a quick test-drive.

Like he knew just what she was thinking, he arched a brow at her, that smile of his widening. His striking eyes twinkling.

"Isaac," he said, reaching for her hand. His palm covered hers on the table. Warm and seductive, his thumb circled softly across the sensitive skin of her wrist.

"T-Toni."

"What are you doing here?" His tone, deep and rich, was as soothing as the way he stroked her flesh.

Good question. Headache forgotten, her pulse raced. *Looking for you.* "My ex-friends. They think I need a man."

"Do you?"

Desire chased the heat across her skin. *I need you.* She laughed, answered, "Yes," then smoothed her bottom lip with her tongue.

His smile faltered. He groaned and shifted in his seat, though he didn't remove his hand from hers. "And you'll find the one you *need* speed dating?"

Uh-huh. "I might," she replied, adding a smile and hoping her tone was as suggestive as she'd meant it.

His jaw tightened. Grinning, she met his stare, heat dripping through her panties. Unable to shift her gaze from his mesmerizing eyes, which mirrored her lust. The gray darkened, clouding over the blue. After a moment, his gaze went slowly downward, settling on her mouth, then drifted lower where she knew her pulse danced along her throat. She swallowed. Hard.

He laughed, bringing his eyes back to her face and turning her hand in his so his thumb seduced her, drawing circles in her palm, much like he'd move against her clit.

Completely enthralled by the sound of his laughter and the warmth of his touch, Toni struggled to breathe. Trying to find composure, she glanced at her watch. Just over a minute left to look at him. To get to know him. "Why are you here?" she whispered, wishing she sounded more poised.

"My brother." He slanted his head toward a man sitting a couple of tables away. "Newly divorced."

Toni glanced at him. He'd been one of the dorks at her table a few cycles before, though not as bad as most. His sad eyes had told her he lacked the confidence his brother seemed to have in abundance. The blatant sex appeal.

"He was nice."

"Nice?"

His attention was fixed on her, but there was a mere hint of jealousy in his tone as he arched a brow and questioned her about his brother in a way that made Toni smile. "Yes, nice."

"He's had enough heartbreak."

She tried an offended look, but knew he wasn't buying it. "And I look like I break hearts?"

Hell yeah, she was a heartbreaker all right. No doubt about it, Isaac thought, wishing he'd worn boxers rather than the damned too-tight briefs constricting his hardened cock. He'd been rocked up since the moment he sat down. Throbbing from the second he'd touched her.

With long blond hair that curled softly around her face and a figure that'd make Playboy Bunnies jealous, she was most men's fantasy. But it was the intelligent gleam in her brown eyes that made her *his* fantasy. Warm and caressing, they packed as much dynamite as her perfect-ten body.

Her flirtation was seductive rather than pushy, unlike that of so many of the other women he'd sat across from during each three-minute cycle. Their suggestive body language and desperate eyes offered casual sex. Toni's promised deeper pleasures.

She smiled, licked those make-a-man-beg luscious lips, then glanced at her watch for a second time. "We have about a minute."

"A minute?" His gaze lingered on her wide mouth, his mind caught up on images of those full lips wrapped around his dick. No blood left to think.

"Of our date." Her laugh was lyrical, the sound tightening his chest until he could hardly breathe. Watching the time meant she was either bored or dreaded the thought of their cycle being over too damned fast when the others had dragged on forever.

He laughed, trying to recall the last time he'd felt this excited about a woman. This turned on from hand holding, a sensual smile, and a look of passion in her chocolate eyes. His cock bucked hard against his pants.

Unable to stop himself, his smoothed his hand up her arm, sliding his fingers beneath her soft sweater. She trembled, but didn't pull away. Melting brown eyes engaged his gaze, the connection a million-watt jolt of electricity. Judging by her racing pulse beneath the pads of his fingertips, she was just as affected.

Grinning like a complete idiot, he inhaled, catching the pureness of her fragrance. "You must've heard before, you're as beautiful as an angel."

"You must've heard, you're as handsome as the devil."

Shaking his head in mock shame, he bit back laughter. "I feel like I'm in high school." Not knowing what else to say, alarmed by how acutely he wanted her.

"Really?" A feminine giggle escaped her kissable mouth, but her stare was smoldering. "I never wanted what I want right now when *I* was in high school."

Oh, God. Isaac held back a groan, cuming in his pants a real possibility. His sac drew up close to his body, his flesh aching with unfulfilled need. One little sentence and he was breathing heavy.

He pushed the words out, his throat tight. "What do you want right now?"

She grinned, her delicate fingers curling around his forearm and teasing him into a miasma of lust. The outline of her dark areolas ringed her beaded nipples beneath her thin sweater, causing his mouth to water. He swallowed, then held his breath as he waited for her reply.

Ding.

She startled slightly. Beneath his hand her pulse jumped,

but her smile didn't waver. Their connection remained unbroken.

Their three-minute date was over. Now he was supposed to stand up and walk away from her. Hell, one false move and everyone in the room would see he was sporting an impressive hard-on.

Chair legs scraped against the floor. The voices around them increased, yet neither of them moved. Neither said a word. Isaac willed the blood from his dick. The final cycle had come and gone. The speed dating was over. A cocktail party followed for anyone who wanted to stick around and get to know one another better.

He'd only met one woman he gave a damn about getting involved with. Hell, he'd just come as moral support for his brother. Now all he could think about was getting into the naked kind of involvement with Toni.

A sweet sigh cast her honeyed breath across his face. She shuddered, then slowly scooted back. He rose as she did, not wanting her out of reach. Not wanting to give up the satin of her skin. Not wanting to give up her soft alluring fragrance.

After a moment, she released his forearm and tentatively reached over to brush at a string on the lapel of his jacket. Isaac dropped his hand away and shoved it into his pants pocket to keep from reaching for her. To keep from dragging her across the table so he could feel her pressed against him, feel the lushness of her breasts, taste the sweetness of her lips.

At the bottom of his pocket, his fingers brushed one of the little candy hearts his nieces had given him earlier. He gripped it in his palm.

"Thank you, Isaac," she whispered, her eyes on his mouth in a way that told him she was thinking about being kissed. Settling his free hand on the back of her neck, he guided her forward, then lowered his head to give her what she wanted. This wasn't the place to claim her as he'd like to. A simple kiss to show his interest would have to do until he could get her alone. *And naked.*

He caught more of her mouth than he did of her cheek, her lips slightly parted. She tasted of bubble gum and something else equally sugary that he guessed was her skin.

"Isaac." His brother's voice invaded their space, but it came from far enough away that it could be ignored for the moment.

"Thank you," Isaac said against her lips, reluctant to move away. She was smiling at him when he did, her eyes shimmering with the same raw desire pouring through his system. She started to move back, breaking the link that'd been infused with sexual energy since he'd arrived at her table.

He reached for her hand and pressed the heart-shaped candy into her palm, then winked as he turned toward his approaching brother.

Toni stood there for a moment, leaning a hip on the table edge. A single step in her stilettos and she'd topple over; her legs ached to be wrapped around his waist so bad. Inhaling deeply, she ran her tongue across her lips, longing for the lingering taste of his kiss and watching him swagger confidently across the lounge.

When he started talking to his brother she looked down and uncurled her fingers to see what he'd placed in her hand. A Valentine's Sweetheart candy, PICK ME etched in blue into the pale yellow treat.

Oh shit! With a gasp, her gaze shot to her hemline. Was her skirt too short? Had she been sitting wrong? Her heart leaped. Breathing stopped.

With a knot in her stomach, she glanced across the room to study him, trying to determine if he was the type who'd have sneaked a peek and seen her tattoos. Not likely. As fine as he was, he wouldn't have to sneak; women would be offering it up.

His dark, cropped hair—mussed as if combed with his fingers—the mesmerizing blue-gray shade of his eyes, and the texture of his kiss weren't traits many women would be able to refuse. And were ones they'd never forget.

Everything about him was memorable.

With heat skittering across her skin and arousal puckering her nipples, dampening her panties, her body ached for a night with him.

Her skin burned. A chill shimmied down her spine. Unless he had Superman's X-ray vision and looked right through the small wooden table, there was no way he could've known about her two small candy-heart tattoos. The pink heart with 4 U in blue graced her really low on the hip, just above her manicured pubic line. The other was a mint green that said MINE in red on her upper inner thigh.

Coincidence that he'd give her a Sweetheart? It had to be, she thought, glancing down at the tiny PICK ME heart in her hand. Taking a breath, she rolled the little heart between her thumb and forefinger as another thought occurred. Her gaze traveled gradually from one woman to the next, checking to see if they all had a candy. Maybe dropping sugar was the way Isaac charmed his way into a woman's bed.

But not a single other woman appeared to be either holding or sucking on one of the candies. Inspection complete and suspicion eased, Toni tucked the tiny yellow PICK ME heart into her purse.

Pick him, he'd better believe she would. Purpose drove her

across the room, weaving through the mingling wannabe couples, formerly known as single dweebs. His brother caught sight of her first, his eyes bulging, his look surprised. It must have been his reaction that caused Isaac to turn in her direction.

She walked right up to him, unprepared for his towering height that the table between them had disguised. Bold now, she tapped her fingertip to his lips, then smoothed downward across his chin.

"Do they make hearts that say *Come with me*?" She curled her finger in a come-hither way. The thrill of desire and the promise of passion had her asking questions and making demands.

She pursed her lips when he shook his head and grinned. Dropping her hand to his chest, she curled his silk tie around her wrist and gave a little tug. His smile faded. Shades of gray darkened his eyes, obscuring the blue. Flesh hardened and throbbed against her belly.

Inching closer, she pulled his head down farther, and lifted on her toes so she could finally get the kiss his body had promised earlier. She feathered her mouth across his, then whispered, "Come with me."

His jaw tightened. A deep groan rattled up from his gut. "Anywhere you say."

Two

"This isn't exactly what I thought you had in mind."

"No?" She arched a golden brow, then lowered her lush lips to the frosty mug and sucked the head off the beer, the little slurpy sounds sending blood rushing to his dick.

Isaac was smart enough to know when he was being toyed with, and Toni was doing a damned fine job. Judging by the way she worked her little pink tongue along the glass edge, then dropped her rich brown eyes to the shadows shielding his hard flesh from view, she had a pretty good idea what sort of effect the action was having on his body.

When he remained silent, she lifted her face and licked those plump lips of hers. "What'd you think I had in mind?"

He tossed a glance around the bar. Neon beer signs hung behind the long wooden counter, reflecting against the top-shelf liquor bottles. Small buckets of peanuts sat on each table, the shells discarded on the floor, their salty aroma filling the air. People sat in clusters, laughing and talking. Several groups of men gathered around the two TVs, watching the featured game.

Shrugging, he did everything he could to appear nonchalant, like he wasn't nearly as desperate as he was feeling. Not nearly as needy. "Someplace more private." *Where we could be fucking instead of drinking.*

"Private," she whispered, her gaze fixing on his mouth with the same hunger pouring from her eyes that he'd seen earlier. Reaching across the table, she touched his hand, then with one fingertip feathered down his index finger. She seductively circled the nail. "What would we do in private that we can't do here?"

Arousal slowed his response, all his focus on the way she stroked her hand over his. "We could think of something." He swallowed hard, ignoring the throb of his cock that begged for the *something* he was implying.

She moaned, a little breathy sound that she followed up with her tongue moistening her lips. "If I had beer at my place, we could catch the game there." Sliding back in her chair, Toni looked at the TV set mounted to the wall above the bar. "What the—that was a foul!"

"I'll buy a six-pack."

"Tempting." She didn't turn back to him, but kept her attention on the screen. "But . . ." She paused as if contemplating her reason. ". . . game's almost over."

Screw buts. Although he'd have looked at the TV to check the score if he'd been able to tear his gaze from her. Her delicate fingers had moved to the top button of her sweater and worked the little pearl through the tiny hole. One popped free, then a second. Isaac struggled to breathe as more of her creamy skin appeared. The cadence of his pulse drummed in time with the beat along her slender neck.

"You don't mind, do you?" she asked, not pausing her little striptease. "I just had to get out of there. Besides, by the time we made it back to my place, I'd have missed the game."

Mind? Hell no. *You're taking your clothes off.* He wanted to be anywhere she was, though in a bed and naked would be better than sipping brew and watching the game at the only sports bar within walking distance. Still, Toni half-dressed was better than a roomful of desperate speed daters, and watching the Kings-Lakers game beat pushy come-ons no matter who ended up with the win.

Isaac eased back in his chair, careful to keep his rocked-up cock from becoming the center of attention. Taking a long drag from his beer, he watched as she peeled off the thin sweater and draped it over the back of her seat, leaving her in nothing but a thin satin camisole, the material strained over the fullness of her breasts.

No bra. Through the pale tones of pink, he could see hardened nipples and the russet shade of her areolas. He took another drink, just to wet his throat, which had gone desert dry.

The cheers from the TV-watching crowd erupted. Toni leaped to her feet, throwing her hands above her head and screaming, "Yes! Score."

With her hands over her head, the hem of her top crept up, leaving her belly exposed. The floral scent of her bare skin washed over him. A sparkle of jewelry caught his eye. Centered amid sun-kissed skin that shimmered softer than silk, a diamond stud pierced the flesh of her belly button. The most exotic image he'd ever seen. Isaac struggled to rein in his desire. To keep his needy groan low. To keep from dragging her out of the bar, seducing her out of her clothes, and sexing her when she was wearing nothing but that diamond.

Taking another drink, he smiled as Toni leaped to her feet again before she'd even settled back down. Appreciating her enthusiasm for the game, he couldn't help being surprised by the sweet, feminine package hiding a sports fanatic.

"Three! Count 'em up, baby."

With her arms in the air and the backlighting from the bar, her thin top was nearly transparent. The full curves of her bra-less breasts jiggled with excitement just as they'd do if he were thrusting into her. He groaned. "Keep that up, and I'm going to have you flat on your back." Though he'd never been a light-weight, it had to be the beer talking, Isaac thought, his gaze moving from her perfect tits to her full lips.

She went perfectly still, hardly even breathing. Time crawled as she turned toward him and grinned. Though her milk-chocolate eyes sparkled with humor, her smile faded and she pursed her lips into a tempting pout. "Keep what up?" She glanced at the TV, then brought her attention back to him. "This?" She cheered again, her gaze fixed on his and not the game.

"Mm-hmm . . . ," he mumbled with a nod.

"Oh, really?" She sat down and leaned forward, giving him a clear view of lush breasts crowned with puckered tips and a valley of cleavage his fingers itched to memorize. His mouth watered. He swallowed. She was testing him. If he leaned across the table and took a beaded nipple in his mouth, would he pass or fail? To hell with her shirt. To hell with the crowded bar. He wanted her. Now.

Toni didn't mean to be teasing him the way she was, but she couldn't help it. There was something in the depths of his gray-blue eyes that intrigued her. The way the color shifted made her heart race. Made her body ache.

Swallowing hard, she struggled to distinguish between the haze of lust and the buzz from her beer. The desire was definitely stronger. She wanted him. Bringing him here had only been an attempt to prolong the evening, but she had every intention of bringing him home with her.

Though a one-nighter was the ultimate way not to start a meaningful relationship, it was a way to meet her body's needs, despite her heart's yearnings for something more lasting. Her heart would have to be put on hold for the night so her body could enjoy Isaac.

She tossed a quick glance at her watch. Hell, it'd already been nine months, three days, and *eighteen* hours. She didn't know if she could wait long enough to make it nineteen. She didn't want to.

Easing her foot from her stiletto, she allowed it to clunk to the floor. The *on your back* comment had done it. She had to touch him. Now. Lifting her foot to his chair, she wedged it between his muscular legs until the heat of his solid hard-on stopped her. The throb of his dick against her sole was answered by arousal seeping through her panties.

"Oooh," she said, her mouth rounding into an O. Curling her toes, she rubbed against his impressive length and watched the storm take over his eyes. Beads of sweat dotted his brow. She longed to smooth them across his skin with her fingertips, learning his texture. To muss his hair. To see those broad shoulders without his shirt and jacket. To see the erection she stroked with her toes naked and ready to enter her.

She wanted it all. And she hadn't even kissed him. Not really. "Is that a promise?" Moving her foot, she measured him, met his throbbing. Stoked it. Hardly able to breathe, at that moment Toni couldn't think of a single thing she wanted more than the fulfillment of his words. "What else can I do to end up *on my back*?" she asked, her voice dropping to a throaty whisper barely audible over the hum of the bar.

His stare intent upon her, he settled his warm hand on her bare foot, his long fingers curving around her. His thumb stroked along the arch. He held her foot steady against his erection. "You feel that?" he asked as he rocked his hips into her. "I'm past playing games."

He moved his cock against her again, and Toni nearly moaned. She blinked slowly, concentrating on bringing her desire under control. Her clit swelled against her thong panties, the ache between her legs begging for the same movement her toes were getting.

"Who's playing?"

A growl rumbled up from his gut. With nostrils flared, he moved from her foot, stroking sensually over her ankle and up her leg. His touch was gentle, but insistent. "I'm going to need a cold shower after this."

"*We* may need a shower, but it won't be cold." Toni tucked her bottom lip between her teeth to keep from grinning when she felt him pulse against her heel. The smoldering intensity in his stare told her she better not be teasing. And she wasn't.

"Now who's making promises?"

"I am."

Around them cheers went up, so loud they blocked out the broadcaster's announcement of the final score, but she noticed them only in contrast with Isaac's brooding silence. She didn't know him well enough to know if it was anger or lust that had thinned his lips. Tightened his jaw. Feeling him rock hard against her sole and his massive body pulsing with energy, she wondered for the first time if she'd made a mistake, and second-guessed her judgment.

Though the way he caressed her leg was tender, there was something dangerous about him—like when he fucked her, it'd be fast and hard, only a moment spared for her pleasure. He released a shuddering breath that carried the hint of barley and hops, and when he smiled, any doubt she'd had fled.

"I hate this table," he said, the hoarseness of his voice surprising her.

"Why?"

"It's between us."

Wiggling her toes against him, she giggled. "I hate your pants. They're between us, too."

"I hate this bar."

"Why?"

"Too many people."

"And no bed."

He arched a dark brow, dropped his gray-blue gaze to her chest, and smiled just as Toni felt her nipples pucker further. "Exactly."

"Want to get out of here?"

Isaac didn't reply. The words would've been a clichéd *Your place or mine?* Instead he eased her foot from between his thighs and shoved his chair away from the table, not giving a damn if a spotlight highlighted the way his dick remained hard.

On his feet, he rounded the table, scooped up her sweater, and waited as she fiddled with her stiletto beneath the table. Hell, he'd suffer through that cold shower if she said no, but he didn't want to give her the chance to. Instead he planned on seducing her until she begged. Until the only *no* she could think of was when she was telling him not to stop.

When she was standing, he entwined his fingers with hers and, without so much as a single word, led her toward the exit. She didn't protest, but caressed his palm with a manicured fingernail.

Outside the early-February night swirled a fine mist of ocean fog around them, the cold biting against his skin. Toni trembled beside him. It was unusually cool for southern California, but the dampness of living by the sea was something he'd grown used to. Gripping her sweater in his free hand, he turned to offer it to her, but paused the second his gaze settled on her.

The breeze whipped at her blond curls, showing off her slender neck and breasts that were reacting to the cold, but her eyes were on fire. The creamy brown filled with desire. She shivered. He groaned. "Brrr . . ." She reached toward him for her sweater, licking her sensual lips.

That did it. He had to taste her. He turned on her, put his fist holding her soft sweater behind her neck, and tilted her face up to meet his. The first brush of her lips made him forget the cold. Forget the bar. Forget their lack of privacy.

His only thought was getting inside her. Smoothing his tongue across her mouth, he tasted the hint of beer, and feminine sweetness that could only be Toni.

She whimpered softly. Pressing firmly against her, he backed her up until she was up against the building's wall. Pinned her there with his much-larger body.

She parted her lips and he swept inside, thrusting into the sultry heat of her, stroking in a rhythm he'd use to make love.

She met his kiss with an eagerness that thrilled him. Excitement rolled in his gut. Blood filled his cock, sexing her soon the only option. Releasing her hand, he slid his between them and covered her breast with his palm, flicked his thumb across a pert nipple. She moaned, slanted her head, and touched her tongue to his.

A few minutes more of this and he'd embarrass himself by cuming too early.

But it was Toni who reduced the fury of the kiss. She nipped at his tongue, sucked on it gently, then allowed cold air between them by putting a hand to his chest and shoving him away.

"Get me out of here now." The words were raspy. Her breathing labored.

He'd damn near lost his mind, aroused past thinking. Glancing around, Isaac dragged in a breath and struggled to get his erection to cooperate by easing off a little. He stepped away from Toni, handed over her sweater, then shoved his hands through his hair to keep from touching her again—here on the street corner.

"Your place or mine?" he asked, then groaned at the stupidity of having actually used such a tacky line.

She laughed, the sound whimsical and alluring. "Mine." She fit her hand to his. "Come with me."

Isaac chuckled. And followed.

Three

Toni's hands shook, fumbling the keys as she attempted to open her door. A tremble that had nothing to do with fear or anxiety or any doubt at all about bringing a man home, and everything to do with her need to get Isaac inside. And naked.

Even now she could feel his heat behind her, smell the scent of his cologne, hear him breathing. She longed to lean back into him. To have his strong arms embrace her, hold her tightly against the solid length of his muscular body, and finally touch her the way his leisurely caresses had promised during their short walk from the bar to her apartment.

Long fingers twisted into the hair at her nape, stroking his thumb in small circles against her sensitive skin. "Need help?" he whispered, his breath dancing warmly across her ear.

Toni shook her head. *Yeah, baby.* She needed help, but

not with the door. She needed him to help her out of her clothes, to ease her poor toes out of her stilettos, to toss aside her damp panties and finally take care of that ache deep inside.

Suppressing a shiver, Toni jammed a key in and gave a twist, only to find it was for the mailbox, not the front door. She tried another, but inserted it upside down. Isaac was the problem, his presence a distraction. Her lust for him causing her to think only of what she'd do to him once through the door and not about what she was doing.

"If you don't hurry, I'm going to fuck you against the door." His fingers tightened in her hair, giving a little tug that caused her to gasp for breath, surprised, not injured.

His demanding tone raced down her spine, tightening her nipples and causing desire to swell her clit. "There you go again, making all those promises," she whispered between pants that were in tune with the jingling keys.

And then he was on her. His large body pressed into her back, forcing her to step forward until her flushed cheek was against the cool wooden door. One forearm rested a few inches from her face; his other hand remained twisted in her hair.

"You don't know me well enough to know if I keep my promises." He rotated his hips so the hard length of his cock throbbed into the small of her back. "You don't know that when I say I'll fuck you against the door, I mean it." He thrust his hips forward again, and used the pressure on her hair to angle her head to the side.

Toni closed her eyes, gulping down the rise of emotion tightening her chest at his mention of how little she knew of him. Focusing on the feel of his hard-on, she reminded herself that this one-night stand was about a good time and offered no assurances of a future. No chance of getting to know him at all, other than the way he screwed.

As if to illustrate he *was* a man of his word, his mouth settled on her throat, lips open, searing. Wet. Flicking his tongue along her pulse, he wedged his leg between her thighs, pushing up the hem of her skirt until the clasps of her stockings were revealed, little pink bows holding up the silk.

His muscles bunching against her drenched panties, he settled into a jolting rhythm. His leg between hers and his erection working against her ass—she'd have let him shove the cloth aside. Let him enter from behind, hard and fast. Let him prove just how right he was—if not for the ding of the elevator.

Isaac's movements stopped, his body going perfectly still behind her. Squeezing her lids closed, she tucked her bottom lip between her teeth to keep herself from begging Isaac not to stop, despite the possible intrusion. So caught up in her need to get his dick inside her, Toni had allowed herself to get carried away in her apartment building hallway.

Breathing a sigh of relief, then sobbing in frustration, she slanted her face to the ceiling and sucked in several more breaths. Shaking her head, she attempted to clear her brain of her stupor, but wits had deserted her. Every cell in her body solely focused on how he touched her, her weight supported on the muscular thigh she rode.

Isaac recovered more quickly. Cool wisps of air slid between them as he shifted away from her. His fingers untwisted from her hair, smoothed down her body, and casually pulled the hem of her skirt back into place. She couldn't bite back the whimper.

"Don't worry, sweetheart, it'll be off in a minute," he whispered against her ear as he moved the arm he'd been leaning on against the door in front of them. His large hand, warm and slightly callused, covered hers. With little effort, he had the key flipped and the lock giving way. The knob twisted. The door swung inward.

Isaac followed Toni inside, then stepped past her when she paused to relock the door. He had to put a little distance between them. Had to clear his head of the floral scent of her skin, the sweetness of her arousal. Dampness seeped through his slacks from where her pussy had pressed hot and wet against him.

Just as he'd suspected from the passion shimmering in the chocolaty depths of her eyes, she'd gone from teasing to melting with a few simple strokes. All those little mewing sounds mixed with breathy moans were just from foreplay. His sac drew up tight, cum gathering at the base of his cock as he thought about how she'd respond to lovemaking.

Groaning, he tightened his jaw and rolled his head on his shoulders as he glanced around the room. The exterior wall was made up of large windows, allowing night to seep in past shades that'd been left open. Outside, the illuminated cityscape twinkled in the distance.

He heard the keys dropping to a hard surface. He could hear the softness of her breathing. He wanted nothing more than to feel her breaths rush across his naked skin, to capture them with his mouth.

What he needed to do was step farther into the room. Put more space between them so if she had any doubts about tonight, she'd have time to voice them.

"Isaac."

The way she said his name, low and raspy, had his dick throbbing in his briefs. Standing perfectly still, he waited for her to go on. Waited for her to tell him this had been a mistake. That'd he be going home to that cold shower.

"Isaac," she repeated, this time louder. More insistent.

He turned toward her, not sure what to expect, but holding his breath just in case she gave him the boot. Standing before the door, she wasn't smiling. Her gaze was warm and seductive. He shook his head; he could get lost in her eyes.

She'd removed her sweater, the thin camisole revealing the slopes of her bare shoulders. Even with the shadows, he could see how her nipples puckered beneath the thin material. His mouth watered.

When he just stood there, she giggled and stepped forward. "Isaac," she said again, grabbing his tie and tugging his head down as she wrapped it around her wrist. She touched her lush lips to his, but didn't open. And didn't linger.

"Yeah, sweetheart?"

Pressing kisses to his skin, she moved slowly to his ear, then traced the shape with the hot little tip of her tongue. "Don't you have some promises to keep?"

He groaned, but wanted desperately to hear her say it. "Promises?"

She laughed, then stepped back, pulling him with her by his tie. "My skirt. The door."

"This skirt?" Placing his hand on her hip, he bunched the material in his fist, to test how difficult it'd be to get it off her. It wouldn't respond to pulling, he realized, and released the cloth to smooth down her flat lower belly. He touched the hem, stroking his fingertips along the edge, then pushed upward to caress the naked flesh above the silk of her stockings. Her inner thighs quivered against his palm.

The heat of her drew him to the wetness dripping from her pussy. He stroked his thumb across a patch of lace, pressing and circling against her clit. She responded to the movement by yanking hard on his tie until his mouth hovered just above hers. He brushed his lips across her skin, felt her body tremble before him. Repeating the light kiss, Isaac increased the pressure of his thumb until a shudder swept through her body and her lashes lowered over her rich brown eyes.

"Kiss me," she whispered, lifting on her toes to pull him closer.

He grinned as he pressed his mouth to hers. Nibbling her bottom lip, he touched his tongue to her pouty mouth, then claimed her when she opened with a gasp.

Slanting his head, he angled over her and invaded completely, pushing his tongue past her teeth into the sultry velvety depths. Sweetness invaded his senses, the subtle taste of hops and something sugary. He drank in the little sighs of pleasure, stroked across her tongue with his, learning the texture.

And she kissed him back. Swirling her tongue, she followed his lead with none of the awkwardness associated with a first kiss. Nothing timid about the way she took charge, or rubbed her body against his so the hard tips of her tits pressed into his chest. Until his dick was cradled against her belly. With full lips open, her mouth was wet and hot, her tongue eager and curious. She moved along the edge of his teeth, lapped at lips. Made him dizzy.

Isaac circled her back with his arms, his fingers finding the zipper that held her skirt in place. The damn thing fought him a little, snagging before it gave way. He put a hand on each hip and pushed downward, over the roundness of her ass. His fingertips skimmed over her skin and thin strips of her lace panties. The skirt slid down, then dropped to the floor in a soft swoosh of fabric.

Caressing the backs of her legs, he broke the kiss and moved his mouth to her neck. He touched his tongue to her pulse, licked her collarbone, slanted her back, and closed his mouth over a tight beaded nipple, feeling it pucker further even through the satiny cloth.

He nipped gently, scraping his teeth across her flesh, pausing to enjoy her responses.

The way her body shook, the way she softly said his name.

"Isaac." Her hands moved up his shoulders; her fingertips stroked across his neck, then slid into his hair and gripped.

Suckling at her nipple, he swirled his tongue across the peak, silently cursing her thin shirt. Thanked God she'd gone braless.

He brought his mouth back to hers, and fought the driving need to rip the shirt from her and caress her naked body. Isaac struggled to breathe; lust tightened his chest. Turned his cock rock hard. Throbbing.

Putting his hands on the backs of her thighs, he lifted them over his hips, forcing her to straddle him at the same time he stepped forward. "This door?" was mumbled between kisses as he pressed her spine against the door with enough force to cause the hinges to rattle. He ground his hips against her center, only his pants and a tiny strip of lace keeping him from her pussy. Wet flesh he wanted to get inside of.

Toni absorbed the solid feel of Isaac's body before her. "Yeesss." On her shirt, the cooling wet spot where his mouth had been sent a chill racing across her skin. The cold wood behind her contrasted the heat of his erection that pressed firmly between her thighs.

Rotating her hips, she wanted his pants off. Wanted him inside her already. His lips were back on her, his tongue searing below her ear. Lolling her head to the side, she reached between them, found the button that secured his slacks, and popped it open.

Pushing the elastic waistband of his underwear downward, Toni touched his head, felt the dewy ball of cum that seeped from the tiny slit. Like velvet over solid muscle, his length throbbed against her palm. She curled her fingers around him, judging his width. Surprised by how thick he was.

Stroking upward, she smiled when air hissed between his teeth.

"Damn, girl," he said, his voice raspy.

"You going to fuck me against this door?" she asked, the rhythm of her caresses increasing. A tempo that mimicked the ache inside her body. She gulped for air. "You keep your promises, right?" Tightening her thighs, she held him to her, and rotated her hips until she felt the muscles on his back bunch.

Tucking his fingers beneath the lace, he gave one firm yank and the panties gave way. "Is this what you want?" His thumb smoothed across her manicured hair, swirled in the slickness of her desire. "Is this how you want it?" His mouth was on hers again, silencing any further comment. His tongue thrust at the same speed he worked his thumb in circles against her clit.

Toni felt climax tightening deep in her gut, the heat spreading across her skin, the tension building. As much as she wanted to orgasm, a good hard fuck was what she had in mind, not a finger banging. She closed her hand around his erection, and tore her mouth from his, panting. "Dick, Isaac. I need it."

A growl rumbled up from his chest as he leaned his forehead against hers and sucked in breaths. "Damn, sweetheart, I don't have anything."

"Not in your wallet? Don't men carry them bad boys?"

"Not in a long time, baby." His body shook with strained amusement.

Isaac's laughter warmed her. Releasing his hair from her fist, she smoothed her palm down his forehead, feeling the dampness of sweat, the heat of his skin, the texture. Lightly touching his face in the dimness of the room, she wanted to feel his smile. Remember it.

"I'll go to the store."

Fire flamed across her cheeks. "No, I have something." Toni bit her lower lip and slanted her face away, not wanting him to see her blush over having condoms.

"Yeah?"

She nodded. "On the table, by my keys." *Within reach*, she almost added, tightening her legs so he wouldn't step away.

With one hand tucked under her ass, his muscular body cradled between her legs, he slanted to reach in the direction she indicated. The keys clanged together, then dropped to the floor. A moment later he was facing her, the box of condoms in his hand.

"Preparing for your speed date?" He arched a brow, and Toni could swear she heard laughter in his teasing words.

She clenched her teeth, feeling heat lick across her cheeks. "My friends."

"The ex-ones?"

"Yep, them good for noth—"

He laughed aloud, then kissed her full and fast on the lips. "Good for something," he said, slanting his eyes toward the box.

Toni resisted the urge to roll her eyes, thinking about the losers she'd met before Isaac. If he hadn't ended up at her table, the condoms her ex-friends had insisted on would have gone to waste. With Isaac, she planned on using the entire box of three.

Smoothing her fingertips down his abdomen, she moved a hand beneath his shirt. His skin was warm, the muscles beneath taut as she scraped her nails up the line of hair that dripped from his belly button to the base of his cock. She touched the small indent, outlined the lines of his six-pack, moved higher to the curve of his pecs. Flicking her nails over his small beaded nipple, she asked, "Can we talk about my friends later?"

His mouth was on her neck now, his lips working magic, his tongue caressing her in ways she hadn't guessed could be so erotic. One large palm covered her breast, his thumb circling the hardened tip. "Anything you want, sweetheart." He spoke against her skin, sending vibration straight to her wet pussy.

"Anything?" She lolled her head, giving him better access.

"Tell me what you want."

She tightened her hand around his erection, the blood throbbing hard. "Put on a condom."

Toni felt him chuckle more than she heard it. What she did hear was the thin cardboard box tear, the crinkle of foil. Glancing down, she watched as he touched the latex to his dick, put the coiled rubber over his head, and unrolled it with one hand. She was soaked, just watching, her arousal perfuming the room. Heat dashed across her skin. Her nipples tightened, vying for just a little of his attention.

He looked so delicious, all those muscle-carved inches, latex draped over his plum-shaped head, veins pulsing in beat with her ache. Then there was the intent look in his gray-blue eyes that warned he was having a hard a time holding off fucking already.

She yearned to prolong the moment, to savor every second. But need was working here, lust in full command. "Oh, baby, is all this for me?" She smoothed her hand down the latex-swathed length of him, the throb fierce. She rubbed his erection against her clit, then fit his head just inside her. The condom was cool at first, but within a heartbeat his dick had warmed in her juices. Her inner thighs ached.

"Yeah, sweetheart, for you." And then with one long thrust, he was all the way in her, his cock pressing against her womb. Pubic hairs tangling.

Toni arched her back away from the door, crying out as her body adjusted to the fullness. To the intense, incredible feel of being connected with him. Isaac—a stranger.

His lips settled over hers, the kiss short and sweet. "You okay?" He withdrew an inch, pushed forward. Withdrew a bit more, again rolling his hips forward to fill her with his cock.

Toni smiled, sliding both hands beneath his shirt and skimming upward to rest her palms against his chest. "I like my friends again," she said, crossing her ankles behind him to drag him closer.

His only response was to increase his rhythm, going from smooth and languid to hungry and volatile. He settled his mouth on hers, suckling her bottom lip into his mouth, biting softly. His tongue caressed her. Whereas his fucking was hard and strong, there was something gentle and tender about the way he kissed.

The combination alarming.

Sweat shimmered on his body as he continued to work into her, his cock pure magic. The muscles of his back, shoulders, thighs, and abdomen bunched and strained as he kept her pinned to the door, the wood rattling with each forceful thrust. Her body just as frazzled, every nerve aware of where he touched her.

Moving from her mouth, his lips touched her eyelids, caressed the sensitive skin beneath her ear. "Do you like me?" he asked, his voice raspy. Raw almost.

If his dick weren't buried in her tight pussy, he'd mock himself for such a stupid question. At such a stupid time. *Like me?* Emotions had no place here. This was about sex. The best damned sex he'd had in ages. Maybe ever.

Sliding a hand between them, he found her clit with his thumb, circled it. Hoping like hell she'd forget he'd asked her anything other than if she was liking *it*.

"Yesssss." Her cry filled him with pride, some strange male-ego satisfaction. Cum tightened his nuts, hot at the base of his cock. He held it back, driving to bring about her pleasure before he lost control.

"You like this?" He plunged in harder, driving as he worked his fingers against her. His tongue caressing her skin, he felt unsure why her answer mattered so much to him.

"Yes. Yes." A shudder moved across her skin, her muscles trembling. "Yes, baby," she said, her back arching as her pussy clamped down around him. Tight and wet and hot.

And he lost it.

Giving her everything he had—and some. Climax fierce, the cum shot from his dick, filling the condom. Draining him of his sanity.

He collapsed onto her, the door supporting both of them. His breathing heavy, Isaac inhaled the sweet scent of her orgasm, touched his tongue to her racing pulse, twisted his fingers into the long strands of blond.

After a few minutes his lungs were able to drag a full

breath. His body began to cool. But hell, one fuck hadn't rid him of his desire for her.

"How many were in that box?"

She took a deep breath, the movement causing her firm breasts to jiggle against him. "Three."

Too damned alluring. "Give me a minute."

Toni giggled. "Promises, promises."

Four

The theme song from *Kill Bill* hummed through Isaac's sleep. He tried to ignore it, tried to focus on the feel of Toni's body curled against him, warm and supple in slumber. But the familiarity of the music seeped into his consciousness, bringing him awake slowly and with reluctance.

His cell phone.

When he cracked his lids, a puff of long hair hindered his vision from taking in the room, but he could see enough to know that night had finished up hours ago and morning was full on them. Sun crept through the wall of windows, the thin drapes doing nothing to shield them.

Pressing his face to the strands of blond, he inhaled deeply the flowery fragrance of her shampoo and the lingering aroma of lovemaking, a scent brought about only by deep arousal, lots of sweat, and multiple orgasms.

He caressed her bare shoulder, her skin smooth and soft. And warm. She sighed in her sleep, leaning into his fingertips. Even in her dreams, hungering for the way he touched her. The single night of sex hadn't cured her *either*.

Morning wood wasn't his only problem. Hell no, her simple reaction spurred his lust, causing his daily hard-on to throb for a fourth go-round. Isaac closed his eyes, conjuring images of icebergs and cold water. Anything to get the intensity of his erection to ease off a bit.

The cell phone started up again, complete with the *Kill Bill* ring tone.

"Just as well," he mumbled, gently removing his arm from beneath Toni's head and replacing it with a pillow. It wasn't like a morning after had been part of the promise, he realized, rolling across a span of cool sheets, then standing nude in the cold morning air. He looked down at her. Her lush lips were puckered, a slight smirk he yearned to kiss off her. Her cheeks were rosy, her skin touched by sunshine.

He'd given her all night, even though it wasn't asked for. She'd said nothing of what—if anything—would be between them when the three condoms were gone. And they were gone, *that* was for sure.

He took a deep breath. Glancing around her bedroom, he was surprised by the decor. Given how feminine Toni was, he'd have suspected a pink flower-filled room, complete with fluffy pillows and plenty of frills and lace. Exactly what the room wasn't, confirming how little he knew about this woman. He hadn't noticed in the darkness the night before, but now he saw her bedding was a dark blue silk, the furniture simple straight lines and contemporary. The only flowers in the room were several large photos done in black-and-white—close-ups of roses.

With the caller not giving up, Isaac turned toward the

doorway and left her room to get his phone before the noise woke her. He followed the music to the front door and his discarded clothing, then dug in his jacket pocket, pulled out the phone, and flipped it open.

"Yeah?"

"Yo, man, I picked up the U-Haul truck an hour ago. You ready, or what?"

How could he have forgotten Collin? Isaac pinched the bridge of his nose with two fingers, holding off the slight blur of a headache. Too many beers, too much energy, not enough damned sleep. He grinned. *It was worth it*, he thought, glancing toward the open doorway leading to Toni's bedroom. To where she slept. Naked.

"Not yet." He cleared his throat. "What time is it?"

"Ten seventeen. You sleep with her?"

He thought about lying to his brother, but Collin wasn't stupid. He'd be able to put together Isaac's leaving the speed-dating event with her and being late to help him move this morning.

Isaac chose to ignore the question, knowing that not answering was all the confirmation Collin needed.

"You dog . . ."

His brother kept talking, but that was all Isaac heard. It wasn't like he'd made long-term promises to Toni. Had never mentioned commitment, but she was fun and he liked her. Something clenched in his gut when he thought about not seeing her again. That the one night had been just that—*a one-night stand*.

". . . so what do you think?"

"Huh? Um, yeah. Sure."

His brother swore under his breath, but Isaac heard it. "You weren't listening. Shit, man, you get *any* sleep?" He went on without waiting for an answer. "So, I'll pick you up on the way to the storage unit."

Isaac held back his groan, knowing what was coming. "I'm not home."

His brother's laughter had him holding the phone inches from his face. "Hey, man, I can get someone else to give me a hand." He laughed again. "If you'd rather stay there."

Oh, he'd rather, that was damned sure. But he couldn't. Not when helping Collin out was so imperative. Isaac had been the one to convince his brother to move from their parents' home—where he'd lived since his now ex-wife had thrown him out—and into his own apartment. He was the one who'd told Collin that moving on was the most important step to getting over.

Seeing the move through, helping get his brother settled into his own place, wasn't something Isaac could flake on. Shrugging into his slacks with one hand, he glanced back toward her room. *No matter how much I want to.*

But the least he could do was leave his number. Let her know that the ball was in her court. If she wanted to play more, he was game.

"I'll meet you at the storage in thirty minutes." He clicked the phone closed before his brother had any more smart-ass comments. Gathering up the rest of his clothes, he got dressed, wishing that this had been any other Saturday. Any day he didn't have plans in the morning and he could have spent the afternoon getting to know the woman he'd made love to all night.

Checking out the rest of her apartment, he realized the living area was done in the same fashion as her bedroom. Plain black leather sofa and chair. Contemporary side tables and lamps. A flat-screen plasma mounted on the wall, along with more of those black-and-white prints.

Glancing about, he looked around for where she might keep some paper and something to write with. He found nothing in the main room. As he strolled across the room, he stooped several times to pick up the tossed-about condom wrappers, gathering all the foil corners and the box, then carried them to the bathroom to throw away.

As he left the bathroom, he noticed a half-open door to his left. He pushed it inward, revealing an office. Isaac stood frozen in the doorway, wondering if Toni had been married or was involved with someone and hadn't said anything.

The room before him was every man's dream.

The walls were dark green, or what he could see of them. Every inch of the wall facing him seemed to be taken up with different framed photos of sports heroes, all originals. All one-of-a-kind shots he'd never seen before. All signed. Some frames held authentic jerseys, also signed by the wearer.

On the floor against the wall were stacks of magazines and several black bags with tons of little zipper pockets. He momentarily took them in, his gaze moving to the bookcase.

Behind a large desk, the back wall was covered with shelves of priceless memorabilia. A helmet signed by Joe Montana. In a glass case, a football signed by legendary Eric Dickerson. A Babe Ruth baseball, complete with a mitt resting at the bottom of the case. A basketball signed by all the 1986 Boston Celtics, the last year they won a championship.

Damn, a man could get hard just being in a room like this. He stepped forward, aware of the faint smell of expensive cigars, but his attention on the single item that was completely out of place. A pair of purple fluffy slippers peeking out from beneath the desk, where Toni must have left them.

Grinning like an idiot, he strolled to the desk, found a pen on a marble stand with her business cards—RAY STUDIOS, her name, business address, and phone number. He slid a card into his jacket pocket, then found a pad of paper next to a stack of smaller black-and-white rose pictures just like the ones on her bedroom walls. Looking around the office, he realized Toni was a mix of contradictions.

Blood poured to his cock as he thought about the fun it'd be trying to figure her out. He ignored the rise of lust, and jotted down a quick note.

Reluctant to leave, he forced himself to stand and carried the paper back to the room where the goddess he'd spent the night fucking hadn't batted a golden eyelash. Looking at how the blue sheet draped over her perfect body, one dark nipple half-exposed, he thought it'd be easy to strip off his clothing and get back in bed with her. Hell, even with Collin waiting, he was tempted.

He swallowed down his desire and stepped forward to put the note beside her in bed where his body should have been. Taking a step back, he slid his hands into his pants pockets to keep from reaching for her, his fingers coming in contact with more of the little hearts his nieces had loaded him up with.

Impulsively, he closed his fist around them and scattered a handful around his note on the dark blue sheets. Smiling, he retreated and let himself out.

Toni didn't want to open her eyes, despite the sunlight she felt falling across her face. Though she knew it, she didn't want to see she was alone. *That Isaac was gone.*

It wasn't like she expected him to be there still. The truth was, he'd stayed all night—a lot longer than she'd thought he would. Not that she minded, but she was just a hit-it-and-quit-it one-night stand. With all those yummy promises, not a single one had included anything beyond the single evening. One night of incredibly delicious, burn-off-her-beer-calories sex.

Keeping her eyes closed and her body perfectly still, she inhaled the scent of him lingering softly in her bedding. *On her skin.* The muskiness of his cum, the saltiness of his sweat, the spice of his cologne.

Toni took a breath, then swallowed down the lump clogging her throat. Refused to acknowledge the sting behind her eyes. "Get real, girl." *It's too late to get sentimental about this shit.* So what, she'd screwed him? Her body had needed it.

But her soul. Her heart. They needed commitment. They needed something more lasting than an empty bed in the morning. And though Isaac Brett had been the most amazing lover, speed daters rarely turned into anything serious. Especially not when she'd given up the goods during the one-nighter.

Shoving her hands above her head, she arched her back off the bed, stretching all the muscles that hadn't been used in a while, but had been worked last night. Three times over.

What she needed to do was get a grip on her raw emotions—probably brought about by lack of sleep. Isaac might have been a bang-and-never-see-again guy, but one thing he'd done for her was show her that she was ready for a man. Ready to not be alone anymore.

Funny thing was, she'd never had a problem with dates. She'd played them, used her looks and body to her own end, and never once thought there'd be a time when she'd want a man and there wouldn't be a good one available.

Taking a few deep breaths, she stretched again, then reached to the side of the bed where he'd slept during the night, just to see if any warmth lingered on the sheets. Just to judge how long he'd been gone.

But the sheets weren't smooth. Instead her palm slid across a bunch of little bumps and something that crinkled. "What the hell?" Her lids popped open, but she paused as her pupils adjusted to the sunlight streaming through the wall of windows.

Scattered on her sheets were a couple dozen of the little candy hearts just like the one he'd placed in her hand the night before, with an array of cute sayings.

Her flesh tingled around her two small tattoos. The images a college dare, but now so fitting to the way Isaac made love. With passion, yet so sweetly. Toni slid a hand down her body, her fingers hovering over the 4 U pink ink just above her pubic line. With the lights off during each of three encounters—against the door, on the floor, in the bed—she doubted he'd seen the tattoos that were identical to the Sweethearts he left in his place on her bed.

Grinning, she lifted one between thumb and forefinger, flipped it over, and read the message. U R CUTE. With a giggle, she plopped the heart into her mouth, smacking her lips as sugary sweetness melted onto her tongue.

Toni was smiling as she reached for the note he'd left mixed in the candy. She unfolded it, saw it was from the pad in her office, and read.

Toni—

Sorry to leave without waking you, but I had something to do this morning. Call me—555-4321. I'd like to see you again. You're beautiful asleep.

—Isaac

Biting her bottom lip to keep it from trembling, Toni cursed the rise of emotion, though she wasn't sure if she was going to laugh or cry. She sat up, swinging her feet over the edge of the bed, then scooped up all the candy. Padding naked, she carried them to the kitchen and dropped them into a ceramic bowl, tucking his note in between them.

It felt good that he thought enough about her to leave the note, but she doubted she'd use it. They had great sex. He wanted more of it—what man wouldn't? And the truth was, part of her did, too.

But the other part of her was aware now more than ever of all those little pangs that had been haunting her, the longing for something lasting, special. It was time she found a man she could be serious about. *Serious with*.

And speaking of serious, she thought, glancing at the microwave clock, she was going to be seriously late to the game if she didn't get a move on it.

She had just enough time to take a shower and still stop by her studio for freshly charged batteries and empty memory cards. Plus, she needed to pick up her long-range lens and make sure UPS had dropped off her darkroom supplies. On Saturdays Lexi, the woman who owned the flower shop next to her studio, usually signed for them. Or when Toni was out of town on assignment.

Heading toward the bathroom, she knew she needed to be on the road by two o'clock if she was going to make it to Los Angeles for the Lakers' tip-off in time. With a feature being done on Kobe, *Sports Illustrated* would be expecting great shots.

Time to think about business and put Isaac—and all the pleasure he gave her—out of mind. Playtime was over.

Five

It'd only been six days since she'd been with Isaac, but already her body ached to fuck. Closing her eyes, Toni rested her forehead on her steering wheel and took a couple of slow breaths. A long nine months had passed without sex, and in one night Isaac had shown her exactly how much satisfaction she'd missed out on.

Now her body was primed up and ready to go, and although she'd tried to deny it, it was Isaac she wanted. During all the games she'd shot, all the hours on airplanes, and all the time she'd spent going through her digital files making sure the pictures were good, her too-cute speed date—who made love with passion and left candy hearts in her bed—had lingered in her memory.

Memories that made her panties wet.

She lifted her chin and rolled the tension from her shoulders as she tried to forget the way it'd felt to have his hands on her naked flesh.

With an exasperated sigh, Toni opened her car door and got out, ignoring the slickness on her inner thighs. She was glad to be back. She reached in her car, grabbed her camera bags, and flung them over her shoulder. As much as she longed to head home, shed her clothing, and climb into a bubble bath, she had a ton of work to do. Files that had to be downloaded, sorted, and e-mailed.

Not to mention the rolls of film she'd taken of lush white lilies in the hotel atrium that she was eager to develop to see how they turned out.

Feeding a couple of quarters into the meter, Toni headed across the narrow street to her studio. Lexi was just about to open the door, a few UPS envelopes tucked under one arm, but looked up with a smile on her face when she noticed Toni approaching.

"Hey, girl. I was just going to leave these for you." She handed over the envelopes.

"Thanks. Is this all of it?" She waited while Lexi nodded. "Shoot, I was hoping for a shipment of chemicals."

"Sorry, hon. You doing okay, Toni? You look a little flushed."

"Just tired." Tired of being horny and manless. Tired of going to bed alone and finding pleasure with her fingers. Just plain tired, since for the last six nights her dreams had been consumed by a lover. She pasted on a smile. "How about you."

"I'm good," Lexi said, staring down at the new wedding band adorning her finger. Toni had taken the pictures for Lexi and her husband, Jackson, a few months back. The newlyweds were blissfully happy, which until now she thought was sappy. Now she couldn't help feeling a bit envious of having a steady man to share life with.

Trying to forget about the pangs in her heart, Toni adjusted her bags and reached for her keys just as the door pushed open and Jenna came bustling out. "Oops."

"Oh!" She was forced to take a step back to get out of Jenna's way.

Though she loved developing her own pictures, she used her darkrooms less and less as the advances in digital photography made working in that medium more practical. Because Toni hated thinking of them sitting empty and unused, she rented darkroom time to other photographers. Jenna was one of them, and over the last year had become a good friend—the friend who'd supplied the condoms.

"Sorry to plow you over, I'm just so excited about showing these pictures to a friend," Jenna said, holding up a small stack of newly developed photos.

"No problem."

Jenna embraced Toni lightly. "When are you going to have time to gab? I'm dying to know if you met anyone on your speed date."

Toni felt her face flame, and slanted her gaze away, knowing her friend would know too much by the telling look in her eyes. "It was all right. Mostly dorks." Hey, that was the truth.

"Toni, if you're looking to get set up, I'm sure Jackson has some friends—"

Toni put up her hand, cutting off Lexi before she was hooked into a series of blind dates. "I'm not." She forced a laugh. "I'm not sure how I got suckered into the speed-date thing, but I'm glad that's over."

Jenna put her hand on her hip. "Well, that's too bad you didn't meet someone. . . ." Her voice trailed off, her gaze intent on Toni's face. "Oh, my God. You did. Who is he?"

Damn, the trouble with girlfriends—sometimes they knew you too well. Letting a breath rush between her teeth, she glanced at her watch before replying, "Another time, ladies, I've got to get some stuff sent before I can think about men." She resisted the urge to roll her eyes. All she'd done for days was think about men. A man. Isaac.

Jenna embraced Toni again, kissing her cheek briefly. "We'll catch up soon." She moved away from the door, but before she reached the street, she looked back. "Oh, Toni, speaking of men, there was a hottie here to see you. You missed him by a few minutes." She did a quick wave and was gone.

"Probably the UPS guy."

"Huh?" Toni asked, her mind drifting to the only hottie she'd met recently.

Her friend's dark brows plunged together and her smile was mixed with a little smirk. "The UPS guy. He was just here."

"Oh, right. Thanks for signing, Lexi. I'll talk to you later, okay?" She could smell the distinct scent of developer now and the darkroom was calling to her. The roll of film burning a hole in her pocket.

"See you, girl," Lexi said, turning back to her flower shop.

Focused on getting her film developed, Toni entered her studio, and headed to her office to put down her camera bags and mail, her mind on the tasks needed to ready the chemical baths for developing her newest photos.

Distracted, Toni was about to drop the UPS mailers on her desk when she noticed the scattering of candy. Not just any candy, but Isaac's little Sweethearts. "Isaac," she whispered, putting her things down in her leather chair so she wouldn't disturb the sugar hearts.

Picking up a single heart, she read the message printed on the pale green candy. LONG 4 U. Arousal spilled hot and heavy through her system. Her nipples tightened. "I want you, too, baby." She popped the heart into her mouth and sucked until the treat dissolved on her tongue and spread sweetness across her palate.

She chose a peach shade and read the message. LET'S MEET. She ate the second candy, enjoying the flavor, her pulse racing as she thought about Isaac being here in her office and leaving these for her. Although she couldn't help wishing she'd been there when he had. *I would have rewarded him for the effort.*

Unsure if it was the rush of sugar or adrenaline, Toni felt more rejuvenated now than a soak in the tub could've offered. Giggling, she grabbed a third candy and read the message on the way to plop it in her mouth. CALL ME. She paused, the Sweetheart suspended at her lips.

Call him?

Worrying her bottom lip between her teeth, Toni should call herself a liar for thinking she'd never use the number he'd left beside her in bed. If she'd meant it, she'd have thrown the note away without so much as a second thought, but the truth was, she'd kept the note and committed Isaac's number to her cell phone memory.

Isaac—and relief for her lust—was but a phone call away. She took out her cell and scrolled until she found his stored name, but her thumb hovered over the SEND button.

Although sex between them had been fierce and delicious, would a man who just wanted a second night of screwing go through all the trouble to come to her office and leave her candy treats? Her hand shook. Was it possible that maybe, just maybe, he wanted something more?

She hit SEND.

During the moment of silence while the satellites connected, her throat went dry, her chest felt tight, and fear had her closing the phone just as she heard the first ring. She swallowed. Swallowed again, trying to get her pulse to slow, her hands to stop trembling.

After just one encounter, an itsy-bitsy piece of her heart was already invested in this man. It'd be easy—too easy—to lose herself completely.

Toni opened the top drawer of her desk, dropped the phone inside, and closed it again so she wouldn't be tempted to use it. Forcing herself to turn away, she fished the rolls of film from her pocket and left her office to go to the darkroom.

She couldn't call him now. As horny as she'd been, she doubted she'd be able to keep her hands off him. She wanted him so badly. Control—a whole lot of self-control—kept her walking toward the darkroom no matter how her body protested.

Standing on the sidewalk outside the plate glass door, Isaac again stared at the caller ID on his cell with a sense of satisfaction. No doubt about it, the call had come from Ray Studios. *From Toni.*

Even if she'd hung up before saying a word, at least she'd called. Flipping a U-turn hadn't been a problem, even with a couple of passing drivers laying on the horn. He was damned well headed back to her office, where fifteen minutes before, he'd left her candy . . . and something else. His pride and part of his soul.

He acknowledged he was an asshole for leaving her bed without saying good-bye. But he hadn't wanted to say good-bye at all and had hoped she'd use the phone number. She hadn't. And the week was one long, miserable hard-on. And a whole lot of too-damned-cold showers.

Desiring more than just sex, he wanted to see her again. Wanted to know what she ate for breakfast, what she hoped for in the future, what she slept in when she was alone. Wanted to admire her smile, and enjoy her enthusiasm for basketball and beer.

The fact that he'd also cleaned out the drugstore's condom supply meant he wanted to get to know her better between the sheets, too.

Shrugging his shoulders, Isaac set aside the torture of the last six days and pulled open her studio door. Aside from the music—smooth and soulful—drifting across the front room and her office door being open, things looked about the same as they had a quarter of an hour ago.

No Toni. "Toni?" he called out, looking at the two doorways that were covered with what looked like dressing-room curtains. When she didn't reply, he said her name louder. "Toni, are you here?"

Only John Legend's lyrics answered him, but after a moment the song faded and he heard the sweetness of Toni's voice. "In here, Isaac."

She knew him by voice alone. He knew he was grinning like a fool as he strolled to the curtain in the direction her voice had come from, and twisted his fingers into the material. He paused before he yanked it open, a distinct chemical smell coming from the other side. "Can I come in?"

"Yeah."

Isaac pulled the curtain aside, stepped through, then let it fall back into place. He stepped into a short hallway with walls painted black, illuminated only by the faint glow of red light. He turned twice and finally entered a ten-by-ten room, with counters on three sides and the sound of running water.

And Toni. She wore sweatpants and a T-shirt, but in the red light it was impossible to tell the color. The long blond strands of her hair were pulled back into a braid, showing the beautiful mouth he wanted to be kissing, and large chocolate eyes that held him completely mesmerized.

She watched him, a slow smile turning her lush lips, her melting gaze at once warming his gut and causing his dick to go solid. "Hi, Isaac."

Hell, the way she said his name had him throbbing, lust so fierce he was actually dizzy—all the blood drained from his brain to fill his erection. "You called," he said, knowing how stupid it sounded.

"You brought me more candy."

He took a few long strides forward, yearning to get her within arms' reach. Longing to touch her. "I was hoping you'd be here. I've wanted to see you."

"I've wanted *you*." A low moan escaped her luscious mouth, but she stifled the full effect by tucking her lip between her teeth in much the way he yearned to.

It took a second for her words to sink in, but his cock reacted instantly, straining behind his button fly. He swallowed. "Oh, yeah?"

"Ooooh, yeahhhh." Her words were spoken softly, but he felt them clearly. She touched the hem of his shirt, then tucked her hand beneath. She scraped her nails across his skin, caressing his navel and swirling her fingertips in the line of hair that dripped from beneath it downward to the base of his dick.

He forgot to breathe.

"Thank you for the candies," she said, reaching her other hand for his shoulder and lifting on tiptoes.

He helped her out, bending to greet her. Supple lips melded to his, her tongue stroking across his mouth. She nipped at his lower lip, then sucked it in a rhythm that mimicked fucking. Groaning, Isaac took control of the kiss before her seduction had him cuming too early.

He slanted his head, thrust his tongue past her lips, and was met with a rush of sugary sweetness. She was warm and pliant, the velvety depths intoxicating. "You taste good, sweetheart," he mumbled against her mouth. *She's eating the hearts.*

"I bet you taste good, too, baby." She ended the kiss, her hand beneath his shirt working free the first button on his fly. She lowered to her knees before him, and worked the next two buttons free.

Isaac groaned, closed his eyes, and turned his face to the ceiling as he sucked in a few sharp breaths to gather his control. Control that damned near snapped when he felt her warm tongue on his flesh. She kissed the triangle of exposed skin, an open wet mouth moving down the thin trail of hair.

"Is this what you want, Isaac?" she asked, curling her fingers around his cock, encased in denim. She squeezed until she forced a jagged breath from him, then stroked the length through his pants with the featherlight touch of her fingertips. With her other hand she worked free the last couple of buttons.

Nostrils flared, he clenched his fists at his sides, and spoke through clamped teeth. "You don't have to do this, Toni." His body throbbed in protest, hoping she wouldn't stop.

With an open mouth and wet tongue, she caressed him,

each kiss longer than the last. "I want to." She eased down his pants and briefs until his swollen head was exposed to the cool air. With one languid stroke, she licked the slit where a pearl of pre-cum glistened like a ruby in the red darkroom light.

Air hissed between his teeth as her mouth closed around him, her tongue defining the ridge of his cock, lapping against the vein running the length of his erection.

With the sweetness of candy hearts lingering on her tongue, she wanted nothing more than to absorb the taste of Isaac's flesh. Toni put one hand on each of his thighs and pulled his jeans farther down, exposing a few more inches of his hard-on. She could feel his abs quiver, hear the way his breathing changed, sense the tension building in his balled-up hands, and it turned her on. Her nipples beaded; her panties went from damp to soaking wet.

With her inner thighs aching, she appeased her lust with the taste of the masculine saltiness of his skin, the bittersweetness of his arousal. She took his head between her lips, opening wide to ease him down her throat, her hands pulling his pants again until they slid down his legs and fell around his ankles. Closing her eyes, she took more of his thick cock, then slid back as she added suction.

His dick bucked, his sac drew up tight, and his hands settled on the back of her head. Keeping her eyes closed, Toni focused on his reactions and tried to slow the racing of her heart as his fingers tangled in her hair. His touch was gentle as he caressed her, but she could tell he was holding back from putting on some pressure and pumping into her.

She allowed his dick to slide from her mouth, looked up at him, and smiled when he grumbled. "Is this what you want?"

Placing her hand around him, she stroked him from base to head, lubricated by her saliva and the liquid evidence of his arousal.

"Do your best." His voice was strained, but held the subtle hint of challenge.

She increased the tempo of her caresses, her fingers curled around him. Each time she stroked, she brought his head to her lips and touched her tongue to him as she thrust upward. "My best? Hmmm?"

She took his cock into her mouth, matched the rhythm of her hand, and allowed his erection to slide down her throat, never missing a beat as she went from hand job to a good sucking.

"Aw, hell." His knees shook. His entire body trembled.

Tightening her cheeks, she stroked down his cock, her tongue working the ridge of his head as she moved up again. In and out, she sucked, never allowing him entirely from her mouth. Her body swayed as she worked him, the lace of her bra abrasive against her sensitive puckered nipples. Each long stroke of her mouth resulted in a rolling of her hips that brought her clit into contact with her panties.

Clamping her thighs together to make the sensation more intense, she worked his dick, finding her own pleasure in every movement. Her breaths shortened. Heat skittered across her skin, and beneath her palms she could feel the sheen of sweat covering Isaac's body.

Moving from his thigh, she closed a hand around his balls. "Aw, hell, Toni," he groaned, his voice raspy and broken. His hands tightened in her hair.

Against her tongue she could feel the pulse of his climax building in the base of his rocked-up dick. She could taste the beginning of his orgasm with each hot, wet stroke. It fueled her own. With one final dip forward of her hip, one more tug of cloth against her clit was all she needed.

"Oh, God." He tried to pull out, but she sucked deeper, not slowing her rhythm or the suction of her lips around his cock. Closing her eyes, she allowed climax to claim her as she swallowed his—a slick ball of fire gushed down her throat. A violent shudder clamped down between her legs.

When his body stopped throbbing, she moved back and took a breath, orgasm still pulsing through the walls of her pussy. Cum seeping onto her inner thighs.

He stood before her for a few moments longer, sucking deep breaths into his lungs. His body shuddered, and he reached down to her, lacing their fingers as he helped her to her feet. Her cheeks felt warm as he tucked his fingers beneath her chin and slanted her face toward his. She licked her lips, realizing they felt slightly swollen and tasted of his climax.

His touch was gentle, his hands framing her face, his fingers extending into her hair. He brushed his mouth across her lips, then touched his forehead to hers. "Wow."

She smiled, turning her face into his palm, enjoying the intimacy of the encounter. "You liked that?"

He kissed her again, this time a little longer and deeper. An expression of gratitude? "Sure as hell beat all the cold showers I've had this week."

She looked at him, the gray blue of his eyes reflecting her own smug little grin. "You've been taking cold showers?"

"Yeah. Don't do that to me again."

Toni's heart thumped hard, but she pretended she didn't know what she'd done. Her hand slipped under his shirt, smoothing her palm across his taut flesh. "Me? What did I do?" She flicked her nail over his flat nipple.

He groaned. "You didn't call me."

"I called you."

"Today."

"I still called," she said, scraping her nails down his chest, enjoying the way his body trembled in response.

Isaac touched her on the chin, his strong thumb smoothing across her lips. "Sweetheart, don't make me wait another six to see you again."

A battle waged, the part of her that'd been desperate to see him again ready to agree, despite some lingering fear she was jumping too high, too fast. A quiet moment passed before she took a deep breath, then exhaled slowly. "I won't."

"Promise me."

She nodded. Pursing her lips, she tilted a hip to the side. "Want to find out if I keep my promises, too?"

He laughed. "Yeah. Go out with me tonight." Before she could reply, he kissed her, silencing any protest with his tongue. But he slowed the kiss before she was able to fully develop it. "I'll bring more candy."

Smiling, she pressed her cheek to his chest and wrapped her arms around him. It felt damned good to hold him close, to feel his chest against her cheek, to smell the spiciness of his cologne. "Okay," she said softly, "but only for more Sweethearts."

Six

Toni closed her eyes for a moment, aware of Isaac behind her as the people jostled around them, the solid wall of his chest warm and comforting. She inhaled the subtle hint of his cologne, a scent she'd become accustomed to during the last ten days. A fragrance she'd gotten to know when she had her mouth pressed to his skin, when they'd made love, and when he wasn't there, by cuddling up with the pillow he'd slept on.

She opened her eyes, laced her fingers with Isaac's, and led him through the Staples Center crowd. Moving with confidence, she knew the ins and outs of this building and could have avoided most of the crowds by using her press pass, but tonight wasn't work.

Being with Isaac was purely for *pleasure*.

Suppressing a whimper of need, she tightened her hand and grinned when he squeezed back, then stroked his thumb across her palm in a way that made her nipples pucker and her breath catch in her throat.

Focused on getting to their seats by tip-off, she led him around the concession lines, past the pro shop, and down the stairs leading to the court. Some people had already taken their places, so when they reached their row—two back from the floor—they had to sidestep past knees to get to theirs.

"No camera tonight, Toni?" a man asked, lounging a few seats away.

Just about to sit down, Toni turned with a smile toward the man, knowing his voice well. Speaking loudly to be heard over all the people still shuffling into their seats, Toni replied, "I'm not working, Jack." She leaned across a few empty chairs and they kissed in greeting, but she felt Isaac tense behind her. "I'm on a date."

Jack swung his gaze to Isaac and assessed him much the way a father would. After a moment he stuck out his hand. "Jack."

Glancing over her shoulder, Toni couldn't help smiling at the look on Isaac's face as he shook Jack's hand and intro-duced himself. A mixture of awe and suspicion.

Turning his attention back to her, Jack said, "About time you get to just watch the game."

"Tell me about it." It'd been months since she'd been able to use these seats. Her daddy had been a season ticket holder for years, first at the Forum and now at the Staples Center. At so many of the games, she'd given away her tickets to friends because she was usually busy moving around the arena with several cameras draped around her neck.

Toni was just getting settled when she felt Isaac's light touch on her cheek. He brushed her hair back with his knuck-les, then leaned over and whispered in her ear, "Jack Nicholson kissed you." His breath was warm as it rippled across her skin, but his tone had Toni struggling to keep from laughing.

He was jealous.

"He's a Lakers fan," she said, watching his gray-blue eyes darken. His jaw tighten.

Part of her itched to touch his face with her fingertips, to smooth the slight frown from his lips with a kiss, but the other part of her damned well wanted to watch the play of emotion in his storming gaze.

He bent toward her, brushing his mouth against the lobe of her ear. His voice dropped. Low and raspy, he asked, "If I say I'm a Lakers fan, can I fuck you tonight?"

Her clit tingled, and her panties felt damp as the ache she felt for him increased. Grinning, she thought about how to answer. They'd be fucking later either way, but she was enjoying teasing him.

"Depends."

"Oh." He nipped her lobe with his teeth. "On?"

"Are you a Lakers fan?" She knew he wasn't. She'd seen his 76ers hat.

He groaned. "No."

She pursed her lips. "Hmmm."

Isaac sat up, put his head back, and laughed. If they hadn't been in such a public place, he'd have kissed that smirk right off her face. "Doesn't sound promising."

She shrugged. "We'll have to see." She tucked her arm beneath his, then curled her fingers around his hand. The music went up, the beat strong as the Laker Girls took to the floor. The crowd quieted and they sat in silence for a few minutes watching the dancers work it out.

When the music went down and the girls cleared the floor,

he could hear Toni sigh as she leaned into him, resting her cheek against his shoulder. Sharp teeth nipped at his flesh through his shirt. "Guess we'll have to see who you root for."

Isaac glanced down at her and she winked at him, her chocolaty eyes making promises—promises he knew she'd keep. Blood rushed to his cock, rocking him up with one simple hint of what was to come later.

One suggestive blink of her eye.

His heartbeat throbbed in his dick, though he tried to relax, tried to ignore his reaction to her whenever she was close. And now, here among tens of thousands of other people, she was curled against his side and he had a hard-on barely held in check by his pants.

Even in the crowd—people around them drinking beer and eating—he was completely aware of the floral scent of her shampoo, the feminine sweetness of her skin. The sugary aroma of Sweethearts on her breath.

Isaac inhaled deeply a couple of times, trying to settle down, trying to enjoy the game rather than just thinking of what he planned to do to Toni when he got her home. By the end of the first quarter enough blood had returned to his brain for him to at least think straight.

By halftime his cock wasn't making its presence known to anyone who bothered to glance at his lap. Leaning back in his seat, he watched some ads play across the big screen while the players were in the locker rooms.

A *Sports Illustrated* cover with Kobe leaping in the air flashed on the screen and the fans screamed. Isaac grinned, recognizing the picture as one Toni had taken. He'd seen it on her computer proofs while she worked on her laptop in bed earlier that week, and he'd tried to distract her with kisses.

"How'd you get that gig?" he asked, slanting his head

toward the screen promoting the feature on the Lakers' star player.

"*Sports Illustrated*, you mean?"

"Yeah. How does a woman like you"—he brought her hand to his mouth and kissed her palm when he saw the protest heat her eyes—"end up shooting pictures of athletes?"

She seemed appeased by the swipe of his tongue to her skin. She smiled, then sighed. "It just happened."

"How's that?"

Toni leaned back, then angled her body in the seat to face him. He held her hand in his, his thumb tracing circles against her palm where a moment before his lips had been. There was something arousing about the way his thumb moved against her skin, something that had her aching to have him work the same way against her clit.

But there was something equally arousing about him asking about her, wanting to know more than how she felt between the sheets. He asked questions about what she did. Who she was. What yearnings she held in her soul.

Her throat felt dry, emotion swelling as she looked at his face, so intent on what she had to say. Taking a breath, she thought back over her career, trying to decide how far back to begin her story.

"I've always had a thing for pictures. Used to borrow my mom's camera as a little girl. From the time I was about eight, I'm no longer in any of the pictures."

He laughed. "Because you were taking them?"

"Good guess."

"Like my mom."

Toni wondered about his mother, what sort of woman she

was. If she'd ever have a chance to meet her. She swallowed, trying to wet her throat, feeling like a fool. Those thoughts were for a serious man—one you had a future with. She blinked away the burning behind her eyes and cleared her throat.

"So, for high school graduation, my grandma gave me a really nice camera. I ended up putting myself through college as an assistant at a studio that does weddings and parties."

"How'd weddings turn into sports?"

"I used to take a lot of pictures of my brother, Nathan. He played football for the University of Southern California Trojans. Now he's an assistant coach for the San Diego Chargers." She watched his face for the connection to be made, knowing he was much more a fan of football than basketball.

He arched a dark brow. "Nathan Ray is your brother. Hmmm. Are you two close?" Isaac asked, brushing a lock of hair from her face, then skimming his fingertips down the pulse racing along her throat.

Toni grinned, thinking about how she'd pestered Nathan to let her tag along with the rest of the ballplayers when he played for USC. "Yeah, Nathan's my best friend." Isaac didn't need to know it'd been her brother's friends' attention that had built her confidence with men.

Those same guys who taught her by their treatment of their girlfriends how to use her looks to get what she wanted from a man. But using her body's charm left her soul empty and her life lonely. "Until you, I spent most of my free time with him. He's wondering about you." Her chest ached, her heart pounding heavily as she waited for his reaction to her brother's wanting to meet him.

"Whenever you want, sweetheart. Did you tell him I'm your man?"

"I told her you're my friend."

His hand settled on the back of her neck, his fingers tangling in her hair as he lowered to whisper in her ear. "Was I just your friend when I fucked you against the door? Was I just your friend when I came down your throat?" He paused for a moment, the words suspended between them. "Will I be just your friend when I wake up tomorrow to you riding me?"

His tongue slid along the shell of her ear, his breath deliciously hot as it slipped beneath her jersey and skittered down her spine. She trembled, arousal pouring through her blood, her insides clamping down with a need to be filled by his long, thick cock. "No." *Not just a friend.*

"No. I'm your man."

Toni bit her bottom lip, studying his face as he leaned back in his seat with a gleam of satisfaction brightening his gray-blue eyes. His smug arrogance about their relationship was the best aphrodisiac she'd ever had. She wanted him. Now.

Sprawling casually in his chair, he caressed her leg with one large hand. "So how'd college pictures end up making your career?"

He shifted gears so quickly, Toni had to shake her head and recall what they'd been talking about before he about made her cream her pants. Oh, right, being a photographer. She took a couple of deep breaths, gathering her composure.

"Some of my pictures made the school papers. Then when they made the national-championship game, I was contacted by *Sports Illustrated*, who wanted to buy some photos. Progressed fr—" The crowd went nuts, drowning out the sound of her voice as the Lakers came back onto the court.

Toni got to her feet, yanking Isaac by the hand to stand with her and cheer. She threw her hands in the air, waving them from side to side, wishing she'd remembered her pompoms when they'd driven up from San Diego, but Isaac had distracted her.

Swaying to the beat of Destiny's Child, she screamed for the dancers and rocked her hips, slowing only when his large hand settled on the small of her back, slipped beneath her Devean George jersey. His hand was strong, his touch seductive against her skin.

The importance of the game faded, the second half no longer holding as much appeal as the man standing beside her. The seats—the seats she used so little—could be abandoned for all she cared at that moment. She wanted nothing more than to be at home, naked, with Isaac touching her, stroking her, fucking her.

Her nipples beaded, chafing against the lace of her bra. Her panties were soaked and she was glad she was wearing jeans to keep the slickness from her thighs.

Toni slanted her head and glanced into Isaac's eyes. The intensity of his gaze had her knees feeling weak, had her struggling to breathe.

There was something fierce and possessive in his look that had her yearning for something more. This gaze was filled with a different type of promise, which she hoped was kept like his others.

"Isaac," she whispered, "you're a pretty good Laker fan."

He chuckled, the look in his eyes telling her he knew just what she was talking about. His gaze drifted downward to her puckered nipples, sweeping as much heat across her skin as if he'd caressed her. "To hell with the Lakers, sweetheart, I'm here for you."

A little louder and he would have gotten his ass whooped, Toni thought. Wondering how many people around them heard

Isaac's comment, she glanced toward Jack, but he was watching the referees start the second half of the game.

Putting one hand behind his head, she urged him forward, lifted on tiptoes, and kissed his mouth. One glide of her tongue—just a taste until later—then she ended the kiss and stepped back, giving him a wink when he groaned in dissent.

"Shhh." She pressed a finger to her lips. "For me. Then sit down and enjoy the rest of the game *with me*."

Nodding, he reached into his pocket, withdrew a few hearts, and glanced down to check out the messages. He laughed, arching a brow as he selected one, then dropped the rest back into his pocket. "Anything for you, Toni. Just promise me one thing."

"What's that?"

He took her hand in his, turning it palm up, then placed the yellow candy heart there.

Toni looked down and read. L8R.

This wasn't exactly what he'd had in mind when he'd put that L8R heart in Toni's hand, Isaac thought, settling into the booth across from her cute, smiling face. Hell no, he'd meant the *later* to be in bed, not a Mexican restaurant over a plate of nachos.

He studied her eyes, his gaze then drifting to her lips as they closed around a chip piled with salsa. "I thought I was a good Laker fan tonight."

Her tongue smoothed across her bottom lip, swiping away a chunk of tomato. "You were." She'd reached for another chip and was busy swirling it in the bowl of chopped tomatoes and peppers, but glanced up at him from beneath long lashes. The provocative look was meant to tease—and it worked, blood rushing to his dick as she licked her lips for a second time.

He cleared his throat, finding words hard to form when his body needed release so badly. Needed her. "What are we doing here, Toni?"

She kept her head down, but he could see her shoulders shaking with laughter. "We're eating." He heard the amusement in her words, her voice so sweet, so alluring. Hell, she *was* a tease, knowing exactly what she was doing to him.

Two could play this game. Getting to his feet, Isaac moved to her side of the booth and slid in beside her. Her chocolaty eyes opened wide as he reached for her hand and settled it over the erection straining in his pants.

"Is that for me, baby?" she asked, her fingers curling around him, her eyes settling on his.

"It's for you." He leaned closer, enjoying her nearness as much as her touch. "I'm learning to live like this."

"Why?" Her words were low and soft, her breath warm against his skin.

"Because I'm always thinking about you." Her chin tilted up, and there was something in her eyes that went dull for the briefest moment, like she wasn't thrilled by what he'd said.

With one hand holding her palm against his rocked-up cock, he used his free hand to reach for a chip, loaded it with salsa, and held it to Toni's lips. The warmth had returned to her eyes, a smile touching her lips just as she closed around the food.

"Something's going on."

She chewed, not responding, though her thumb smoothed continuously across his flesh creating a throb he felt clear in his gut.

He swallowed to ease the dryness in his throat, then went on, torn between the distractions of lust and an emotion he wasn't ready to name. "There's something between us."

"Kem-sty," she said over a mouthful of chips.

Isaac grinned. "Amazing chemistry."

She nodded.

Hell, yeah, he liked the way that fit. What happened between them *was* sparks and flashbulbs, easily explained by their chemistry and the charge their bodies created together. There was a connection between them he'd not felt with other bed partners. Other lovers.

But with others it'd always been about the sex. With Toni there was something more. He wanted to know her, and stranger yet, he wanted to share parts of himself.

Though his body still demanded release, blood keeping his cock solid, he felt his shoulders relax as he lounged next to Toni and allowed their conversation to slip into the topic of their favorite foods. Felt content as they fed each other, laughing about shared interests between nibbles of chips and bites of nachos.

He could tell by the feathering of her movements that the motion was absentminded now, but her fingers continued to caress him through the cloth as she asked him of his education, career, friends, and family.

Inhaling the floral sweetness of her skin, he told her of his sister and two nieces, of his brother's struggles being newly divorced, of his parents' long and happy marriage.

He hadn't noticed how long they sat talking until he reached for his plate and found the food cold, their glasses empty. His gaze swung in her direction; her face turned toward his, her perfect lips plump, just begging to be kissed.

"So, Laker fan, you want to come home with me?" Her

hand tightened around his hard-on, her gaze slowly lowering to where the table's shadow shielded their fondling.

"You did promise me *L8R*." The throb of blood was heavy now. Sucking a few deep breaths, he willed it away in order to stand up.

She pressed her mouth to his lips, her tongue tracing over him. She didn't linger as long as he'd have liked, and allowed her fingers to fall from his crotch as she ended the quick kiss. "I'll do better than just later. I'll give you the rest of the night."

Seven

Didn't matter how he angled them, the two boards weren't going to fit together. Annoyed, Isaac set the pieces of wood aside and reached for the directions, knowing damned well that if he'd been thinking straight, he wouldn't need them.

"Any luck?" Collin asked, setting a bottle of beer down next to him.

"You couldn't buy a preassembled CD cabinet?" At least the glass was cold, droplets of condensation wetting his skin as he brought the drink to his lips and chugged some down, grateful for the respite from distraction. The distraction of constantly thinking of Toni.

His brother took a long drink from his own beer before answering. "Cheaper this way, and I've got a lot to buy."

Isaac nodded, his gaze shifting around the close-to-empty apartment. Nothing of his brother's former life remained with him, all taken by his ex-wife. Setting the half-filled beer bottle aside, Isaac squeezed his lids closed and rubbed the bridge of his nose between his thumb and forefinger, his mind dwelling on earlier that morning.

On the sweetness of Toni's smile as she'd cooked him breakfast and brought it to him in bed. How she'd laughed between bites of pancakes and eggs, telling him about the assignment she was leaving for a few hours later.

Sexy as hell, she sat with the sheet pulled up over her breasts, one dusky nipple partially exposed, and licked syrup from his fingertips, making suggestive comments that had him yearning to replace his digits with his dick.

But what kept his body wrapped up in knots and an anxious rhythm pumping in his heart was the way she'd kissed him good-bye when he'd driven her to the airport. Tender and loving, that kiss couldn't have been any better. Couldn't have sizzled any hotter.

Opening his eyes, Isaac once again glanced at his brother. It was hard to image Toni raking him over the coals the way Collin's ex had. Reaching for the cabinet instructions again, he knew one thing for certain. He never wanted to give her a reason.

He cleared his throat. "I think there's some missing pieces." He held out the paper, tapping his fingers against a labeled part that he couldn't find in the package of supplies.

Collin looked at the instructions for a minute, then nodded. He took another long drink from his beer. "You still sleeping with your speed date?"

Isaac scoffed. Speed date—there wasn't much fast about the way he'd been fucking Toni. Not that he'd be giving his brother details. "Toni. I'm still seeing her."

His brother snorted, his grin turning into a goofy smirk. "You like her. Holy shit, Isaac, you *like* her."

Gritting his teeth, he was damned glad he was holding the paper in one hand and a board in the other. It'd keep him from curling his hands into fists. Keep him from revealing just how much he cared when he knocked the wind from his brother's body. "Yeah, I like her."

"Isaac likes a girl. He really, really likes her," he chanted, in the tune of the Life cereal commercial. He was smug now, with a grin that Isaac would've enjoyed pounding off his face—just to show a little brotherly love.

"What's wrong with me liking Toni?"

"Not a thing, little brother. It's just you don't usually like them. You just like to screw 'em and lose 'em."

Rolling his shoulders, Isaac kicked over the box the cabinet had come in, hoping he'd missed something inside. He needed to do something else, because the truth was, he couldn't deny his brother's words even had he wanted to.

He had never lacked for dates, but he'd never given a damn about making anything from a single one of them. Never would have guessed that a three-minute encounter with a stranger could leave him craving her. Leave him dreading the following days that she'd be out of town on business.

Tension tightening in his gut, he took a couple of deep breaths before turning back to Collin. "What else you got that needs putting together?"

Better that he do something, be physical and helpful, than reminisce about each of their dates, all they'd talked about and shared, all the passion they'd made love with. Better to focus on the here and now than to get lost in four days of lonely desires.

In thirty-two years, he'd never once thought of himself as a romantic.

Until now.

Adjusting himself in the sand, Isaac leaned back on one elbow and watched Toni across the small blanket, her lids drooping, her gaze turned toward the waves rolling onto the beach ten yards away. Her hair was pulled back from her face, giving him a chance to study her profile, her small, perfect nose, her pouty full lips, the sensual slope of her throat.

In the four long days she'd been out of town on assignment, he'd thought he'd go crazy from wanting her so bad. There hadn't been a moment she wasn't on his mind; not a second passed without him needing her in his arms. In his bed.

Four days that changed his life.

Without her beside him, he'd realized something. *He wanted her to be.*

Isaac took a deep breath of the cool salty air, the fine spray of the ocean mist doing nothing to chill his body's fire. Never in his life had a woman made him think of beyond tomorrow. But Toni—oh, fuck!

I'm in love with her.

His gut clenched up tight; his hands fisted into the cool, damp sand beside him. She made him think of their future, made him want things he'd never given much thought to before.

Permanent things.

Just over a month since he'd stepped up to her speed-date table. Three minutes later his fate had been sealed by a quick kiss and a Sweetheart.

Beside him, Toni exhaled, putting a hand over her mouth to try to stifle a yawn.

"You're tired."

Her gaze slid slowly away from the Pacific, her chocolate eyes looking darker as the sun dripped over the vast ocean.

"Yeah, and a little jet-lagged." She spoke softly as she put her hand on her shoulder and massaged her nape.

"Come here, let me do that for you," Isaac said, sitting up and brushing the sand from his hands. He set aside the remains of the picnic—a picnic he'd packed to welcome Toni home after her four-day absence, but the truth was, the picnic was for him. He wanted her alone, where he could look at her.

Hold her.

He put out his hand and she took it, her fingers warm against his skin. Helping her ease across the blanket, he spread his legs; with his heels in the sand he bent his knees so she could sit between them. She sighed as she settled in the V created, and leaned against him, her back to his chest. A hand rested gently on each of his thighs, sending sensation straight to his dick. His sac drew up.

Ignoring his erection, he rubbed Toni's shoulders, rotating his thumb in circles down her spine. "You get good pictures?" He worked his fingers along her shoulder blades, the knotted-up muscles eventually giving in under his tender manipulations.

"Mmhmm. I'll show you later." Her lashes fluttered down to rest on her cheeks.

His fingers skimmed down her back and Toni whimpered, her head lolling to the side. He smoothed lower, settling his palms about her waist.

Toni giggled, "That tickles, baby."

"Do you want me to stop?" he asked, leaning forward to claim her neck with his mouth. He dusted kisses along her pulse, touched his tongue to her skin beneath her ear until she trembled in response and her breathing shortened. When she moaned, he wrapped one arm around her and tugged her toward him so she could feel his hard dick throb at the small of her back.

"Please. Please . . . don't . . . stop."

Exactly what he wanted to hear. "I've got something for you."

"This?" She reached behind her, curling her delicate fingers around the jeans encasing his hard cock, then squeezed until air hissed between his teeth.

He clamped his jaws together, working to remain in control. It'd be damned easy to lay her back on the blanket, strip her out of her clothes, and fuck her the way he wanted. Hell, he'd even packed condoms. So what, they were on the beach? Sunset in late March, they wouldn't be noticed. No one was around even with the Coronado Island beaches being a prime tourist destination.

"Later," he managed, though blood for thinking had abandoned him. Isaac reached into the basket and pulled out a candy heart instead, then held it where she could read it. "This." U R CUTE.

She laughed. "So are you." She angled her head back in order to look up at him.

Her plump lips parted oh so temptingly, he covered her mouth, thrusting his tongue past her teeth into her warm velvety depths. Slanting over her, he stroked her sleek heat, then found a rhythm with his tongue like he'd like to pump with his dick.

Her hand tightened around his hard-on and matched his movements. A languid pace, slow and leisurely, as he found pleasure in her touch, in the scent of her arousal mixing with the ocean breeze, in the throaty whimpers she made each time his cock bucked against her palm.

Just when the tempo began to pick up speed, Isaac slowed the kiss and released her mouth. He had to slow down or cum in his pants before he was able to get Toni off.

"Kiss m—"

"Sshh . . ." He brought the U R CUTE candy up and smoothed it across her lower wet lip, then plopped the heart into her mouth. Moaning, she licked away the sugar with the little pink tip of her tongue.

He touched his hand to her waist, found the hem of her blouse, and slid his fingers beneath the fine material, the silken texture of her skin much softer.

With his thumb, he found the shallow indent of her belly button and the diamond piercing. He flicked a nail across the gold and rock.

She shuddered, then rolled her hips back against his groin. "Stop playing, Isaac, and give me something."

Knowing exactly what she wanted, he grinned with satisfaction as darkness settled around them, the last splinters of sunlight shimmering pink along the horizon.

Soon. Soon he'd be inside her.

He reached for another Sweetheart, holding it up for her to read before he placed it to her lips.

BE MINE.

"Isaac, baby, I am."

Toni blinked hard to hold back tears, the heart melting on her tongue. It'd been a miserable trip, the longest stretch they'd been apart in the last few weeks. She'd been distracted and restless, wanting only one thing: Isaac's hands on her, his cock in her pussy moving against her clit. Yet it was more than just the sex she'd missed, but being with him.

She covered his hand with hers, then guided his palm

lower, across where butterflies fluttered, to the waistband of her capris. Not wanting to think about the implications of the Sweetheart or her reply, she directed his hand over her 4 U candy-heart tattoo to the manicured line of her pubic hair.

The message on his Sweetheart held subtle promises, the first she doubted Isaac had any intention of living up to. Although she was having a good time with this one-night stand turned fling, serious wasn't on the menu. Only candy hearts were. He never mentioned a future, so if they were living for the moment, she wanted to enjoy it to the fullest.

"For you," she whispered, leading his forefinger in an outline of her tattoo, then farther. The short hairs were wet with arousal as she eased her knees apart and pressed his fingers to her clit. Her breath caught in her throat, but she forced it out with a soft murmur of need.

"For you, Isaac. I'm wet for you." She rolled her hip, bringing her knees up some so she could open herself for his touch. "Do you want me?"

His erection jerked hard against her, his body shaking. "Yeah, sweetheart, I do." He slid his other hand beneath her shirt and with deft fingers unhooked the front clasp of her bra with one quick twist. His palm brushed over her tit, the puckered nipple straining for his attention.

He cupped her breast, his strong hand squeezing firmly, then rolled her beaded nipple between his thumb and forefinger. When she moved against his hand, he tugged the tightened tip to a flash of surprise before soothing away the sting with the featherlight caresses of his fingertips.

"Oh, God, you feel good," he mumbled, his voice strained, as he thrust two fingers inside her, his thumb circling her clit rhythmically.

He pressed a wet, openmouthed kiss to her shoulder, his

tongue flickering along her pulse until she trembled and tightened her hand around his dick, wanting him to feel the same consuming lust.

A growl rumbled from his chest and vibrated across her skin, as he thrust his fingers in deeper, easing her lips apart and coaxing her juices from her. Her fingers were there, too, drenched with her arousal, touching Isaac's as he thrust in and out her of her body. Urging him to go faster.

Swallowing down the emotion of being held by him, she stared out at the black choppy water, watching how the reflection of the Hotel del Coronado lights danced along the waves in time with their heavy breathing and broken pants.

The wind had picked up; cool and damp, it soothed her skin, which burned from the inside. Toni tilted her chin to the sky, and lowered her lashes to focus on the coil of building climax.

She touched his thumb, pressing it more firmly against her clit. Making his circles faster.

He chuckled. "You like that?"

"I missed you." It was a whisper and she was unsure if he'd heard her until he answered a few moments later.

"Good. Prove it." He held her captive, one hand over her tit, the other working her pussy. "Cum for me." His hand plunged into her, his thumb tapping against her clit.

The tremors started, first on her inner thighs, then deep inside her. She nodded, gasping for breaths, unable to answer as orgasm flashed powerfully through her. On her own fingers, she felt the spasm around his hand, the slickness of her juices pour from her body. She felt the need to clamp her legs closed and hold him there.

To draw the sensations out.

"Ah . . . oh, Isaac." Air whooshed from between her lips

as she grasped his upper arm with her free hand to anchor herself as her body shook with release.

"Sweetheart, I've got you." He held her close. Abandoning her breast, he stroked her hair, touched her cheek, and pressed gentle kisses to her closed eyelids.

Toni wondered if her heart would burst; it thumped so hard. His touch was so gentle. More than sex, his caresses made her feel cherished. Her body still throbbing, this path of emotion was too raw to deal with at the moment. Taking a breath, she opened her eyes and slanted her head so she could look up at his face.

He was smiling when he kissed her briefly on the mouth. "You okay?" he asked, holding up a candy heart that said the same thing. U OK.

Toni laughed, drawing up her knees so she could turn in his arms. "Yes." She pressed a quick kiss to the V of his collarbone where his button-down shirt gaped open. "Where do you keep getting these hearts?" She took U OK and stuck it in her mouth.

"My nieces. My sister's the director of marketing, so her two little girls keep me supplied."

"Cute. How old are—" A yawn overtook her words.

"Let's get you home."

Toni nodded, sleepiness making her movements slow and heavy.

"Don't fall asleep on me, Toni. I'm not done with you yet."

She couldn't help smiling. "You making promises again?"

"Hell, yeah."

Eight

Isaac put his hand over Toni's when she reached for the light switch. "Leave them off."

He dropped the suitcase he'd carried up from her car on the floor by the door, then turned her in his arms and held her against him. The scent of the ocean lingered in her hair.

Tucking her head beneath his chin, he inhaled the floral scent of her skin, reveled in the feel of her small hands on his back, rejoiced when she sighed and snuggled closer.

And he felt it then, the subtle but undeniable shift in the way he looked at life and his future. While he'd dated—and slept with—his share of women, holding her this way was the first time he knew what he'd been missing, that the part of his heart held apart had been saved for Toni.

Only Toni.

He took a breath, sliding his hands across her shoulders,

down her back, over the rounded slope of her ass. She shivered against him, then held him tighter as she turned her face and pressed her mouth to his chest. Kissed him where his heart throbbed. For her.

"Leave the lights off? You going to love me?" she asked between soft kisses, but he could feel the heat of her lips even through his shirt.

. . . *going to love you? Baby, I already do*. And the little bit of emptiness in his soul filled by his loving her. By his admitting it.

Isaac bent, putting a hand behind her knees, and scooped her into his arms, held the lush curves of her body cradled against his chest. "Yeah, sweetheart, I'm making love to you."

In the dimness of her apartment, the only light came from the city twinkling across the bay. He could see her luscious lips turn into a smile, her dark eyes on his face. Her arms wound around his neck and she sighed, a little happy sound he intended to make louder.

His cock swelled with blood as he strode across the room, pushing her bedroom door open with his foot. The thin drapes hanging over her wall of windows were pushed to the sides, affording them the same incredible view of San Diego. The perfect setting for what he had in mind.

Making Toni his.

Though he hated to put space between them, he slid her down his body to her feet beside the bed. He skimmed his hands over smooth long hair, framed her cheeks with his palms, curled his fingers around her neck, moved lower to the hollow of her throat.

He grazed his fingertips along the collar of Toni's blouse, dipped beneath, where her skin was warm.

She moaned. "Hurry," she whispered, reaching for the buttons of her shirt.

Brushing her hands aside, he put his hands on the first tiny pearl button. "Let me." He worked it through the hole, kissing her softly on the tip of her nose, on closed eyelids, at the corners of lush lips, along the delicate line of her jaw.

She moaned, rolling her head to the side to give his mouth better access to her neck. One by one he worked each button free. Touching the slopes above lace-covered breasts caused her to tremble. Isaac smiled, nudging the loose material over her shoulders and replacing it with his lips.

Her soft skin was warm and held a hint of rose fragrance. He groaned against her skin. He slid his tongue downward. Over lace straps, then he closed his mouth around a pert nipple straining for freedom. Her back arched; her head fell back. Long blond hair floated over his hands as he stroked down her arms, over firm breasts, then with a flick of the snap had her bra off and falling to the floor with her shirt.

Her capris were next. He worked them down her hips, over the nicest ass he'd ever seen, down legs he intended to have wrapped around him. Soon. They fell to her ankles and she kicked them away impatiently.

"You're too slow, Isaac." She touched his cock beneath his jeans. "Get naked with me."

Grinding his teeth together, he struggled to hold off the ball of cum working its way from his sac to his dick. He swallowed the lust burning in his chest, the need churning in his gut.

Tonight was about Toni. Showing her how much he loved her.

But he could be—and should be—naked to do that.

Reaching into his front pocket, he pulled out a handful of

Sweethearts and tossed them to the bed. The little hearts scattered over her dark blue comforter. The condoms he'd stuck in there earlier joined the candy, the foil wrappers picking up the reflection of the lights outside the window.

He allowed her hands to caress his erection, the movements purposeful and sensual. Didn't stop her when she worked his button fly free and shoved the denim from his body. Then his T-shirt and briefs joined the pile of clothing on the floor.

But he put an end to her exploration when she curled her hand around his rocked-up cock and stroked him up and down a few times. Slid her thumb across the bead of pre-cum glistening in the low light.

And when she moved to lower before him, he put his hands on her upper arms and halted her progress despite how his dick bucked in protest. He wouldn't be able to handle her mouth on his burning flesh.

Not without blowing his wad.

"Isaac, please." Her whimper of objection turned into a moan of frustration when she reached for him again, but he rebuffed her touch. "Are you trying to make me suffer, baby?"

"I'm suffering, too, but tonight I'm taking my time." He scooped her into his arms and lowered her to the bed.

The candy hearts pressed into her skin, cold in contrast with the heat pouring off Isaac. Toni reached for him, opening her legs as he settled above her, supporting himself on his forearms. The head of his cock nudged against her clit. She pulled up her knees, rolled her hips, trying to complete the contact.

Trying to get him inside her.

"Sweetheart," he said, putting a hand on her hip and easing

away from her, "we're going slow." He moved downward, his palms sliding across her thighs, her calves, the arches of her feet. Lifting one leg, he kissed her ankle, flicked his tongue across her sensitive skin.

Toni shivered, her gaze on his face. He was watching her. The blue had vanished from his eyes, leaving them gray and smoky. His nostrils flared as he opened his mouth and settled his lips—searing and deliciously wet—against her flesh.

"Isaac." His name seeped from her lips, her back arching off the bed, her nipples begging for some of the tongue action he was giving her calf.

"I'm right here." He reached to the bed and picked up a candy heart, then dragged the pale yellow heart across his tongue. When it was soaked, he removed it from his mouth and touched it to her skin. It was warm at first, but cooled as the heat of his mouth dissipated. Damp, the pressed sugar melted, leaving an almost chalky trail as he dragged the heart up her leg and followed with his tongue.

"Isaac."

"Hmm?" he mumbled against her, the vibration echoing and intensifying her need. Taking her leg, he draped the back of her knee over his shoulder, then reached for a second Sweetheart. Again he wet the baby blue candy in his mouth, then touched it to her flesh.

She trembled as he bent to her inner thigh, dissolving the sugar as he rubbed it on her, pausing when he reached the MINE heart tattoo. "How come I've never seen this before?" he asked, reaching for a third candy and pressing the identical shape to the ink in her skin. He held it there, his intense look moving from hers back to her spread legs.

"We're always in a hurry." *In a hurry now*, but Isaac seemed to be taking his sweet-ass time.

"Mine," he said in a timbre Toni didn't recognize.

She searched his face, trying to understand what he was thinking, but saw only his profile as he stared at the Sweetheart he pressed over the MINE tattoo.

"This is mine." His mouth was on her again, biting into the candy on her inner thigh, his teeth scraping against her flesh and the permanent heart marking. "You're mine."

Toni swallowed the lump clogging her throat and tried to forget the rise of emotion. "Yes. Yes, yours." *But only for tonight.*

Only one more night. She closed her eyes and allowed sensation to lead her back to arousal, back to where Isaac worked magic upon her skin. She was in too deep, and if she was going to keep herself from drowning, tonight would have to be it.

Only tonight.

He had another candy wet and on her, drawing sugar images and licking them up with his tongue. Higher, he trailed the candy over her hip, bypassing her tingling clit.

"Please, Isaac."

"Not yet."

"Baby"—she put a hand on his shoulder and tried to urge him down—"you're killing me." Slickness seeped from her pussy. Her thighs ached.

He chuckled. "I'm going to take you to heaven." Sugar melted into her belly button and he lapped it away, twirling the diamond piercing in his mouth. Clicking it with his teeth. Covering her breast with one hand, he tweaked her puckered-up nipple, pinched slightly, then soothed away the hurt by drawing candy circles that he cleaned up with the heat of his lips and the swipe of his tongue.

"Promises, promises." Her voice was strained. Breathing broken.

"And I keep my promises, Toni. You should know that."

She rolled her hips, tightened her legs around him, attempting to pull him closer. "Then get to it. Fuck me, already."

He ignored her, smoothing another candy across her, focused on the sugar art, then leaving her skin damp from saliva and sweat.

"You taste sweet."

"That's the candy."

"I don't think so." He scooted back, touching his fingers to the line of hair she'd shaved above her clit. The blond curls were dark with arousal, wet with need. "You're sweeter than sugar. Here." He skimmed his fingers downward, easing her apart, then sinking inside her.

"Oh, God," she cried out, arching off the bed. Her legs shook, her body trembling as he started into a tempo she rocked her hips into and prayed would pick up speed.

She could feel the heat of his breath close to her pussy before she heard him say a word.

"And here." He licked her clit, dragging his tongue slowly over the swollen flesh. "So sweet . . ." He lapped at her, then suckled her clit into his mouth with a few rhythmic sucks. Sliding lower, his tongue joined with his fingers and thrust inside her. Deep and fast and repeatedly.

Sensation exploded in Toni. She moved with him now, rolling her hips into his face, working to deepen the thrusting of his fingers and tongue, wanting him to be fucking.

Reaching out to the sides, she grabbed at the bedding, but

her hands closed around candy hearts and a condom packet, the foil crinkling as she tightened her fingers around it. She wanted it on him. Wanted him inside her.

Isaac's dick throbbed hard against the mattress, cum a few simple strokes away. He'd promised heaven, but he was the one about to go there and he hadn't even fucked her yet.

He closed his eyes, inhaling the honeyed scent of her arousal, licked away the cream, touched her clit with the tip of his tongue, then circled and sucked when she cried out his name and thrust her pussy up to his chin.

This was how he wanted her. Writhing and aching and wanting him. Only him.

"Isaac," she whispered.

Keeping his mouth on her, he glanced up and saw her reaching for him. Her fist landed on his shoulders and when she uncurled her fingers, Sweethearts rained down on him.

And a condom.

He closed his eyes, took a deep breath, her sex heavy on his skin, and eased away from her, kissing her belly button, the slight slope of her abdomen, one puckered rosy nipple.

Then he sat back, crouched between her knees, and tore the foil from the condom. The circle of latex was cold when he touched it to his dick. Air hissed between his teeth as he tilted his face toward the ceiling, struggling to breathe.

Then Toni was there, one hand holding him by the base of his erection, the other unrolling the latex downward. The lubricant chilled him, the contrast of her warm hands caused him to throb against her palm.

"Take me to heaven, Isaac," she said, assuming the lead. Her hands were on him, first on his shoulders, then his chest.

Not like he was putting up much of fight, but it didn't take much pressure to have him flat on his back with her straddling him.

She gripped his cock with both hands, rising on her knees above him. Her golden skin was dappled with remnants of sugar. Her sunshine hair was damp around her temples, and floated around them as she fit his swollen cock to the entry of her soaking-wet pussy.

Isaac felt her chocolaty gaze on his face, understood the shocking intensity. He stayed with her, still upon the bed despite his driving need to thrust upward and get inside her tight, wet heat.

With a smirk of satisfaction, she relaxed her knees and dropped, plunging down on his cock, curving her back as every hard inch impaled her.

The tips of her breasts pulled into tighter beads, and jiggled temptingly as she trembled around him. "Ah . . . ah." The walls of her pussy clamped down, gripping him tight, then fluttered as she came, drenching his latex-swathed dick.

He laughed, pushing himself up on his elbows, thinking he'd flip her on her back and fuck her hard until he found the same release.

Wouldn't take long.

"Where you going, baby?" she asked, pressing a hand to his chest. She hunched forward, her body still in spasms, and kissed him fully on the mouth. He knew she could taste her juices when she ran her tongue across his lips. She whimpered. "I'm not done with you yet."

He was throbbing hard, his sac drawn up close to his body. Isaac tried to think of a comeback—but his brain was hazed over with lust. His body taut. Sweat dampened his brow.

But Toni—sweet, feminine Toni—took over complete

control. She went from still to riding him hard. Up. Down. Grind.

In. Out. Grind.

Unable to fight against the motion, he grabbed her hips and drove into her with each downward glide. The ball of cum was there, at the base of his cock, just ready to explode, but he managed to hold back—until he felt the tightening of her second orgasm, heard the tempo of her shallow breaths change, became consumed by the fierceness of thrusts.

"Isaac!" Her nails bit into his skin. "Isaac!" Her body shook violently over him.

And that was it for him. He came. Hard, and in a scant moment of sanity—of rational thought—he knew he'd never be the same.

Nine

Toni awoke before Isaac. She kept her eyes closed, staying perfectly still as she listened to the soft, slow rhythm of his breathing in sleep. It was the sound she wanted to awaken to every morning. Clamping her trembling bottom lip between her teeth, she held back the whimper of dismay, knowing that wasn't going to happen.

She rubbed the sleep from her eyes with the palm of her hand, took a deep breath, and eased away from Isaac's warm body. Her body was stiff as she stood and stretched, her thighs sore from the hours of lovemaking the night before. From riding him so hard.

Ignoring the protest of her muscles and squinting against the shimmering sun reflecting off the bay through her eastern-exposure windows, she scooped up his T-shirt from the floor and put it over her head, working her arms through. The scent of the ocean mingled with the lingering of his cologne. Toni wrapped her arms around her middle and inhaled.

Her gaze floated around her room, over the rose-petal black-and-white photos, the pile of their clothing, to the beautiful man asleep in her bed, the sheet at his waist accentuating the lines of his toned body.

To hold back a sob, Toni pressed the back of her hand to her mouth and blinked hard. This was the last time he'd be in her bed, their final morning. Without a commitment—which he hadn't offered—keeping this up held too many risks to her heart.

Turning away from him, she moved silently through her small apartment to her office and retrieved her camera bag, checked the memory card, then went back to her bedroom. *Click. Click. Click. Click.* The high-speed shutter went off over and over again as she reentered her room, rounding the bed. As Isaac slept on his side with one arm tucked beneath the pillow, she captured him from each angle the same way she'd do an athlete in full action. *Click. Click. Click.*

She moved closer, zooming in on his face. *Click. Click.* His jawline. *Click.* The shadows left on his cheeks by his eyelashes. *Click. Click.*

Toni moved the lens downward to his full lips that knew just how she liked to be kissed. Pale blue powder had dried on one corner, candy-heart sugar that he'd licked from her body. A flash of heat spread across her skin and her nipples puckered, but she cast aside her lustful reaction. Instead, she focused the camera and let the shutter take a dozen shots of it; she wanted desperately to hold on to the image. The memory. *Click. Click.*

Moving to her camera bag, she set aside the digital and retrieved the 35-millimeter that contained the black-and-white
film.

Taking a breath, she moved to the side of the bed, squat-
ting so she was level with him, then focused on his face. *Click.*
His mussed hair. *Click.* His hand, fingers limp against the
dark blue sheets. *Click. Click.*

Rising slowly, weight pressing against her shoulders, she
rounded the bed, then focused the camera lens on his back.
The sculpted muscles cording along his shoulders and hugging his spine. *Click. Click.* The slope of his hip, the shadows
the sheets left over his ass, the power of his thighs beneath.
Click. Click.

Isaac would move on with his life, but she'd have these
pictures forever. He'd made so many promises—and kept
them, except the one she truly wanted. *Tomorrow.* Every single one of them. The one promise she needed. She swallowed
hard, the sense of loss overwhelming. The suffocating feeling
of love not reciprocated.

Toni lowered the camera and swiped tears from her cheeks
with the backs of her hands. Tears she hadn't even realized had
fallen.

She backed away slowly until she reached the cold wall.
Her knees buckling, she slid downward and sucked breaths
between her trembling lips.

"I love you, Isaac Brett," she whispered, the tears salty on
her lips. *But I'm ready for serious. Ready to settle down.
Ready for commitment.*

A month and a half ago, forced by her girlfriends—
girlfriends she counted on and whose shoulders she used to cry
on—into a speed-date event, she hardly recognized the symp-
toms of wanting a man for something other than bed sport,

but meeting the man of her dreams, she knew without a doubt what she wanted.

Isaac.

But he wasn't offering.

Sitting on the floor, a camera draped around her neck and wearing nothing but his shirt, she watched him. The way his eyes fluttered, the rise and fall of his chest, the tick of his pulse at his temples. When he rolled to the side, his hand slid across the sheets where she should have been, instinctively reaching for her, and moaned in his sleep when he found her absent.

Pushing to her feet, she put the cameras away, went to the bathroom, and splashed water on her face to wash away the evidence of her misery.

She'd say good-bye with dignity.

"Didn't think you were a coward, Toni," her brother said, putting his hands up and standing in front of her to keep her from getting to the basket.

Toni ignored him, swiping a wristband over her forehead to mop up the sweat as she continued to dribble the ball with the other hand. She shifted, made like she was going one way, then rounded him—juking him out of his shoes—and made a layup.

She shoved the ball at him. Hard. "You call that cowardly, big brother?" Placing her hands on her hips, she sucked in a couple of breaths and got ready to defend against him.

"I'm not talking basketball, and you know it."

It felt good to be hanging with him again. Even if she was missing Isaac like crazy. They would have gotten along well, she thought, glaring at Nathan for bringing him up.

"Shut up, Nathan. What would you know?"

"I know you're in love with him."

She smirked, then attempted to swat the ball away from him. "Ha. Says the confirmed bachelor."

"Fine." He lowered his shoulder and charged. No match for his football player six-four frame, she was forced out of the way as he dunked it over her. The ball bounced across the gym, but neither made a move to retrieve it. He pulled his shirt off and dragged it over his face and shoulders.

He was looking at her, really staring, and Toni was sure there was more her brother wanted to say. But didn't. After a few minutes he turned and stalked to their things on the floor by a few metal folding chairs. He sat down and opened a bottle of water.

Toni joined him, sinking into the chair, the cold metal a relief to her heated body. She grabbed her own water and chugged it. When the bottle was empty she turned toward her brother. "Fine. That's it? You're not going to press me?"

He shrugged. "What can I say, Toni? Only you know how you feel. But I have to ask, if you don't love him, why are you so sad? Why you playing like you want to do me damage?"

She swallowed, wishing there were more water to wash away the sudden dryness in her throat. "I'm not sad."

"Bullshit."

It was hard to speak without letting her brother hear the swell of emotion. "You don't know what it's like."

He tossed back his head and laughed aloud. "And thank God for that."

Toni didn't bother with a rebuttal. Instead they sat in silence, their breathing slowing down and the sweat drying on their bodies.

Nathan yanked her ponytail much the way he had when they were younger. "You are a coward, though, girl."

She shook her head. "Why do you say that?"

"Because you know what you want and you're not going after it."

Not knowing how to reply, she chose to ignore his comment. She stood and stretched toward the ceiling, then bent to her toes. The workout felt good, easing some of the tension sleepless nights had caused. A little more relaxed, she packed up her things. "You feel like lunch?"

Nathan picked up his cell phone and checked the time. "Nah, can't. Meetings."

Toni nodded and flung her bag over her shoulder, then tossed her empty water bottle in the trash like it was a ball. "Check you later, then." She turned away and started walking toward the basketball, which had rolled to the other side of the gym.

"Hey, Toni." When she glanced back he added, "You going to be okay?"

She swallowed. "Yeah. I'll live." But without Isaac's tender kisses, gentle touches, and Sweethearts, living wouldn't be easy.

Ten

With the phone tucked against her cheek, Toni curled her feet beneath the hem of the silk robe and leaned back against the leather of her sofa.

"You should've told me what was going on," Jenna said, her voice low across the phone lines.

"It's not a big deal," Toni lied. Her affair with Isaac had been a very big deal, big enough to change her life.

"You know, girl, we wouldn't have sent you if we thought you'd be hurt." Jenna was silent for a moment, guilt clear in her tone. "We just wanted you to have a good time. To meet someone nice."

"I did." Damn the single hot tear. Irritated with herself, she swiped it away with the back of her hand.

"But Toni, then why are you not seeing him anymore?"

"Because we don't have a future."

"Says who? Is that what he said?"

Toni shifted the phone to the other ear, pushing locks of hair back, too. She took a deep breath, knowing her friend would have the same reaction as her brother. "He didn't offer me anything other than . . ."

Than what? Friendship? Passion? What hadn't he offered her? The answer rang loud and clear through her mind. His heart.

"Toni, honey, you're a grown woman. When you want something, claim it. You can't expect him to offer something if you didn't let him know you were open to accepting it."

The phone slipped slightly. Sucking in a gulping breath, Toni squeezed her lids closed, exhaling slowly through her mouth. "I know, Jenna." Swallowing the thickness in her throat, she ended the conversation, saying good-bye and gently put aside the phone.

A few minutes later, she pushed from the couch and headed toward the shower. As much as she longed to go back to bed, to hide her misery under the warmth of the covers, she still had work to do. A business to keep afloat.

Less than a half hour later, Toni sat at her desk in her home office, staring at the images on her open laptop. The images of Isaac, naked and asleep in her bed. Hitting PAGE DOWN, she watched as each picture scrolled by, and wanted to caress the screen in the manner she would his flesh-and-blood form. Her hands shook.

Near the end of the series, she spotted something on the edge of the bed, so she Photoshopped to make the image larger. The speck turned out to be a white candy heart with mint green writing. I LUV U. Her breath caught and her pulse picked up. After a moment of hesitation she sent the cropped picture to the printer, then tucked the photo in the drawer with some of the candy hearts he'd left her.

Including the PICK ME candy that had initiated their affair.

She closed her eyes and took a few deep breaths, then turned back to her task. When she reached the end of the file, she glanced over at the rolls of film sitting on her desk—the rolls she'd taken but hadn't had the courage to develop yet. But spurred by her brother's taunts of being a coward, she knew today was the day. She grabbed the two rolls, stood, and left her office.

She decided to walk to her studio, needing the fresh air and an alternative to fucking that would burn off the tension.

Coronado was a small island, and Coronado Village— where her studio was located—was just over a mile away.

Toni arrived at the village fifteen minutes later. As she approached she noticed Jackson and Lexi standing outside the flower shop, sipping Starbucks in the sunshine. Jackson nodded at her, and Lexi was grinning extra wide, but they didn't say anything other than a quick greeting as she reached for her keys. They hovered and stared, giving Toni the distinct feeling they were standing out there for a reason.

Waiting for something to happen.

The thought sent a shiver down Toni's back as she stepped inside, pausing to allow her eyes to adjust.

About damned time, Isaac thought, watching Toni stop by the door. She looked good, but tired, he realized, his gaze roaming across her face, firm breasts, hips, long, long legs.

As much as he wanted to go to her, get his arms around her, and demand to know why she stopped returning his phone calls, he decided it was best to wait for her to come to

4 U Sweetheart   213

her office. He'd met her friend Lexi and her new husband, Jackson, and convinced them to let him in. Nice people. But hell, the last thing he wanted was an audience.

Toni's body shuddered as she inhaled deeply and withdrew something from her pocket. Looking down at the item she held, she walked his direction, the sway of her hips making his dick go rigid.

"Hello, Toni."

She startled, her big brown eyes flashing with fire, then melting as they settled on his face. He felt the heat go straight through him. "Isaac," she said, stepping closer, right up to him.

He brushed his knuckles under her chin, slanting her face, then smoothed his mouth over hers, his body rejoicing when she didn't stop him, didn't pull away. "You promised I wouldn't be forced into cold showers."

"And you've been needing them?" she teased, her plump lips curving into that smirk he liked to kiss off her.

"You stopped returning my calls."

Something moved through her eyes—regret, maybe—and she stepped back, causing his hand to fall away. "I'm sorry." It was breathy and filled with pain, twisting hot and sharp into his gut.

"What did I do, Toni?"

She shook her head. "Nothing. Nothing. It's not your fault."

He swallowed, his pulse pounding hard at his temples. "What *can* I do?" He watched her face, needing to know how she felt.

Though he suspected he knew the reason—at least he hoped to God he did—he needed to hear her out. If she admitted to half the amount of feeling he had for her, he knew he'd be okay. They'd be all right. The one-karat heart-shaped diamond burning a hole in his pocket wouldn't go to waste.

"I don't think you can do anything, baby." She shook her head as she worried her bottom lip with her teeth. With a wavering smile, she touched his chest, running her fingertips slowly over his abdomen. "I like you, Isaac."

"I like you, too, sweetheart."

"No. I mean, I *really* like you."

Damned dick of his thought it was time to go, bucking hard against his briefs. He fisted his hands at his sides to keep from reaching for her, from clearing off her desk with one arm and bending her over it with the other.

He clenched his teeth together to suppress a groan. The movement of her fingertips across his body was about to make him burst. "Then why stop seeing me?"

"My friends."

"The ex-ones?"

She grinned. "Yeah. Them. They sent me to the speed date, Isaac. I wouldn't have gone if they hadn't convinced me I'd been long enough without a man."

"I remember how we met."

She smiled again, lightly grazing his denim-swathed hard-on with the back of her hand. "And you've been fun."

Oh shit, could I have been wrong? Was I a plaything she's now over? Staring into her eyes, Isaac tried damned hard to keep his cool, though something fierce was burning in his blood.

She went on, not halting the torment she was causing with the sensual touches and caresses. "But I want more than fun, Isaac. I know now that I need more than that. I need serious. I need long-term." Her nail clicked against his top button; then her fingertips grazed his skin. "Maybe even a lifetime."

Lust was pumping hard now, a dangerous combination mixed up with all the emotion. At least she wasn't saying she was done with him. Her needs he could take care of. "And you don't think I can promise you forever?"

She closed her eyes, her body trembling. Her breath, sweet and warm, washed over him as she gathered herself, but said nothing. He wanted to kiss her long and deep with lots of tongue. He wanted to worship every inch of her body, starting with the beaded-up nipples poking through her shirt, and ending up at the melted honey of her pussy.

Isaac groaned and framed her delicate face with his hands, then touched his lips to hers, holding back claiming her mouth fully. He kissed her closed eyelids, feathered his mouth across her cheeks. "You think I can't promise you tomorrow? Is that it, Toni?"

She had both hands under his shirt, her palms soft as they explored the contours of his body. Scraped a nail over his flat nipple, drew figure eights with the pad of her thumb, followed the trail of hair that dropped from his belly. "No, I don't think you're ready."

Isaac threw back his head and laughed. To hell with not being ready. He'd purchased the heart engagement ring three weeks into their relationship. He was waiting for her to realize that they were meant to be together. Hell, he'd spent hours at his sister's kitchen table with his nieces going through the messages on all the little hearts, looking for just the right one.

Grabbing her wrists, he eased them from beneath his shirt because there was no way he could think straight when she was touching him sweet and sexy like that. He put a little distance between them, scrubbing a hand over his face and back over his hair. The floral scent of her lingered on his clothing, on his skin.

"Toni, I have to show you something." He reached into his pocket, closing his fingers around the heart. Then he placed it on her hand.

Toni could feel the cool sugar treat on her palm, but didn't want to look down. Didn't want to read the message. Instead she focused on his face, watching the gray storm in his eyes, the blue disappearing. His hair was mussed; his lips were pressed into a straight line that didn't let on what he was thinking.

Taking a deep breath, she looked down and read the Sweetheart candy, MARRY ME.

Her hand shook, but he cupped his larger hand around hers and held it steady, his touch warm and confident. Through the blur of tears, she read the heart again to make sure she wasn't seeing things. MARRY ME.

"Isaac?"

He curled her fingers up so the candy wouldn't drop, then put his hands on her hips and lifted her, settling her butt atop her office desk.

He stood in the V of her legs, brushing his fingers through her hair, caressing her cheeks, touching the pulse that throbbed in her neck, kissed the hollow of her collarbone, tweaked her puckered nipple, then dropped to his knees in front of her.

"I can do forever, sweetheart. If you have me, Toni Ray, I can promise you every single tomorrow."

Shaking her head, Toni tried to think, tried to understand what he was saying, but she was scared . . . afraid to believe. "All this because you don't like cold showers?"

He chuckled, the sound drawing her gaze to his once again. The intensity of his eyes didn't waver. "No. All this because I don't want to go to bed every night without being in you. Wake up ever again without you. All this because you're the one for me. All this, sweetheart, because in three minutes, I fell head over heels. All this because I love you."

She was shaking now, breathing sporadic. Toni watched as he reached into his pocket a second time, this time bringing out a gold ring with a heart-shaped diamond. He held it in her direction.

"All this, Toni Ray, because I want you to be my wife."

"Promises, promises."

He grinned, a smile that made her insides heat up and her pussy go wet. "Say yes, and it'll be a promise I keep."

"Yes."

Dipped in Chocolate

One

Nathan Ray had a hard-on for a woman he didn't know. A woman he'd never seen before now. Hell, he didn't even see all of her, just her back side: narrow waist, round ass, shapely legs. His gaze was transfixed on the sway of her hips as she hummed a melody.

And dipped her fingers in chocolate.

He stood there with his body rocked up, his blood pumping, and his brain fogged over with lust. Mesmerized by the delicate lilt of her lyrical voice, he stared as she brought her hand up, tilted her head back, affording him a glimpse of profile, and one by one licked her fingers clean.

Clenching his teeth together to repress a groan, Nathan shifted his stance to make room in his boxer shorts for the rush of need that had his cock filled with blood. Throbbing. He knew nothing about this woman, other than she had a body that could make a grown man weep, and knew damned well how to use her tongue.

Wiping her hands on a small apron tied around her waist, she moved away from the vat of chocolate. "I can't believe this shit," she murmured, pausing farther down the counter. She lifted a handheld hair dryer, flicking it on.

Though her voice was drowned by the echoing vibration of the blower, he could hear her singing again as she picked up something small and dark, then held it in the current of the air. After a few moments, her movements settled into a rhythm of lifting and drying, then setting the object on a tray beside her.

Not sure how to get her attention without scaring her, Nathan moved forward a few steps, close enough to hear her voice more clearly as she sang a few words here and there, humming the rest. Close enough that he could smell the chocolate and an equally sweet shampoo. Deep red curls were gathered atop her head and shimmered in the fluorescent lighting, jiggling when she moved.

Sliding his gaze downward, he studied the feminine fingers wrapped around the hair dryer, and looked for a ring. Grinned when there wasn't one, or any evidence that there'd been. Just a few feet behind her now, he was able to see over her shoulder what she was working on.

Blackberries.

She was drying them one at a time, and judging by the way she cursed every few berries, she wasn't happy about it.

As tempting as it was to stand there all night watching her perfect body wiggle as she sang, muttering profanities that kept his dick hard, he knew he needed to get on with it. To deal with the reason he'd come.

"Excuse me."

"Awhh!" She spun toward him, her eyes wide with fear, the blow-dryer aimed like a gun, blasting him with cool air. The berry she'd been holding was crushed between her fingers and dark purple juice slithered down her hand.

"Didn't mean to scare you."

"What do . . . you want?" she asked between gasps.

"I'm looking for Jayla Brooks."

Green eyes slanted past him toward the door as she turned off the blower and lowered it to her side. "We're closed."

He knew that. The sign on the glass outer door had been turned and the lights in the front had been shut off. In the back he'd seen a shadow moving around. "The door wasn't locked." So he'd let himself in.

She stuck the squished berry in her mouth, the tip of her pink tongue swiping away a drop of dark juice as she jabbed her hand to her hip. "We're still closed."

Nathan shifted his weight, feeling unsettled under the scrutiny of her wide expressive eyes. He didn't know her at all, but he read the fear in her glowing stare. Made him feel like an ass for coming in unannounced like he had.

He put up his hands. "Hey, look, I'm sorry. I'm just looking for Jayla Brooks. I was told to talk to her."

She didn't look convinced that he was harmless by his apology. Her hand tightened around the handle of the dryer and it lifted slightly, like she was taking aim. "Told by whom?"

"Alexis Lyle. Said if I want sweets, Jayla's the one to talk to."

Her cheeks flushed pink. At least hearing Alexis had sent him seemed to relax her a bit. She glanced away for a moment, putting her weapon down with a clunk on the stainless-steel work surface.

"Can you come back tomorrow, *during business hours*, Mr. . . . ?"

"Nathan. Nathan Ray," he said, extending his hand toward her.

Narrowing her eyes, she stared at his hand as if it were offensive. She sucked in a deep breath, letting out a shaky exhale, then wiped both hands on her apron and reached for his. Her touch was light, her skin soft. "Jayla Brooks."

Nathan focused on her face to keep from glancing down, but he'd already caught a glimpse of dusky nipples visible through the thin white tank top she was wearing. Gazing at her face did little to help cool him down. Not when a small chunk of blackberry flesh clung to her full bottom lip and begged to be licked off.

He cleared his dry throat. "I need to get an order in for a bridal shower. Blew it on time"—he shook his head, whistling a breath of air through his teeth—"and have no idea exactly what to order. Those little cake things? Fruits?" His gaze strayed back to her mouth.

She wet her lips and the berry disappeared into her mouth on her tongue. "Come back another time, Mr. Ray—"

"Nathan"

"—I don't have time tonight."

In the morning he was getting on a plane and wouldn't be back for nearly a week. He'd procrastinated too long already. "This won't take long. Can't you just take an order now?"

The hip with her balled fist swayed to the side, a little expression of attitude. She might have been irritated, but the effect failed on him. She looked damned sexy. *Sugar and spice, and everything nice*, hell, yeah, this woman had it going on.

"No, I can't just do it now. You'll have to come back. Or go someplace else, Mr. Ray." Her chest puffed up and a rosy shade stained her cheeks. She glanced toward the door behind him. "We're closed."

"I'm already here."

"I have too much work to do tonight."

"I'll help."

"Please, leave."

Not what he wanted to hear. "Come on. You have a lot of work and I have an extra pair of hands." He held them palm up, then flipped them over and back again. "I'll help you. . . ." He looked at the bowl of wet berries, the blow-dryer, and the tray of dry fruit. He had no idea what she was doing. "I'll help. You take an order. Simple. We both leave happy."

Simple? Who the hell did this guy think he was? She so didn't have time for some overbearing, overmasculine hunk of male. Not tonight. She glanced at the waiting order form affixed with a magnet to the metal table, then back at Nathan Ray, the finest man she'd ever seen.

Tall and broad, he looked like surf and turf: the chiseled body of a performance athlete, the coloring of a beach bum.

Inside she felt like her chocolate, all warm and creamy, just looking at this guy, even if his size was a bit intimidating. If he wanted to force the issue, she wouldn't stand a chance. Good thing his type of pushy didn't seem criminal.

He wanted to stay and help, and truthfully, she wanted it, too. She'd put him to work and look her fill. By the time the job was complete, she'd have had enough time to appreciate his fineness, and he'd have told her what sort of desserts he wanted for the bridal shower.

"Whose bridal shower?"

"My sister, Toni."

"When?"

He rolled his massive shoulders like he was working out a kink. "Sunday, May first."

Jayla counted the weeks forward in her head. The date was just three weekends away, not a lot of time. But not a problem if the order wasn't too large. At the moment, she was without an assistant because the high school girl who'd been working after school failed to show up for four days straight. The girl was so fired.

Undependable, in addition to being irresponsible, her ex-employee was the sole reason she was now pulling an all-nighter. The little twit had failed to log in six dozen milk chocolate strawberries, four dozen dark chocolate blackberries, and five pounds of white chocolate blueberries, all expected for delivery by ten A.M. tomorrow.

Oh, yeah, if Nathan wanted to lend her a hand just so he could place an order tonight, she'd take him up on his offer. The heat that crept across her skin when she looked at him and wondered how good he'd look naked—definitely delicious—had nothing to do with her decision to let him stay.

Too many berries did.

Dragging in a deep breath, she slowly let it out, trying to ignore the way her nipples beaded, knowing she was going to invite him to spend the night there, working beside her.

She turned back to the table and lifted the hair dryer. "You know how to use a dryer, don't you?"

He grinned wide, reaching up he ran his fingers through his short mussed strands. "I usually shower and go." His hand moved over the light brown, golden-tipped hair.

What, after he climbs off his surfboard? She rolled her eyes and he chuckled. A rich sound that sent warmth seeping from the pit of her belly to the juncture of her legs.

She ignored his laughter and handed over the dryer. "Keep it on cool. We're not trying to cook the berries."

He looked over her shoulder. "We're drying all those?"

"That's just the beginning."

"Wouldn't it be faster to use paper towels or something?"

She shook her head, second-guessing allowing him to stay. She didn't have time to give a lesson on hand dipping fruits in chocolate, or the importance of making sure each piece was completely dry.

Decadent Dips, the business she'd started as a way of putting herself through college, had a reputation of quality. She couldn't ruin her tempered chocolate by allowing a single drop of water. And she couldn't ruin the fruit by bruising tender flesh. Air was really the only way to go. If she had more time, she'd have washed them, then set them aside until they were dried naturally.

Tonight she used a blow-dryer. She had neither a choice nor the luxury of time.

"A paper towel can damage the berries." She picked up a plump blackberry and held it up between them. "You need to hold it gently and make sure you dry all sides. Can you handle that?"

"Yeah," he said, taking the fruit. His tanned fingers brushed against hers, the touch fleeting, but the heat remained. He stuck the berry in his mouth and chewed.

"Hey, they're for dipping, not eating."

"Really?" He stepped closer and Jayla fought the need to retreat. His strong hand settled beneath her chin and tilted her face up toward his. With a gentle stroke, he smoothed his thumb across her lips. "That's too bad. They taste good."

It was a test of her willpower to allow his touch while

keeping her lips closed, and not touching the pad of his thumb with her tongue. She wanted desperately to know if his skin would taste as good as it looked.

She blinked hard, repressing a whimper, then stepped back so his hand fell away. "If you're going to help me, no eating. Hold them carefully. Dry them completely. Set them on the tray. You do that, Mr. Ray—"

"Nathan."

"—and we can talk about what you want for your sister's shower. Deal?"

He smiled, charming and confident. She knew then, this whole thing was a bad idea. Her body was on fire. She swallowed down the rise of desire, the need to get his hands back on her.

He reached behind her and set the dryer on the counter. For a minute she thought he was going to leave, but instead he worked free the buttons on his cuffs and rolled his sleeves up to his elbows. And she stood there staring at tanned skin draped over muscular forearms.

Her nipples reacted by puckering tight and a shiver moved down her spine.

Once he was done with his shirt, he reached back around her, brushing her upper arm with his bare skin, then picked up the blower and a berry.

She gulped. "I'll get more fruit," she said. Then she turned away and went straight into the walk-in fridge. The door slid slowly closed behind her, affording her a moment of privacy. But even the chilled air did nothing to cool the desire that had damped her skin.

Two

She'd wasted a good fifteen minutes in the walk-in cooler, trying to cool the heat brought about by one single touch of the
man she had blowing her berries dry. Closing her eyes and
tugging in a shaky breath, Jayla leaned against the metal wall.

"This can't be happening," she said through chattering
teeth. "Not tonight."

There could be only one focus tonight, and that was getting this order done by morning. She didn't have time to be attracted to Nathan Ray, no matter how good-looking he was.
No matter how his smile made her inner thighs ache. No matter how she'd longed to touch his golden skin.

Her business had to be her only concern. Decadent Dips
had paid for college, a cute condo on the California coast, not
far from the ocean, and the freedom of being self-employed.
But she'd nearly lost all that three years ago during a nasty

divorce. Her ex-husband had left her accounts in the negative and her self-confidence in shreds.

Since then, she'd pretty much kept her distance from men, keeping one goal in mind: making Decadent Dips a success. Rebuilding it to the moneymaker it was before she'd lost her head to the wrong man. Before he tried to strip her of her dreams with his secret addiction to gambling.

During the last three years she'd been fine being single, focusing on her career. She didn't need a man. Hadn't been tempted to date and didn't miss male company at all. Not even at night. Even during her marriage when she'd felt the loneliest, haunted by a sexual appetite and needs that weren't met.

Whether it was anger or self-preservation, she'd closed off her heart and shut down her yearnings many, many months ago—and didn't miss them a bit.

That was until a sun-kissed stranger scared the shit out of her, and with one touch made her want again.

Jayla swallowed the lump in her throat and pushed off the fridge wall. Her nipples were beaded up tight, but she'd chalk that up to cold, not desire. At least the dampness on her skin had frozen off.

"Not tonight," she repeated, taking a deep breath. She picked up a flat of plump, red strawberries and headed back to face Nathan—back to work. She wouldn't allow him to open up the floodgates of emotional vulnerabilities, not when the damage could be too great.

The physical part, well, maybe. Once the order was complete, she might be interested in experimenting with the possibility of taking on a lover, especially one who looked like a sculpted god.

"Hey, what took you so long?" Nathan asked when she

entered the workroom. He took the flat of strawberries from her and carried them to the large double sink. "You go hand-pick these?" He winked at her before putting down the box.

"Funny. If you want to crack jokes, just make sure you do it while you're working." Even though she was newly escaped from a cold box, one of Sunshine Boy's smiles had her hot again, damp as a humid day. She moved to his side at the sink. "I'll wash, you dry. You're good at it." He'd completed all the blackberries while she'd hidden in the walk-in.

"What would you do without me?" He laughed, taking the bowl of strawberries she'd just run under the water. "You needed me tonight."

Was she transparent? Jayla turned to look at him, only to catch him staring. *At her breasts* and the damned puckered nipples that wouldn't quit poking through her shirt.

She cleared her throat and he lifted his warm browns slowly to her face. Did he have no shame? Cocky grin firmly in place, he seemed perfectly fine getting caught checking out a woman's chest. He was smug almost, like she should be okay with it, too.

And damn it, her body was. She squeezed her legs together, feeling every single day of the three years of not getting laid.

She ignored the rush of wetness between her legs. Her gaze slid downward, roaming over his toned body to the bulge in his pants. At least she wasn't alone in arousal, she thought, measuring his hardened length through the twill of his slacks.

Berries first. They'd take all night to hand dip. A chill ran down her spine as she tore her gaze from him and finished up at the sink. Shutting off the water, she carried the bowl and set it beside the one he was working on.

Thinking it was a good idea to get her mind back on her job, she asked, "Why don't you tell me what you have in mind?"

He arched a brow and his brown eyes darkened with a hint of mischief. "Um . . . I was thinking about getting you out of that shirt."

Oh, God, she almost said okay and reached for the hem. Dipped fruit be damned, she wanted to dip him.

Her cheeks went hot. A tingle rippled through her clit. She squeezed her lids closed and took a few deep breaths. Getting a grip on her lust before it got out of control, she looked at him, putting her professional face on.

"I was talking about for the bridal shower."

He chuckled, that sexy grin of his making her want things she had no right wanting from him. Namely, him stripped naked and pleasuring her.

Jayla turned away from Nathan, unable to keep from touching him while standing so close. She went to the vat that slowly warmed the chocolate, and checked the consistency.

She'd moved to get away from him, but he followed, standing so close behind her, one sway of her hips would bring them in contact. She didn't acknowledge his nearness as she continued to stir the melted milk chocolate.

"You're the professional. Why don't you tell me what's appropriate for a shower?"

His warm breath feathered through the fine hairs at the nape of her neck and carried the scent of strawberries. He'd been sneaking fruit when she wasn't looking. Her stomach grumbled. She hadn't eaten since lunch and the thought of the berries made her hungry.

Her mouth watered. "Depends on your sister. Does she like fruits?"

"Sure."

"They're my specialty. I started with just strawberries. I've expanded into all sorts of fruits. Cakes. Candies." She glanced over her shoulder. "I've even done grasshoppers a customer brought in."

"You're kidding."

"Nope."

He grinned, tugging a curl off her face. "I'll pass on the bugs." He tucked the strand behind her ear, but his fingers lingered on her skin. His fingertips smoothed downward, following the low-cut scoop of her tank top neckline. "The rest sounds good."

She stirred the vat more vigorously, everything about him disturbing her dipping routine. His hand crept lower, following the line of her body, down her ribs, gently touching her waist, finally settling low on her hip.

"The rest? You want some of everything?" Her voice rose in pitch.

"Yes."

He drew her back as he tilted forward, pressing his hard cock into the small of her back. She almost forgot to breathe and her lungs burned as she absorbed the feel of him, dealt with her body's reaction. The throb at her clit, the way her pussy clenched, wanting him inside.

Sucking in a gasp of air that carried the spicy scent of his cologne, she dropped her ladle. Fat droplets of warm chocolate splashed up in her face. She turned and his arms went around her to pull her close, his erection wedged between them, cradled against her belly.

There were dots of splattered chocolate all over his button-down shirt and neck. She scraped at one with her fingernail, then wiped the stain. The muscles on his chest strained and bunched and she fought the urge to open up his shirt and feel them flex beneath her mouth.

Reaching up, she swiped at another bead of chocolate on his collar.

"Did you want to talk about what I want?" he asked, widening his stance so he didn't loom so much taller than her. His dick throbbed against the apex of her legs.

She glanced up at his eyes, saw the reflection of her lust. A tremor coursed through her blood. "What do you want?" She licked her lips, then held her breath while waiting for his answer.

"I want to know why you didn't lock the door." His hands slid over her ass and he ground his erection into her. "Someone could take advantage of you working here alone."

She slid an arm around his neck and pulled him toward her. "You mean like this?" she asked, licking a drop of chocolate from his skin. She couldn't help it. She was hungry and he was damned tempting.

Nathan closed his eyes, a groan rattling up from his chest as her hot little tongue lapped against his flesh. His cock bucked hard against her flat stomach, the tips of her breasts pressing through his shirt.

She lifted her head slightly, wiped her fingers in another drop, then followed the smudge with her tongue. "Mmmm . . ."

When she pulled back she had smeared chocolate on the tip of her nose, chin, and lush lips. Bending forward, he touched his mouth to hers, running his tongue along the gap between her lips. She was incredibly sweet.

And the way she'd licked him was the most erotic thing he'd ever felt. He wanted her doing it again, except all over his body, and he wanted her naked and dripping with chocolate so he could lick it off.

She put her hands on his upper arms and pushed out of his embrace, leaving cool air swirling against his erection as she moved away. A blush of pink stained her cheeks as she glanced over her shoulder at him. "You still going to help me? It's late and we haven't dipped yet," she said, holding a strawberry by the stem.

"Show me how."

"It's easy, just time-consuming." She moved a tray of dried fruits closer to the vat of chocolate, then set up a second rack. "The sooner this is done, the sooner I'll be able to put some thought into what you need for the shower. Shouldn't take long since bridal showers are fairly standard."

There was still chocolate on the tip of her nose, and her deep green eyes kept dipping to his crotch, letting him know that even though she'd moved out of his arms, she wasn't all business. Nor was she as unaffected as she seemed.

Standard . . . shouldn't take long . . . Her words bothered him. He didn't want her to be able to fill a quick order, then never see him again. He had to think of something else. "I need something else, too."

"What?" she asked, handing him a large berry dangling on a stem.

He had to think fast, not sure exactly what kind of dessert would take longer to plan, but feeling without a doubt he wanted more time to get to know Jayla. Touching her. Having her mouth on him.

"Umm . . . sauce. I need chocolate sauce."

Her brows plunged as she squinted speculatively at him. "I don't do sauce. I dip things. Fruit. Cakes. Candies." She grinned, and her fingers brushed his as she pushed the berry stem into his hand. "Sometimes bugs."

When he glanced down at the fruit she'd given him, his gaze collided with the vat of chocolate. "But you could. Look at all this chocolate. You could make some sort of sauce."

She dipped a fruit, then put it on the rack. "Like something to put over ice cream? I guess I could."

"No, I was thinking body sauce." Blood filled his cock and a throb started as she kept her beautiful eyes fixed on him. The wetness of her mouth lingered on his skin and he couldn't help thinking how good it'd feel to have her run her tongue elsewhere on his body.

Her gaze moved to where she'd kissed chocolate from his skin. Reaching for her, he swiped the smear from the end of her nose. "You mean, like"—she blushed, her voice dropping to a whisper—"sex sauce?"

Out-of-control desire had him pulsing hard, held back by thin boxers and his slacks. "Yeah."

"They make that kind of thing for . . . shops."

"I've seen it. It's not very good."

"You've tried some?"

Nathan shrugged. He hadn't, but he liked how her wide her eyes became. He could lose himself in the pools of green. "Not very chocolaty." He grinned.

She smirked.

"Will you do it?"

"What do you need chocolate body sauce for?" She turned away, and dipped another berry. "Never mind. None of my business."

"The bachelor party."

She laughed. "And what exactly do you do with sex sauce

at a party for all men?" She followed up her sassy question with a wink.

"Nothing. It'd be a favor. A party favor to take home."

"Oh."

"So you'll do it?"

"Let's get these done and talk about it tomorrow."

It worked. She'd see him again, even if it wasn't for the reason he wanted. But there was time for that. "Can't tomorrow. I'm going out of town."

"Okay, Mr. Ray." She put a hand on her hip. "Start dipping and we can set up a meeting next week. I'll get you some samples of desserts I can do for your sister."

He dipped a berry the way she'd done and set it on the drying rack. "And the sauce?"

"I'll see what I can do."

Three

It'd been a few days since Nathan had walked into her work-room and awoken hormones she'd thought were permanently dormant. His arrival in her life resulted in a succession of sleepless nights, days of being on edge. Touching the puffiness beneath her eyes, Jayla knew she looked like hell. She yawned, then swiped the moisture from her cheeks with the back of her hand as she glanced at the digital clock on her nightstand.

3:52 A.M.

Hours before the sun brightened the morning sky. She had passed the night tossing and turning, unable to get comfortable on the mattress without remembering how his hands had felt against her skin. Unable to close her eyes without seeing Nathan's face, remembering the promises in his incredible brown gaze.

Taking a deep breath and kicking the tangled sheets off her legs, Jayla rolled from her bed, finding it useless to lie there and imagine how Nathan's golden body would feel against her. A fantasy she'd been dealing with since he'd helped her deliver the dipped fruit they'd worked on all night, then arranged for a tasting the following week.

Their meeting was scheduled in three days, but spring was one of her busiest order seasons. She'd hardly had time to think, let alone do the proper planning for a body paint she'd never tried before. Getting together a sampling for his sister's bridal shower wouldn't be an issue. She kept the walk-in fridge and pantry well stocked at Decadent Dips.

It was the chocolate sauce, and its sexual nature, that had her mind working over ingredients. She'd already tried two different recipes, but the first had hardened as it cooled, like a topping over ice cream. She'd added more butter to keep that from happening, but was having a hard time judging how it'd react when introduced to body heat.

And body heat was the problem *she* was suffering from, a slow smolder of desire she'd felt ever since he'd touched her. Ever since he'd caressed her cheek to swipe away the stains of blackberries on her lips. The smoldering need had her restless and unable to sleep. And lack of sleep wasn't making it any easier to do her job efficiently.

A shiver running down her spine and her nipples puckering, she stalked to the bathroom, pulling her curls up and securing them back. She took a few calming breaths as she slid her arms into a terry cloth robe, then splashed cool water on her face.

"Get a grip, chick," she murmured, smearing a clay skin-rejuvenating mask across her skin. The cool, sweet scent of melons and cucumber wafted around her.

If she couldn't sleep, she might as well spend the time working, she decided, moving to her desk by the eat-in kitchen and powering up her computer.

As the mud mask dried, Jayla cruised through her book-marked recipe sites, scribbling notes on a pad of paper on her desk. She followed a couple of links, ending up at recipe sources she hadn't tried before. She searched for different methods of getting the right consistency for her sauce while keeping the chocolate from getting firm when it cooled.

She'd already run a search for all different types and brands of sexual chocolate and chocolate body art, then spent a few hours running around to several different sex shops in the San Diego area to pick them up. She needed to know, after all, what she'd be compared with. Heat rushed across her cheeks when she thought about all the items she'd picked up, not all of them chocolate. Nope, included in her purchases was a big box of latex. She closed her eyes, and a whimper seeped past her lips. She'd met Nathan once and she was already thinking about fucking him. Had been thinking about it relentlessly.

Better to be prepared, she'd reasoned, and hid the box of condoms in the back of her nightstand beneath a few magazines. She let out another breath, but this time her whimper sounded a lot more like a moan—the thought of being naked with Nathan dampened her pussy and made her inner thighs ache.

It was an odd feeling, to be so aroused after three years without so much as a stirring of desire.

Wanting to know more about her sunshine man, Jayla went to google.com and entered his name, Nathan Ray. Pages of links popped up. Quickly she scanned the sites before following one of the links.

It took her to an old newspaper article featuring a high school star running back named Nathan Ray. It was hard to make out if it was him covered with a helmet and face mask in the black-and-white photo.

She followed another link and ended up on the San Diego Chargers' home page. A photo of her surfer boy listed him as assistant running-back coach.

"Oh, shit." Snatching her hand away from the mouse, she caught her breath, her racing pulse pounding at her temples as she stared at the photo and the short write-up about Nathan Ray.

No way! Please, please, he can't be involved in professional sports. Tears stung her eyes, a few falling from her lashes as memories of her ex, Mark, came rushing back. Of days on end when he wouldn't come home, disappearing to Vegas to place bets.

The sport never mattered. Mark played the odds, gambling on fights, baseball, basketball, football, hockey. Neither the event nor how much he spent mattered. It didn't matter to him that his addiction had damned near cost his wife her dreams and had definitely ended their marriage.

She'd grown up in a household full of girls with an absentee father, so sports hadn't played a major part in her life. She'd enjoyed small doses of exposure over the years—that was, until gambling had become an obsession for Mark. Now they represented bitterness and a part of her past she'd rather forget.

She'd successfully avoided involvement in sports for three years, but now fate dumped a suntanned, muscular athlete into her shop. Into her life. And although Nathan wasn't an athlete, he was involved in a profession where many high-profile players had admittedly fallen prey to the lure of gambling. To her, it wasn't merely a question of high stakes with the wallet, but also with her heart.

Feeling conflicted, she exited the page with trembling hands, then sent her computer to sleep as she went back to the bathroom to wash away the flaking dried-up clay.

Weary, she crawled back into bed at a little before five, hoping to catch a few hours of sleep, knowing that they would be marred with images of golden skin draped over a perfectly chiseled body. There was no denying her body's cravings for this man. It was her heart she was uncertain was ready for emotional involvement again.

But she could take that part slow. Very slow. Assuming he was even interested.

Nathan lounged on a barstool watching Toni in the kitchen, preparing breakfast. A damned late breakfast, he thought, glancing at his watch and seeing it was nearing eleven.

"Just don't go overboard, Nathan. You know I don't *do* frilly," Toni said, stirring batter for pancakes.

He smirked. "You look pretty frilly to me." He arched a brow at his sister. Her blond hair was pulled back in a braid, her skin was flushed, and she was standing barefoot in the kitchen surrounded by flowers supplied by her fiancé.

Toni followed his gaze, then jammed her hand to her hip. "Don't be a chauvinist pig, Nathan. Being barefoot in the kitchen hardly makes me overly feminine. I can make pancakes and still kick your ass in basketball."

"Whatever." He narrowed his eyes, unwilling to admit that she gave him a run for his money on the court. "Where's lover boy? I'm assuming you're not cooking for me."

"In the shower." She ladled some batter onto the pan. "You can join us, though, if you're hungry."

"Nah, I need to head home and take care of a few things"—like buy some condoms so he was prepared if things went the way he hoped—"before I meet Jayla later. I just wanted to let you know I have everything under control. It's going to be special."

Toni flipped the pancake. "Nothing extravagant, really. I want a small, simple wedding. And start talking, big brother. Who's Jayla?"

Lack of sleep had to be making his jaw slack and his lips run free. He hadn't meant to say that, but Jayla had been on his mind ever since she'd left him standing outside her shop last week. He'd had a hell of a time focusing on rookies and viewing game film when the entire time his dick was throbbing from the memory of her nearly see-through tank top and dusky nipples that puckered and elongated. Made his mouth water.

Clearing his throat, he swallowed down the choking lust that had lingered for the past six days.

"Not what you think. She owns Decadent Dips, the place Alexis recommended."

"Is she cute?"

He repressed a groan. *Cute and sexy as hell.* "Yeah, but quit trying to play matchmaker."

His sister grinned as she removed the pancake from the heat, then ladled on another. "You still dateless for the wedding?"

"You don't listen?"

"Bring her."

"I said no matchmaking."

His sister laughed. "It's all the frilliness. Clogs my ears."

Nathan stood, rolling his bunched-up shoulders. Desire made his body tense, tightening the muscles until they throbbed painfully.

"I've got to get out of here." He rounded the counter and kissed his sister's cheek. "Say hi to Isaac for me."

"I will."

He was almost out the door when he heard Toni's laughter-filled voice following after him. "Bring her."

The door closed with a thud, but her words stayed with him. Maybe it was because he had this driving need to get to know Jayla Brooks better. To know the flavor of her lips, the taste of her skin, the sweetness of her arousal.

Maybe because there was something vulnerable and alluring in the depths of her deep, watery green eyes. Something completely kissable about the bow shape of her lush lips. Something pure and undemanding about the clarity of her voice when she sang.

It was strange to want this one woman so badly. In his profession there was never a shortage of groupies and women willing to throw themselves at him for a chance at getting in his bed. Money and position were their goal, and he hadn't been tempted into having those worthless affairs in years.

Besides, as one of the youngest coaches in the NFL, he didn't have time to be distracted by cheap floozies who were overly willing to spread their legs. He had to be serious or get replaced.

Until he met Jayla, he hadn't realized how long it'd been since he'd had a girl. She made him want to be her man—at least for a night. Made him want to know if she'd hum when he was making love to her. If she'd be as passionate while he was up in her as she was when she was dipping berries in melted chocolate.

He'd be seeing Jayla in a couple of hours, and he planned on seeing what he could do to make all those yearnings a reality.

Four

Jayla was sitting on the metal work surface when he entered the back room of Decadent Dips, her focus on a notebook, her feet swinging in time with the tune she hummed. The tone was alluring and welcoming, and Nathan felt his body harden in response.

His gaze roamed over her. From too-short shorts, smooth bare legs shimmering in the overhead lighting, to delicate feet tucked into flip-flops, to toes tipped in pale pink.

The green T-shirt accentuated the color of her eyes and the fullness of her breasts. It was thin enough to show off her puckered nipples, which pressed against the material, but dark enough to keep the peachy shade hidden beneath.

Highlighting her slender neck and the fine feminine lines of her face, her deep red curls were gathered atop her head, and jiggled as she moved.

Her beauty was breathtaking, her sensuality fuel for his body, which was already in overdrive. One glance, and there it was again. *The lust*. The need to bury himself deep within her body. Desire sharp and heavy.

Nathan cleared his throat, and her gaze swiveled from the paper toward him. Her eyes widened at first, but then brightened with a smile as the melody died on her lips.

"You're late," she said, sliding off the counter. "I thought we agreed on right after I close."

He chuckled. "I know." He walked across the workroom, pausing when she was just a few inches from him. Standing so close, he could smell the sweetness of her skin, soft and floral. He inhaled deeply, catching her perfume mixed with the richness of chocolate.

"Sorry," he said, brushing his knuckles slowly across her cheek, following the downward slope of her jaw.

He'd spent a little too much time deciding what kind of condoms to buy, and going over his game plan. He needed to convince her that a little mutual gratification would be worthwhile. His cock bucked against his jeans in response to his thinking about it.

Dragging in a shaky breath, she replied, "That's okay." She slanted her gaze away, but not before he thought he saw the hint of uncertainty.

"Let me show you what I've come up with for your sister's bridal shower," she said, dropping her notebook on the counter and moving to a tray filled with samples.

On display were several dozen assorted varieties of dipped fruits, along with small squares he assumed were chocolate-covered cakes. Each was decorated in pink ribbons and frosting flowers. Delicate like Jayla, but too girlie for his sister, he realized, remembering Toni's warnings against frilliness.

"Do they taste as good as they look?" *Do you?*

"Try them."

Nathan lifted a square to his mouth. Beneath the frosting and dipped-chocolate shell was a moist strawberry cake with a whipped-cream center. It melted on his palate. He lifted another. White chocolate coated devil's food cake inside.

"Damn, they're good." He glanced over at Jayla. Her gaze was fixed on his mouth as she watched him expectantly. Her lips parted slightly, and her tongue licked along the bottom one as he chewed, sending blood pouring to his already-hardened dick.

"Come here," he said, draping his fingers around the nape of her neck and moving her closer. The only way these desserts could be better was mixed with her kiss.

She whimpered as his mouth brushed against hers, but didn't pull away. He pressed more firmly, then slid his tongue along her lips until she parted farther for him. Slanting his head, Nathan swept inside her mouth, stroking past her teeth, exploring the sultry heat.

The chocolaty flavor of her treats didn't compare with the sweetness of her mouth, the tenderness of her kiss. He smoothed his tongue along hers, felt her shudder against him as her hands fisted in his shirt. Her body melting, he supported her weight.

He could lose himself in the luxurious texture of her soft, warm mouth. And she was kissing him back, sucking gently on his tongue in a rhythm his hips begged to emulate. He caressed her shoulders, slid his hands down her back, molded his fingers to the slope of her ass.

With hands on her hips, he pulled her against his erection, knowing she could feel him throb. She answered with a low moan. With a nip of her teeth to his tongue.

Straightening, she ended the kiss. A hint of a blush covered her cheeks and she was breathing heavily. She swallowed, shifting her expressive eyes away from his face, but her hand lingered and she slowly drew figure eights on his chest with her fingertips.

"Nathan," she said, her voice shaking, her warm breath seeping through his shirt to caress his skin. "What are we doing?" She glanced briefly at his face, then rested her forehead on his sternum.

"Sampling desserts." He smoothed his palm down her spine. "You're not okay with that?" Though his heart rate shot up and his body ached with desire, he held his voice steady. Keeping his cheek against her temple, he kissed her along the hairline and breathed in the clean scent of her skin.

She shook her head, causing her red curls to brush against his chin. "No, I'm all right with sampling, Nathan." Her nails flicked across the small puckering of his nipple. She followed the scrape of her nail with a light kiss he felt clear through his shirt. "I want it so bad, it makes me nervous."

His gut knotted up. "Hey"—he kissed her again—"I'm not looking to make you nervous. Anything you feel uncomfortable with, say so and I'll stop."

Nodding, she kissed his chest again, several light brushes of her lips that were driving him insane. "Why?" she asked, between.

"Why what?"

"Why not just order and go?"

Nathan shook his head, then placed his hands on her upper arms and eased her body away from his so he could see her face. He hated the distance it created between them, but he needed to see her eyes. A wide green stare met his. "I'm not sure what you mean, Jayla. I'm just trying to spend some time with you."

"Why? You don't even know me."

"No, but I'd like to."

Jayla closed her eyes, the need to step back into his embrace overwhelming. Instead she sucked in a whistling gulp of air through her teeth and stepped back farther.

"Have you ever been married, Nathan?"

"No."

"I have."

She studied his face for his reaction. He nodded, his brown eyes narrowing slightly.

Reaching for her left hand, he lifted it between them, and smoothed his thumb across her bandless ring finger. "You're not still?"

"Divorced."

He moved her hand higher and lightly brushed his lips across her fingers. Relief shone from his rich gaze. "Okay. You were married. Are you still hung up on him? Is that what you're telling me?"

She laughed. She couldn't help it, even though this was a serious conversation. She'd hardly thought of Mark at all during the last few years and certainly hadn't missed him. Definitely didn't have a thing for him.

Snorting as she halted her laughter, Jayla answered, "No, I'm not hung up on him." Recalling the tough lessons he'd taught her about lies and deceit, she knew she had to tell Nathan like it was. Let him decide if he wanted to walk out the door. Her free hand slid down his muscular arm, then gripped his hand and twined their fingers.

"But you should know, I don't know if I'm emotionally available. I've been down that road and didn't like it."

He grinned at her, with this charming smile that bordered on arrogance. "How about we work on the chocolate sauce together?" He winked. "Spend a little time with me. *Maybe you'll like it.*"

"There's something else."

"Tell me, Jayla. I can take it."

She squeezed his fingers and clamped her lids closed as she drew in a few calming breaths. She wet her lips. "I'm not real big on your profession."

He laughed, smoothing his thumb in circles on her palm. Arching a brow, he released one of her hands and put his hand over his heart, feigning offense. "You don't like coaches?"

Glaring at his hand on his chest, Jayla tried not to smile. He was so cute, so sinfully handsome, his smile could make her forget the reasons why professional sports made her nervous. "Don't be silly. I don't dig sports."

"How 'bout you overlook what I do, and I'll overlook that you don't *like* what I do." He winked at her, his brown eyes twinkling with humor. "Just let me get to know you."

Jayla smiled, allowing a release of air from her tight lungs. "You may not like me."

"I'm attracted to you."

She bit back a giggle as she stepped closer and touched the bulge between his legs, smoothing down the length with the light touch of her fingers. "I can tell, Mr. Ray," she said, laughing when he pulsed hard beneath his jeans.

"Nathan." He looped an arm around her waist and pulled her close, slanting his hard-on into her belly. His mouth found her ear. He smoothed his tongue along the sensitive skin, the wet heat pooling desire against her clit.

"You okay with this?" he asked, tugging her lobe between his teeth, then soothing it with his tongue. "How's this?" His hand slid between their bodies and covered her breast, tweaking an elongated nipple through her shirt.

A tremor ran down her spine. Lolling her head and arching her back, she pressed her breast more firmly into his palm, whimpering when his hand slid away. He replaced his fingers with his mouth, murmuring, "This?" before his lips closed around her beaded tip and suckled it into the incredible heat of his mouth.

Soaked with arousal, her thighs ached to be wrapped around his waist. Deep inside her pussy she felt a painful emptiness, begging to be filled by his dick. Jayla tried to swallow down the rise of lust, to tamper the desire to be taken hard and swift. To slow her heart rate, which throbbed in her clit.

His damned skillful mouth left her nipple, touched the hollow of her throat, skimmed the column of her neck. Licked across her lips. "You okay with this, Jayla?"

His tongue thrust into her mouth, silencing any comment had she been able to form conscious thought or a rational word. His lips tasted of cake and chocolate, sugary. But he kissed with power and authority, stroking against her lips, her tongue, her teeth, demanding her response.

Luring her tongue to press and swirl with his, to undulate in a rhythm mimicked by the rotation of her hips against the yummy length of his rock-hard dick.

Just when she was tempted to rip off her clothing—and his—he slowed the kiss, suckled her lips, then, with a quick peck, stepped away.

At least he was breathing hard and the smirking twinkle in his eyes was gone, replaced with something smoldering and dangerous. Something held by a firm hand of control. At least she could see the way his erection reached for her, bucking against his jeans.

"You all right with all that?" he asked, between jagged pants.

"Yes." *I'm all right with more.*

He kissed her again, just a smiling peck to her lips. "Good." He winked, like he knew what she'd been thinking.

Jayla took a deep breath, then exhaled as she squeezed her thighs together to get rid of the tingle. Licking her lips, she glanced at the steel worktables. "Let's finalize your sister's order. We still need to talk about the sex—um, sauce."

Tossing his head back, Nathan roared with laughter. He had sex thrown at him all the time that he had no interest in. Now he was chasing it. But there was something about Jayla that confused him.

He wanted more than just sex, but also to know about her. Like what her ex did that gave her a distaste for becoming emotionally involved. What secrets lingered behind her dislike of sports? Why was she concerned he might not like her?

If her pussy tasted as good as her lips?

Clenching his jaw, he suppressed a needy groan. "I'll take some of each. Thirty people—you decide how many I'll need." Keeping hold of her hand, he moved them to the tray of samples. "Just get rid of the frills. Toni isn't really the frilly type."

"Do you want something else? Besides lace and icing flowers? I could do lines, or dots, or hearts, or suns"—she slanted her eyes at him and smiled—"or surfboards."

"Can we just do plain?"

"Plain dips can be *very* elegant."

"Settled. Now, tell me about the sauce."

Pink splashed her creamy cheeks, a shade so alluring he was tempted to run his tongue across her skin.

"Come here, I'll show you a few samples."

She walked farther down the counter and removed a sheet of aluminum foil from atop several bowls and a few small bottles of prefabricated body chocolate. That heavy throb in his cock started up again, thinking of where she'd been to get those sex sauces. Too damned bad he hadn't been with her.

Jayla was talking, but it took him a second to focus on her words. ". . . isn't working because it's too runny. I tested it on my hand." She picked up a spoon and dipped into one of the bowls of chocolate sauces she'd made, then spilled it on the back of her hand. "See, it just runs off and makes a big mess."

Nathan bent and touched his tongue to her chocolate-smeared skin. "Tastes good, though."

With a paper towel she cleaned the chocolate from her skin. "Yeah, but it's wrong. I tried to add less cream"—she reached for a second bowl—"and this one seems to be pretty good, except it balls up when—"

"What did you get these for?" he asked, lifting a tiny bottle of the premade sexy-shop supply.

She blushed again. Taking it away from him, her fingers brushed his, sending blood south. She put it back on the countertop. "I wanted to get an idea of flavor and texture. They don't taste like good chocolate. You don't want any of those."

Grabbing the spoon from the last bowl of sauce, she held it up toward him. "See, try this."

"It's body chocolate. I need to try it on your body."

The pink on her cheeks deepened to red, and the lush shade of green in her expressive eyes went from moss to forest. Her body trembled slightly. A splintered breath danced around his face as she slanted away from him and looked around the back workroom of Decadent Dips.

"You're right. If we're going to get the right consistency, we're going to have to mix it with body heat." The tip of her tongue peeked out as she wet her lips. "We're going to have to test these at my place."

Five

Pacing didn't help her nerves, but Jayla couldn't bring herself to stop either. Rubbing her palms down her hips to smooth the material of her sundress, she tossed a look at the clock—the tenth in less than five minutes. Thirty-second intervals sure didn't make time move faster.

And Nathan wasn't even expected for another few minutes, yet every time she heard a car on the street, she walked to the window and looked outside.

There's no reason to be nervous, she reasoned, putting her hand between her breasts and taking a couple of deep, slow breaths. She was completely prepared for his arrival, had been ever since yesterday when they set up the sampling at her condo rather than the shop.

But him coming here was a whole lot more about the sex part of the chocolate than it was about the sauce. She knew what she was after when she invited him over. He was well aware of the offer.

Sleeping had been close to impossible as she'd waited for the sun to rise. Working had been worthless, as she'd watched the seconds tick off the hours. She'd decided to leave early and get the recipes set up and the sauces started.

And she'd prepared for more than just making body paint. Oh, yeah, she'd Naired her legs, trimmed the tight curls into a line, put on a simple sundress with nothing on beneath. She didn't forget about the condoms hidden in her nightstand, moving a few to the catchall drawer in the kitchen so they'd be close by.

She smoothed her dress again to dry her palms, and went to the fridge. She removed a jug of milk, the perfect comple-ment with chocolate, and was about to get two glasses from the cabinet when the *tap-tap-tap* sounded on her door.

Startled, she put the container aside with shaking hands and moved toward the door, pulling it open, eager to get Nathan inside.

He stood on the threshold, holding a bouquet of passion-flowers and baby's breath, the setting sun highlighting his golden-tipped hair and tanned skin. He wore slacks and a for-mal shirt, but he'd lost the tie and unbuttoned the first few buttons.

"For you," he said, stepping inside and kissing her softly on the mouth.

Accepting the flowers, she allowed the door to fall closed behind him. "They're gorgeous."

"Lexi put it together for me."

Jayla smiled. "She's talented." And she was. She and Lexi had done a lot of events together, supplying flowers and desserts.

Walking toward the kitchen, she felt Nathan fall into step behind her. "You brought me flowers like we're on a date." She put the bouquet on the tile countertop, then looked for something to put it in.

"We are."

Smiling, she glanced over her shoulder and caught him looking at her butt. "Really? Hmmm . . . thought this was work."

He chuckled as he smacked her ass hard.

Jayla gasped, but the slight sting was chased away with a soothing caress and a gentle squeeze.

"I'm cool with mixing business and pleasure." Nathan leaned back on the counter, his stance wide and casual.

"Great." She tossed him a bag of chocolate chips. "Add these to that pot. And don't turn up the heat under the double boiler."

"Double boiler?"

"This. So the chocolate doesn't burn." Picking up a spoon, she began to stir as he added the bag of chips, the lumps slowly starting to melt.

He moved closer. Reaching around her, he covered her hand with his, and helped stir the chocolate. But Jayla's body had stopped giving a damn about the stove as soon as he stepped up behind her. She was unbelievably aware of every incredible inch of his rock-hard erection pressed against the small of her back.

Whimpering, she lolled her head back against his chest, allowing him to support some of her weight. He bent, his mouth touching her neck, lips open and wet. "Isn't this sauce too hot?" he asked against her skin.

Drawing a shuddering breath, "Yeah. I have another recipe already cooled that we can try." Though reluctant to leave his heat or the feel of him muscular and broad behind her, she also wanted Nathan Ray dipped in chocolate. And she meant to have him.

"Here." Leaving the stove, she moved to a large center island and removed a kitchen towel from over a ceramic bowl. Dipping a finger into the room temperature chocolate, she watched his brown eyes follow as she brought the dipped finger to her lips, licked, then sucked it clean.

She dipped two fingers and he stepped in her direction.

"That's a nice suit, Nathan."

"Thanks."

"It's going to have to come off."

His golden brows plunged together, and his eyes narrowed. She lifted her two fingers, dripping with rich sauce. "Right." Shaking his head as he chuckled, he started working free the remaining buttons.

Thinking she was about to get a glimpse of tanned skin over a perfectly chiseled chest and abdomen when he pushed his shirt off his shoulders, she was disappointed to see the plain white T-shirt beneath.

"That, too."

Laughing, he tugged the cotton T off and tossed it in the same direction he had his other shirt. "Better?"

Oh, yeah, better. Just looking at the carved muscles as he stood naked to the waist made her pulse speed and arousal seep from her pussy.

"Hmm?" She teased, catching a drip of chocolate from her fingers with her tongue, then licking the slither of sweetness that slid toward her palm. "The pants, too, Nathan. Can't ruin them."

There wasn't a moment's hesitation as he reached for his belt and worked it free. "You're wearing a dress."

She smiled. To keep him from noticing the tremble in her hands, she put her fingers back in the bowl and swirled. "True, but I'm the *dipper*, not the *dippee*."

The top button of his fly was next; then the jagged teeth of the zipper gave way. Staring at the bulge hidden behind boxer shorts, she felt her knees turn to jelly, and the tingle at her clit became more prominent as the throbbing of his hard-on caused the V of his pants to widen.

"I'm the dippee?" Shrugging out of his slacks, he kicked them to the side, then tucked a thumb beneath the waistband of his boxer shorts. He arched a questioning brow.

"Mm-hmm . . ." Closing her eyes briefly, Jayla tried to calm the tempo of her heart. "I'm the one who needs to check consistency." There was something incredibly intimate about standing in her home with a man wearing nothing but under-shorts. Aside from occasional handymen, Nathan was the first man who'd been in her condo for years.

Wetting her lips, she glanced at him. Mostly naked and sporting an impressive erection beneath thin satin, standing in her kitchen, his presence was oddly disturbing to her soul, profoundly arousing.

Swirling her fingers in the bowl, she ignored the tightness of her nipples and the wetness slick on her inner thighs. "Those can stay. . . ." Scooping chocolate sauce, she stepped toward him. Touching her hand to his chest, she smeared the richness over his flat brown nipple. "For now."

Nathan growled, his body shaking as she followed the smudge of chocolate with her tongue. One touch and he damned near came. His dick was throbbing hard, and a hot ball of cum built at the base.

Reaching behind her, she pulled the bowl closer, then

dipped several fingers in again. "Very chocolaty. Nice rich flavor." She touched her dipped hand to his mouth, swiping chocolate across his lips. "Good?" She smoothed the rest across his pecs, the touch of her hand light and alluring.

"Yeah."

"It's better on your skin." And then her lips were on him again, mouth open, tongue lapping at the sauce, getting mostly his skin. She sucked it off his nipple, followed the curves of his muscles with swiping licks of her talented tongue.

Jayla had worn her long wild curls down around her shoulders, gorgeous hair he wanted to grip while he was fucking her slow, but right now they hid the erotic sight of her mouth on his flesh.

Putting his hand beneath the mass of silken hair, he brushed it away from her face, then watched her eat from his skin. His jaw ached, the cadence of his pulse pounding at his temples. One hand holding her hair back, he smoothed his other palm down her spine, over her rounded ass, and yanked up the material of her dress.

Pantiless. His hand caressed smooth firm flesh, kneaded the globe. Rolling his hips forward, knowing there was nothing beneath her dress, he wanted her closer, wanted to feel the damp heat of her pussy. Wanted to get inside her.

Pre-cum seeped from his tip. A hoarse moan escaped as she undulated with him, dick to clit, separated by cotton, not latex. He trembled, control waning.

Awh, hell, she's a tease.

Smiling, she stood shaking her head. "This batch isn't right."

"Huh?" The only head thinking was his cock's. Thinking about one thing. Sex. With Jayla. *Now.*

She scooped more, then let the sauce slide onto his skin at his navel. "Your skin is hot, making the sauce warm."

"So?" He watched her plump lips, fighting the desire to claim them.

"Makes it thin."

"So?"

She giggled, her green eyes meeting his. Her fingers swirled in the line of hair low on his abdomen, teased and danced, the back of her hand brushing against his cock several times.

Breaking eye contact, she knelt slowly before him, drawing down his boxers, the waistband being chased by fat droplets of dripping chocolate. The warm sauce seeped around the base of his hard-on, his sac drew up tight, and his shorts fell to his ankles.

"You're dipping me?" he asked through clenched teeth.

"Yes." Chocolate-coated fingers curled around him, sliding up to the ridge of his cock, then slid to his base and back in a slow steady rhythm. She dipped one finger of her other hand, and touched it to his head, drawing circles around the drop of pre-cum.

Looking down, he could see right into the gaping neckline of her dress. Firm breasts, rosy beaded nipples. With her thighs slightly spread, he caught the sweet scent of her arousal.

His chest burned as he held his breath, waiting. Anticipating. A test of willpower to keep from speeding up her tempo by thrusting his hips.

Getting more chocolate, she soothed it around the ridge, then angled him to her lips. Warm and titillating, her breath caressed him. His hands balled into fists at his sides.

"Mm-hmm, better on your skin," she whispered, licking the pre-cum, then closed her lips around his head.

Air hissed between his teeth, his body trembling from the force it took to stand there and allow her to suck him, while stroking up and down his dick with chocolate-coated fingers.

"Jayla—"

She tightened her cheeks, adding suction, as she took him deeper into her mouth. Deeper. Angling her hand so her thumb stroked along the vein running down the underside of his cock.

Slanting back, she looked up him, her eyes shining with appreciation. Though her lips were wrapped around him, he could see her smile in her expressive gaze.

"You're killing me, Jayla." He thrust his hips, the smile doing in his restraint.

The beat quickened as she slanted back to his hard flesh. Up and down she moved before him with her hand. Up, down. Up. Down. And her lips were there sucking him in the same in-and-out tempo, the same driving rhythm.

The movement of her tongue as she sucked chocolate from his cock caused beads of sweat to form on his forehead. The motion exotic, the beat mesmerizing.

The ball of cum moved higher, orgasm a few quick sucks away. He could feel the pulse of release. It beckoned to him, but he struggled to hold it at bay, to hold off for a few more strokes.

But she seemed to sense how he grappled for control. Not slowing her movements, she tightened her lips, and cupped his sac, massaging gently.

"Jayla!" He tried to warn her as the hot ball of cum shot up his dick, tried to pull back, not knowing if she was ready or accepting of it. But she followed his retreat, coaxing the climax.

"Oh, God!" He pumped into her mouth and came.

A violent tremor moved through him as he pulsed hard, emptying himself into her luscious mouth. Turning her gaze to his, she allowed him to ease from her lips, holding his semi-hard dick tenderly. The last pulses of orgasm looked opal against her chocolate-dipped hands.

A few quiet moments passed, the silence broken only by his harsh uneven pants.

He could hear the laughter in her voice. "Are you happy with this recipe?" She stood, wiping her hands on a dish towel.

"Yes!" The word hissed between his teeth.

Her lips went pouty, but her green eyes teased. "Oh."

He chuckled.

"But to make it perfect, we're going to have try a few more."

Six

Jayla turned on the bathroom sink, bending to put her hair in the flow of water. "Look what you did," she teased, wetting her hand and working free the clumps of chocolate tangled in her curls.

He chuckled. "Wasn't my fault."

Nathan's laughter drew her gaze upward, to catch his reflection in the mirror. Wearing nothing but his boxers, he stood behind her, his brown eyes twinkling with humor, his kissable lips curved into a smirk.

"Oh, no?"

"Nope." He stepped forward, putting his hand on the back of her thigh, then slowly slid upward, over her ass. His finger crept beneath her sundress, pushing up the hem as he caressed her flesh. "You were distracting me with this."

Jayla giggled. She'd been humming while stirring a bowl of

cooling chocolate body sauce when he'd come up behind her. He'd nudged her hair out of the way with his chin and had been kissing her neck when he reached around her and dipped his hand into the warm chocolate.

Next thing she knew, his hand was gripping her hair and angling her head to give his lips and tongue better access. And her hair ended up a chocolaty mess.

"Distracting you how?"

"You have any idea how sexy it is when you wiggle your ass while you sing?"

"I never remember words. I hum." She pushed a few curls into the water, her fingers working melted chips that were now starting to harden.

"Singing, humming, you were still shaking it."

Grinning as she caught his gaze in the mirror, she wiggled her butt for him, earning a groan. She laughed. "You got it in my ear, too."

He swatted her flesh a couple of times, somewhere between a pat and a smack, before his hand dropped away and he moved to her side. "Let me help."

His much larger hand joined hers in the flow of warm water, his fingers spanning out across her scalp. With her head to the side, her face was inches from his bronzed abdomen, each muscle sharply defined. When she inhaled, the scent of his skin wafted around her, mixing with the sweetness of the chocolate, and the lingering saltiness of his climax.

She wanted to forget about the mess in her hair, her mouth watering, her gaze fixed in the line of dark hair that trailed from his navel to his dick. His golden perfection was marred simply with a few remaining smudges of chocolate she hadn't licked clean.

His voice was low and hoarse when he spoke. "Stop breathing."

"What? Why?"

"I can feel it. You're making me hard." He tilted his hips, showing how he was lengthening in his shorts.

She giggled. "Oh." Rounding her lips, she blew a long steady breath against his skin.

"Brat." He shut off the sink. Then with her hair wrapped around his fingers, he urged her to stand. "Too much chocolate for the sink."

"Great." She touched her wet, matted hair, feeling the lumps of chocolate. "I don't think this recipe works."

He released her hair and shrugged massive toned shoulders. Stepping around her, he moved to the shower, opened the glass door, and turned on the spray. Back at her side, he was sporting a gleam in his eye that bordered arrogance.

The tempo of her heartbeat sped; her breathing shortened. "You got it in there. You going to wash it out?" She angled her hip and pursed her lips.

"Damned right." Both his hands settled at her sides and gathered the material of her dress in his fists, then yanked up, and dragged it off her body. "Too bad you're not wearing a bra and panties."

Jayla swallowed. His brown eyes had darkened and stared with so much intensity at her breasts that her nipples puckered up and her knees threatened to buckle. "Why?" she whispered.

He tweaked a nipple between his thumb and forefinger. "It'd have been fun taking them off you."

Smiling, her gaze headed south to the satin of his boxers and the hard length of cock beneath. Her skin felt damp, moisture slick on her inner thighs. She swallowed the dryness in her throat, then wet her lips with her tongue.

Self-control was a discipline Nathan prided himself on, but Jayla seriously put that in jeopardy. Drawing in a deep breath, he put his hands on her upper arms, her body so sweetly feminine, he had the desire to gather her to his chest and protect her from the hurt and uncertainty he witnessed on occasion in her expressive eyes.

To love her so thoroughly that the insecurities in her deep green pools would be vanquished permanently.

Mustering the last bit of his restraint, he turned her away from him instead, and gave her an encouraging push toward the shower.

Glancing once over her shoulder, her eyes said *Come to me*, the sway of her hips sensual and alluring. Curved just perfectly, her hourglass figure was made to be adored. She walked to the shower, touched the stream of water with her fingers, then stepped inside.

Shrugging out of his shorts, he picked up the condoms from the counter where he'd tossed them when he'd reached to help rinse her hair. Looking at her now, her creamy skin wet and glistening, he was damned glad he'd grabbed them from his pants pocket when he'd followed her to the bathroom.

He followed her now, into the shower, then closed the glass door behind him. She turned toward him, water streaming over her body, over her shoulders, down firm rosy-tipped breasts, dripping off elongated nipples.

Putting the condom packets on a built-in tile shelf that held shampoo and conditioner, he stepped beneath the spray of water.

7

3

Her gaze had followed his movements, her eyes widening, and her cheeks went pink. "Two?" she asked, putting a hand on her hip and slanting it to the side in that sassy way of hers.

Laughing, Nathan moved closer. "You never know." Sliding his hands behind her back, he pulled her close, wedging his rocked-up cock between them.

Her delicate hands settled on his chest; her palms stroked over him, then upward to curve around his neck. The tips of her tits were teasing his skin, causing the throb in his erection to become more pronounced.

Humming, she swayed against him, rotating her hips in this sensual manner that incited his need. Tightening his jaw, he was determined to wash the chocolate from her hair before he tore open one of those condoms and drove into her.

Smoothing his hand from her hip, up her spine, his fingers tangled in her long, wet curls. Using a little pressure, he angled her head back, putting her hair beneath the strongest force of the shower.

Her eyes closed and her back arched over his arm as she relaxed in his hold. With his free hand he reached for the shampoo and squeezed it onto the wet strands, then used both hands to work up a lather.

"That feels good," she whispered, long lashes casting damp shadows on her cheeks, head lolled back.

Tiny iridescent bubbles slid down her body, snaked across her breasts, and gathered around her beaded nipples. Pointed upward because of the arch of her back, her nipples begged for attention.

As liquid sluiced Jayla's hair, he covered her breast with his palm, kneading the flesh, her skin slick with water and floral shampoo. He circled her areola with his thumb, rubbed back and forth across the bead.

She moaned softly, barely loud enough to be heard above the spray of water. "That's good, too."

Nathan's gut knotted up; his chest went tight. There was something about her honest responses in her expressions of joy that made him think about this being more than a fling. A more serious thing.

Gulping in a breath, he tried to check his need. Rein in his demanding desire. To keep the cadence of his pulse from throbbing in his dick.

But Jayla wasn't playing along with his struggle to go slow.

She stood and wiggled from his hold, stepping back into the harder jet of water. Fine droplets splattered around them. She reached for him, caressing his erection with a gentle touch, with a tenderness that had him bucking and holding back orgasm.

"Your dick is so beautiful," she said, her fingertips smoothing over his head and feathering down his length, then back to his head again.

He chuckled, thrusting his hips and pressing his hard-on more firmly into her hands. "Beautiful? Ha! He's mean. Dangerous. He'll make you scream."

He'd meant it as a joke, but the blush on her cheeks deepened as she reached for one of the condoms.

Jayla's thighs ached. Arousal mixed with the water running down her legs. Her beach bum was covered with golden skin, his body unbelievably toned, each twining muscle defined. From biceps, to pecs, to his washboard stomach, every cord was distinct, shadowed, and outlined.

And there was power that pulsed beneath his skin, a magnetism that made her clit tingle, made her pussy desperate to be filled.

"Make me scream?" She tore open the condom, allowing the foil packet to fall to the shower floor. She wanted him so badly, her hand was shaking. "Yes, please."

Nathan growled. And she laughed as she touched the latex to his head, fitting it over him, then rolling it down his cock with both hands.

He moved forward, his hand cupping her ass, then sliding down to the back of her thigh. "You're sure about this?" he asked, his voice strained.

"Nathan, I'm begging." But she couldn't breathe. A tremor of need seeped through her body. She rolled her hips toward him. "Please."

Groaning, he backed her to the tile wall, and pulled her leg up to drape over his hip. On tiptoes on her other foot, she was open for him. Open and soaking wet.

She touched his chest, ran her palm across the disk of his nipple, followed the angles of his body with her fingertips, swirling in the water.

His hand closed around the base of his dick and he angled toward her, touching her with his tip. Giving her not even an inch, when she ached to have him hard and full and deep inside.

Panting, she tried to tighten her leg around his back, to use her foot to force him forward.

He gave her another inch, and her body stretched, then clamped around him to encourage him farther, to keep him from leaving. Whimpering, she licked her lips.

She felt the movement of his chuckle more than she heard it, and then he was there, thrusting into her.

"Awh!" Her back arched away from the shower wall. He was pulsing inside her, every throb intensifying the tingling in her clit. Dragging in a shaky breath, she lifted her other foot and wrapped her leg around his back, her weight supported by the wall, anchored on his dick.

With the cold tile pressed against her back, the water was hot enough to generate steam, but it felt merely tepid compared with the burn he created. She pressed a kiss to his collarbone. "You feel good." Each word was said between her lips to his skin.

His body was shaking as he stood there, buried in her tight, wet heat. Her body felt so small naked and wet and held against him, but her pussy—she molded around him, stretched, and accommodated his entire length. And as much as he needed to thrust in, he held back, waiting for her, wanting to know she was okay being fucked by him.

Her teeth scraped his skin. "Make me scream."

That's what he needed. Holding on to her hips, he withdrew nine inches, leaving just his head inside, then drove into her hard.

She cried out, her back arching and her breasts shaking with the force of his movements. Her legs tightened around him, urging him to give her more.

He repeated, withdrawing, then pushing inward. Jayla cried out again, but he captured the sound with his mouth as he thrust his tongue between her teeth in the same wild rhythm he worked his cock into her accepting, slick heat.

Bending his knees slightly, he pressed into the shower wall, driving into her at just the angle she'd need to hit the right spots, to rub the base of his erection against her clit.

The sweetness of her mouth was driving him crazy as she swirled her tongue with his, meeting his thrusts by holding him with her thighs.

In and out he moved, cum building, ready to blow. Her

breath tasted of chocolate, her skin scented with floral soap, the air perfumed with arousal, with impending orgasm.

One long thrust and her body shook, her nails bit into his skin, and her pussy clamped down hard around him. Breaking the kiss, she screamed as enthralling and violent shudders wracked her body.

The way her pussy fluttered around him released his control. Cum shot up and he came hard, filling the latex. Every muscle straining, he collapsed against her, pinning her body to the wall, their jagged pants mixed with the sputtering of the shower spray.

The water cooled. The shower causing chills rather than comfort was what caused them to untwine their limbs and separate. Nathan bound an arm behind her back to steady her, then shut off the spray.

Grinning and feeling more content than he had in a long time, he pressed a kiss to the tip of her cute nose. "You all right?"

She blushed, but her eyes smiled. "Perfect."

Seven

After he'd kept her awake making love last night, Nathan didn't blame Jayla for falling asleep. If his attention and focus weren't required on the narrow, winding highway, he'd easily be lulled by the motion of his Lexus and the plushness of the seats.

Rotating his neck on his shoulders, he allowed a contented breath to slowly seep from between his lips. Well-sated and completely relaxed, he looked forward to spending the day with Jayla, to spend time talking to her, listening.

And he looked forward to the light in her green eyes when she saw what he'd planned for the day. Shifting his gaze off the road for a moment, he glanced at Jayla. She was curled slightly on her side facing him, a hand tucked beneath her chin, long, thick lashes leaving shadows on her creamy cheeks.

Her luscious lips pursed slightly in her sleep, bringing back memories of the night before and the way those plump lips had pleasured him. Blood poured to his cock, perpetuating his constant semiaroused state.

But the sweetness of her face and the gentleness of her slow even breathing did more than incite his desire; it tightened his gut and made his chest ache with an entirely different need.

Shifting his attention back to the road, Nathan thought about the last few weeks, and how quickly life had changed. Since the night of tasting chocolate and ending up in the shower, he'd pretty much spent every night the following week at Jayla's—in her bed, under her sheets, and welcomed between her thighs.

Before he stepped into Decadent Dips he'd been a single man, and happy that way. Now . . . now he had to wonder if that was what he really wanted. His throat went dry.

Last night had proved just how important she was to him. He'd had to go out of town again, to a meeting about preseason training camp for the Chargers. But after their week together, his hotel room bed had felt lonely and cold. In such a short time, his body had become accustomed to the release she offered, and he'd been heavy and rocked up after three nights without her.

But it wasn't until he'd seen her smiling and waving at him at the airport yesterday that he realized it was more than just her pussy he'd missed. He'd missed the tenderness of her soul. He'd missed the joy of her voice, the happiness of her laughter.

Shaking his head to clear the fog of yesterday's memories, Nathan took a few deep breaths to slow the wild beat of his heart. To quiet the roar of his pulse in his ears.

Easing off the gas, he took the exit off the highway, following the directions he'd checked out earlier. The road narrowed further as they passed beneath a stone archway and through huge iron gates. As he continued up the drive, both sides of the road were lined with vineyards, rows and rows of grapes.

Slowing to a stop, he parked in front of a large stone winery, and shut off the ignition.

"Jayla," he said, touching her shoulder. "Jayla, sweetie, we're here."

Her lids fluttered, then opened slowly. He could tell it took her a moment to figure out where she was, but when her gaze settled on his, her lips curved into a smile. "Hi . . ."

"Hey." He smoothed his palm down her arm, across her soft skin.

She arched her back, stretching her arms above her head. "I fell asleep."

"Yeah, I guess I wore you out."

She blushed as she adjusted the seat back to an upright position, and looked around. "Where are we?"

"Stone Ridge Winery."

"A winery?"

"Toni told me about this place. I guess Isaac brought her up here for their wine-tasting tour."

"We're drinking wine"—her lips went pouty as she returned her gaze to him—"not eating chocolate?"

Simple words, but they worked him over, making his dick hard. "I could turn the car around. Go back to your place."

She giggled, her attention dropping to his lap and the growing bulge. "We'll do that later. This place looks like fun." Reaching for the door, she adjusted her skirt as she slid out of the car, then closed the door behind her.

Nathan closed his door and rounded the car to Jayla's side. "This way," he said, taking her delicate hand in his and leading her toward the wide stone stairs that opened to a large patio and massive oak doors.

Jayla followed behind Nathan, his touch warmer than the brightness of the midday sunshine. Vast blue sky was marred only by a few wispy high clouds, and the air smelled fresh and clean. Like earth and grapes rather than ocean, and she wondered how long she'd slept while he'd driven away from San Diego.

Hours, she guessed, judging by the grumbling in her stomach. They'd made love all night and skipped breakfast. After the way Nathan had sexed her, she was in desperate need of nourishment.

"Is it just wine, or do you think there will be some food? I'm hungry and with no food, the alcohol is going to go straight to my head."

He paused, drawing her close to him, and brushed his mouth over the sensitive skin beneath her ear. "If I get you drunk, can I have my way with you?"

She laughed. Turning, she kissed the corner of his mouth and pressed their joined hands to her belly. "Feed me, Nathan, and you can have anything you want."

Jerking away from her, he tugged her after him, up the stairs and across the large patio. "Let's find you something to eat."

Inside was cool and dark, very atmospheric with rock walls and oak floors, but there was something alluring about the rustic elegance. To the left was a long wooden bar, polished to a shine, lined with wineglasses. Farther down was a row of tables and several people dressed in uniforms setting out trays of finger foods.

Her mouth was watering as they walked toward the tables of food, the aromas appetizing.

"Do we help ourselves?" Nathan asked one of the employees, a thin man who looked to be in his late forties.

"Yes, yes, please do." He pointed toward the dishes. "If you're here for the tour, it doesn't start until two o'clock, but please feel free to make a plate and roam about."

"Thank you."

With her stomach growling now, she loaded her plate. Nathan did the same; then they reversed their steps, heading back outside and down the stairs. It was too glorious a day to be wasted indoors.

Instead they strolled down a narrow path where tall grapevines were staked up on either side. Tiny green clusters of grapes were just beginning to form.

"Tell me about your sister," Jayla said, reaching over to take a skewered shrimp from Nathan's plate.

He smacked her ass, and laughed when she reached for another. "I'm beginning to think you like that."

"I do." She wiggled her butt for him. "Now, tell me about Toni."

He shrugged. "Not much to tell. The little brat is crazy about sports and has a passion for photography. She's a photographer for *Sports Illustrated*."

Jayla noted the pride in his voice. The love. Swallowing down the marble in her throat, she slanted away from him so he wouldn't see the way her breathing changed. The way she struggled to fill her lungs. Squeezing her lids closed for a moment, she reminded herself that it was the betting, not the events, that caused so much damage.

Shoving away the burning behind her eyes, she looked

back at Nathan and forced a smile. "Sports seem to be a theme in your family."

"Yeah, athletics have been pretty important." With a wide grin, he flexed his arm for her, winking when his biceps bulged.

His muscles pulsed beneath golden skin, and her hand itched to touch where he flexed, absorb the warmth of his flesh. Slowing her pace, she steadied her breathing and wet her lips.

"Do you ever make bets on games?"

He shook his head, the sunshine dancing on the tips of his cropped hair. "Never cared about gambling, I just loved to play."

"Oh." She popped a little muffin in her mouth that turned out to be some sort of crab cake.

They walked onward in the quiet stillness of the day, a gentle breeze rustling the grape leaves, the occasional whistle of birds floating on the zephyrs.

His hand touched her upper arm, pausing her movement. "These aren't as good as yours"—he held a chocolate-dipped strawberry to her lips—"but have a bite."

She took a chunk between her teeth, the juice filling her mouth as she chewed. "You're right." She licked her lips and smiled. "Not as good as mine."

"Maybe this'll help." And his lips touched hers.

Jayla parted for him. Holding the plate to the side, she moved closer, drawn by his heat. On tiptoes, she wound her free arm around his neck and fit her body to his as his tongue invaded her mouth.

The chocolate melted, but the flavor of the berry remained. The lingering sweetness reminded her of their first kiss. Whimpering, she touched her tongue to his, stroked against him, brushed across his lips and teeth. Took pleasure in his groan, and the throb of his cock, which pressed against her clit.

His fingers twisted into her hair, smoothed down her throat, caressed the arch of her spine, pulled her closer as he ground into her through their clothes.

"You taste good, Mr. Ray," Jayla whispered into his kisses.

He nibbled at her lips, stroked his tongue across them, licked at a piece of chocolate, moaned when their tongues collided over the same bead of berry juice.

He kissed the corners of her smiling lips, her cheeks, her closed eyelids. "You make me *feel* good." He pressed his mouth to hers in a firm but quick peck. "Happy."

"Oh, yeah?" She stepped away from him, her hand sliding down his arm until their fingers were joined. She swung their hands between them. She wanted to dance, there, surrounded by vines and blue sky, and admiring brown eyes. "Tell me how."

"You make me laugh." He lifted their hands and angled their fingers so she'd spin under his arm. And she did, giggling, then stood before him again. "So don't hate me when I make this confession."

"A confession? Wait, don't tell me you *are* married."

He shook his head. "Not yet."

"You're gay."

He yanked her forward until her body was flush to his, and he thrust his hips forward. "Not hardly."

As if on cue, his erection throbbed against her. She laughed and glanced down. "What, then?"

"The chocolate sauce. I didn't need it."

She released his hand and stepped back, swaying her hip to the side and jamming her fist to her waist. "Well, you rat.

There will be consequences, surfer boy." Her attention slid from his face to his erection. "Hmm . . . how should I make you pay for wasting my time?"

He laughed. "Hey, no waste. I'm going forward with the order. But I lied about needing it, so you'd spend some time with me."

She tapped her foot and wet her lips. "You could've asked."

"I'm asking now, Jayla. Spend some time with me."

"Well, all right, but only because you fed me." She took his hand and twined their fingers. "What were you saying about drinking too much wine?"

He tugged her along after him, chuckling. "Yeah, let's go see about getting you drunk."

They'd moved down the path back toward the hall when Jayla squeezed his fingers. "By the way, I knew you were lying. You don't have much of a poker face."

He kissed her hand. "I'm glad you understand." He added a wink.

Eight

He moved in her lazily, his strokes slow and languid. In, he filled her, lingered with his cock pressed to her womb, then slid out with a mere roll of his hips. In again, with a graceful flexing of his ass. Out unhurried.

Jayla closed her eyes, arching her back. She lay sprawled naked on the sheets, Nathan fitted between her thighs, her knees bent slightly, her legs angled around him so her feet rested on his muscular calves. A cool ocean breeze danced through the open window, the dawn sea fog losing out to the rise of late-morning sunshine.

"This is the one," he said. Supporting his weight on one forearm, he used his other hand to spread smooth chocolate sauce across her nipple, drawing the flesh tighter. He nipped, then soothed with temperate kisses.

The sauce chilled her skin, having sat out on her bedside table all night, but he warmed it with his tongue. With deliberately somnolent licks and drowsy swipes. With lips that teased and nibbled, with a thorough mouth.

"Mm-hmmm . . . a good recipe." Stretching her arms above her head, and angling her hips toward him as he entered her again, she hummed the melody of a love song, completely contented with the languorous pace of how he was sexing her. The notes seeped from her subconscious, escaped her closed lips.

"I love it when you sing for me, Jayla." He pushed deeper inside her, filling her with every hard inch.

Jayla's breath caught, the song fading away, as she focused on keeping the burning behind her eyes from turning into liquid. The tears gone, she became totally absorbed on the feeling of fullness, on the lazy cadence against her clit.

"Why'd you stop?" he asked, using his fingers to soak her skin in chocolate, and the wetness of his kisses.

"You make me unable to breathe, Nathan."

"I'm too heavy." He shifted slightly, taking more weight onto his side.

"No, not that." Banding her arms around his massive shoulders, she held him to her before he could roll away, and squished the chocolate he'd been licking from her breasts between them. She pressed her feet to the backs of his legs and tightened her thighs.

It wasn't his weight that caused her breathing to halt, her lungs to burn, her throat to go dry. No, not the largeness of his body, but his heart. Because of the gentleness of his love-making. The tenderness in his kisses.

She hadn't known there was anything missing in her life,

but Nathan had stepped in and proved how huge the void had been. Her heart ached. Now she wasn't sure she'd be able to go back to the quiet days and lonely nights of her former life.

"My dad used to call me Jayla Bird," she said, wanting to share something of herself with him. Wanting someone to finally know her soul.

He chuckled. She felt the vibration all the way into the damp heat of her pussy.

"Jayla Bird? I like it."

"My ex didn't. He didn't like my singing."

"Your ex is a damned fool!" His thrust held a force the previous movements lacked.

She gasped.

"What did he do to you?" He kissed her softly at the corner of her mouth, touched his lips to her ear as he curved his back and filled her again, pressing the entire length of his erection inward. Drawing out slowly.

She didn't care that they were talking about her ex-husband while they had sex. It was part of the sharing, part of the blending of bodies and souls. Her flesh stretched to accommodate him, as did her heart. Emotions she'd thought were dead when she'd realized she'd never really loved her ex the way a woman should love her husband.

Though she'd pledged her life and commitment, she'd never envisioned a forever with him. Yes, she'd been hurt by his deceits and the ending of their marriage. But she'd never been devastated.

Sliding her palms up Nathan's biceps, she felt his muscles bunch and strain beneath her fingertips, felt the fine sheen of sweat that covered his golden beach-bum body.

"He was a faithless liar. He stole from me."

"Your heart?"

"No." *My ex never had it.* "He stole money, and abused my trust." She brushed her fingers along his collarbone, then his neck. She felt his pounding pulse, and a mimicked rhythm throbbed inside her with each deep penetration.

"I don't cheat." He followed the statement by suckling a nipple into his mouth, lavishing her with the skill of his tongue. His large hand settled on her hip, holding her to the bed as he moved against her, inside her.

Jayla said nothing. Her thighs quivered. Her pussy tightened. Her heart ached. There was no comment to be made over his assertion. In order for there to be a cheat, there'd have to be some level of trust. Commitment. She'd known Nathan for only a month, and didn't know where she stood. Didn't know where she wanted to stand.

He thrust in again, adding a grind against her clit before he moved out of her body, leaving just his plum-shaped head enveloped in her soaked flesh.

"I don't steal," he said, lifting his head and turning his face toward her.

She smiled at the chocolate on his chin and lips. At the determined glint in his brown eyes.

"You're smiling?"

"At this," she said, using her thumb to clean the sauce from his face, then licking it off her finger. Lifting slightly, she pressed her lips to his chin, tasting what remained of the chocolate and the slight saltiness of his skin.

"He gambled"—she kissed his mouth, the brushing of lips light and fleeting—"on sports."

Nathan pretended her statement meant nothing to him personally. That the hopes and plans he'd had for their future didn't threaten to crack. Though his slow thrusting faltered briefly, he picked it back up, entering her in this lazy sort of rhythm.

Although he acted unaffected, her words told him so much. Her actions started to make sense. Questions she'd asked on the odds of winning, and whether he ever kept track or placed bets on big games.

She might not have meant to do it—or even realized what she was doing—but she'd been testing him. Hell, she'd even told him she wasn't big on his profession.

He couldn't change the past, take away her experience. He increased his strokes to a faster pace. There was only one thing he could do: show her he wasn't anything like her ex.

He slid a hand across her ass, up her leg, which curved so sensually around him. Smoothing his palm back across her hip, he slid his hand between them, his fingers finding her clit.

Whimpering, she moved beneath him, her hips rising to meet his, her feet urging him with pressure to the backs of his thighs.

"Nathan," she said, her breathing becoming irregular. "Nathan."

His fingers worked against her clit as he kept up these steady strokes into her tight, wet pussy, the beginning of shudders fluttering around his dick.

"Sing for me, Jayla Bird," he demanded, pressing his thumb to her clit, then moving in small circles. "Sing for me."

Her body moved with his, her back arching off the bed, the sheets becoming a tangled mess. And though it was with broken, heavy breathing and pants, she began to half sing, half hum the melody of the love song that had been drifting from her lush lips a few minutes before.

The soft lilting of her voice caused his sac to pull up tight, the pulse of cum to build heavily in the base of his cock. Holding his jaw tight, he held orgasm at bay, wanting to take Jayla there first.

In he thrust, hard and deep, grinding his thumb against her clit, so the words halted and she cried out instead. The flutters in her sultry heat no longer whispered, but clamped around him.

He moved out, withdrawing until merely an inch was left inside her luscious body. She whimpered in time with the melody, trying to follow him so he wouldn't slip entirely from her.

In again, until she was shaking, and the quivering around his dick held him inside her, then drenched his flesh as she came.

"Nathan," she cried, her body trembling. Her nails biting into his skin.

He was shaking as he moved into her one last time. "I don't gamble." The words were more fiercely spoken than he'd meant, but control was waning. Then gone. With her body caressing and milking him, he gave over to climax, releasing the cum he'd been holding back.

Giving over to ecstasy, orgasm shot up his cock and filled the latex in a violent rush. Air hissed between his teeth, sweat wet his skin, and he collapsed on top of her, barely holding himself on his forearms so he wouldn't crush her.

Trying to catch his breath, he closed his eyes and swallowed the drying in his throat. Inhaling deeply, he was assaulted with the sweetness of her skin and the pureness of her arousal. And chocolate. A sexual chocolate sauce perfected with testing and experience.

Nathan rolled to his side, then flopped on his back, tugging breaths into his lungs. Around them the sheets were damped with sweat and marred with dark, rich chocolate.

Jayla laughed, moving against his side and draping her arm over his chest. "This isn't going to help make a good impression."

"Huh?"

"Being late. I'm going to be late and it's all your fault." She emphasized by tapping her fingers on his chest. He flexed and she giggled. "You not get enough sleep or something? What was up with slow?"

"You liked slow." His hand caressed the slope of her back, smoothing down her spine to the roundness of her ass. He squeezed.

She giggled and moved away from him to the side of the bed. "Yes, I did. Next time do slow when I don't have a wedding shower to provide desserts for."

"Come back to bed." He patted the mattress beside him, knowing she wouldn't. She stood beside the bed and stretched her hands over her head, the creamy skin of her breasts and belly covered in chocolate. "Come back. Toni won't mind you being late."

"I mind."

She was grinning at him, her green eyes roving over his naked body, stalling on his half-roused dick. Interest flared in her expressive gaze, but he saw when he lost her to work for the day.

"You stay in bed as long as you want. I have chocolate-dipped desserts to get delivered and set up." She indicated the chocolate sauce on her skin. "That means I've got to get in the shower."

"Jayla Bird, sing for me while you're in there."

She shook her head as she entered the bathroom. Lying there on his back, breathing slowly returning to normal, he listened as the water went on and the glass door closed behind her.

A few moments later she started to sing.

Nine

Jayla kept her back to the room as guests arrived, her heart rate pulsing in her ears, her lungs burning with each slow breath she sucked between her teeth, then held. Though the displays of chocolate-dipped cake squares were layered on tiers, and the dipped fruits were set up properly, she moved them, shifting their angles, rearranging each piece. For one reason.

Delay.

After Nathan drove her to Decadent Dips and assisted her in loading her refrigerated delivery van, she convinced him that riding together would only lead people to make assumptions—assumptions she didn't know if she was ready to face. Although he'd arrived ahead of her and in his own car, he'd still waited by the door and then helped her carry in her items, lingering by her side as she started to set up.

She'd finally had to shoo him away from her. She was the hired help for the day, paid to be there to provide the desserts. He was a guest. The bride's brother.

Closing her eyes, Jayla steadied her trembling hands. Her ordinary routine would be to set up, then quietly slip away from the event, only to return later to collect her supplies. But today—today she could hear Nathan's voice across the room. Could hear his warm laughter, the low timbre of his speech, and she didn't want to leave. She wanted to go to him. Stand next to him.

Claim him as her man.

Something she had no right to do, especially considering she was the one who'd warned him she wasn't into emotional investments. That deep involvement wasn't available. She swallowed the lump in her throat, the truth undeniable. It was too late.

Wetting her lips, she opened her eyes and glanced over her shoulder, to see that she was being approached. Only it wasn't Nathan making his way to her side, but it had to be his sister.

Tall and slender, she had the same sun-blond hair, the same shade of brown eyes. The same stunning smile.

She hugged Jayla quickly, catching her off guard. The same welcoming personality. "I thought your name sounded familiar when Nathan told me who he hired. Now I know why. We've met already." She looked over her shoulder briefly, then lowered her voice. "And we partied at Lexi's wedding."

"I remember. You're Toni." Heat expanded from her cheeks down her neck. She felt like smacking her forehead for her stupidity. Why hadn't she connected Toni with Nathan? Not only did they look the same, but there was the Alexis connection.

After Toni had finished taking pictures of Alexis and

Jackson at their wedding, she'd sat with Jayla and shared more than just a bottle of champagne. They'd commiserated over being single and over thirty. And as the bubbles got to their heads, they'd complained about how the lack of a man left them with nothing going on in the bedroom.

Amazing how a little booze could turn strangers into girl-friends.

Gulping down the embarrassment of having shared so much with Nathan's sister, she tried to make light of the memory before she drowned in the shame of it.

"Fixed your man problem, I see." She laughed softly.

Toni grinned, slanting a look across the room. "So did you."

Jayla followed the direction of Toni's gaze to where Nathan stood. Watching them. He was pretending he wasn't. He stood with a few other men, nodding now and then, but his rich brown eyes kept swaying in her direction. He didn't smile or react when their eyes collided. Their meshed gazes lingered; then he slowly broke contact, turning his attention back to the conversation going on around him.

"Wh-what do you mean?"

"Nathan. He told me about you, only I didn't know it was *you*, you." Toni picked up a chocolate-covered berry and took a bite. "Oh, yum, these are so good."

She watched the bride-to-be eat the dessert she'd created, enjoyed knowing her work was satisfying. But her mind raced over and over again on the words Toni had spoken. What had Nathan told his sister?

Toni was devouring the berry, but Jayla wished she'd quit eating and start explaining. Nathan wasn't the kind of man to kiss and tell, to share their experiences in bed. The rhythm of her pulse faltered, and she squeezed her lids closed briefly, wondering what sort of info about their relationship he'd be open with his sister about.

"They look great, as usual," a woman said from behind her.

Jayla startled, her pulse leaping. She'd been so deep in thought about Nathan, she hadn't heard anyone else come up. Turning, she forced a smile onto her face that turned genuine.

"Lexi, how are you?" Lexi first hugged Toni, then turned to her and gave her a quick embrace. Jayla kissed her friend's cheek. They hadn't worked together on an event recently, but they'd had lunch a little over a month back. Her gaze drooped to Lexi's small rounded belly.

"I'm good," Lexi said, smoothing a hand over her pregnancy. She picked up a piece of white-chocolate-dipped cake. "You know I'm partial to these. Don't let me eat too many or you'll have to roll me out of here."

Toni reached for the type Lexi was eating. "I haven't tried them yet."

"How far along are you now?" Jayla asked.

"Five months," she said between bites. "I can feel movement now. It's the neatest thing." Lexi's hand continued to lovingly caress her stomach.

Wetting her lips, Jayla tried to ignore the tightening in her gut, the pangs of longing. Maybe because she'd been alone and focused purely on business, she'd never thought much about having a family.

But during the last month, learning the meaning of love by Nathan's gentle ministrations, she yearned for things she hadn't known she was missing.

Jayla laughed lightly, glancing around at the arrangements of flowers, no doubt provided by Lexi. "Doesn't seem like long ago that you were married."

"It wa—"

"It wasn't," Toni interjected, rubbing a hand lovingly over the swell of Lexi's baby. "But it doesn't take long when you're knocking boots regularly."

The three of them burst into giggles.

Nathan couldn't keep his eyes from traveling toward Jayla as she stood clustered with his sister and Alexis Lyle. They were eating chocolate and laughing like they were old friends, but the expressive pools of Jayla's green eyes kept shifting toward him. His sister was no better, tossing him a pointed look a time or two.

Forcing his feet to remain where he stood, he longed to go to her. To find out why his ears were burning, knowing damned well he was being talked about.

It was difficult seeing her here, mixed with his friends and family. She belonged, but she wasn't ready to hear it and he feared she'd end things between them before she realized it was true.

She was skittish, and after learning her reasons that morning, he understood why. She'd been misused, and trust wasn't an easy thing to rebuild. His stomach ached. His shoulders bunched with tension. He held his jaw tight, teeth clenched.

He had two things going for him, though. The fact that he hadn't been the one to break her trust, and that she'd had enough faith in him to tell him about parts of her soul that she'd previously kept hidden.

He stood with a group of men. Isaac and Jackson were talking, including him in the conversation, but he answered with noncommittal grunts and shakes of his head, his attention fixed on the woman across the room.

With bouncing red curls once again secured atop her head, wide green eyes, and plump bow-shaped lips, she looked so young and innocent. But he knew the pleasure of her mouth, knew the perfection of her naked body. His cock hardened. His blood raged toward his dick.

Shifting his stance to hide the erection growing behind his slacks, he took a few deep breaths and folded his hands in front of him, to hide the bulge his willpower wasn't able to control.

She smiled in his direction, nodding her head to something his sister was saying. Then she wet her lips, and even across the room he could imagine the taste, like the chocolate body sauce they'd created—and tested—together.

She wore a black skirt and a simple white shirt. Around her waist she'd secured a green apron with the Decadent Dips logo on the front of it. Toned legs and creamy thighs he planned on being between—he glanced at his watch—in a few hours, feet encased in strappy sandals, and toenails painted red. He was completely captivated by this petite woman.

It was odd really. A month ago he hadn't been thinking of a future, other than one that included football and coaching. He glanced at Lexi's pregnant stomach. Not that he was ready now, but a month ago he'd have scoffed at the idea of being a father and settling down.

Now . . . now Jayla Brooks made him want those things. Eventually.

Their relationship was so much like the melted chocolate— smooth, delicious, lots of fun—but the chocolate was designed for quick dips.

What he wanted was a little more solid.

A hell of a lot longer lasting.

He was in love with her, had been since he first heard her sing. The kind of love he wanted to cherish, to spend a lifetime nurturing.

Nathan felt dizzy. He stepped away from the men around him, a step or two, and put his hand on the back of a chair while he caught his breath. A nerve on his shoulder ticked, tension slithering down his spine.

"You all right, man?" Jackson asked.

He shook off the light-headedness. "Yeah, I'm cool."

Isaac, his soon-to-be brother-in-law, thumped him on the back a few times. "You sure? You look like maybe you need to sit down."

Shaking his head, Nathan squared his shoulders. The last thing he wanted was to go sit down.

Hell, no, what he wanted—what he *needed*—was to go to Jayla and find a way to tell her how he felt without scaring her away. Slanting his face toward the ceiling, he closed his eyes and inhaled a few times to get his thoughts together.

Feeling a little more relaxed, he opened his eyes and walked away from the guys. Their questions lingered behind him, asking if he was sure he was doing all right. He didn't reply, his head, his heart, his body, after one thing.

Making Jayla Brooks permanent.

Turning his attention across the room, he looked at where he'd seen her last, but only his sister and Lexi remained. He scanned the entire room, but when he still hadn't spotted her, his heart started thumping hard against his ribs. His lungs constricted.

Something was wrong. He felt it clear down in his soul. She hadn't merely slipped away to the restroom or gone to her truck for more supplies.

He strode across the room, each movement purposeful

and determined. It'd taken an effort not to run out the door and see if her delivery van was still parked outside.

It wouldn't be. He knew it'd be gone. He swallowed. Jayla was gone.

His hands were shaking when he reached Toni's side. "Where is she?"

Toni shrugged, putting her hands out palm up. "I don't know. One minute we were talking about my wedding. The next thing I knew she mumbles, *'I have to go,'* and just walks away."

He nodded. He knew she was gone. Had known it deep down from the second he'd looked up and didn't feel her glorious green-eyed gaze.

Nathan angled away from his sister, not wanting Toni to see his pain. Not wanting to ruin her bridal shower by throwing a chair against the wall like he really wanted to.

"Aren't you going after her?" Toni asked.

Yes. No. Damn it, he had no idea what he should do. What the right thing would be for both of them. He knew what he wanted—Jayla naked and accepting his body. Jayla laughing at his jokes. Jayla teasing with her expressive eyes. Jayla Bird singing when she came.

Hell, yeah, he was going after Jayla, but first he had to be prepared. He needed a ring. A diamond. He needed to properly offer her forever, but the odds weren't in his favor.

Ten

She suffered from misery of her own making. It'd been nearly a week—six dark and lonely days—since she'd seen her sunshine boy, since she'd been warmed by his solid flesh and glowing smile.

He hadn't called or dropped by, but why should he? She was the one who'd left without saying good-bye.

Jayla squeezed her lids to keep the burning behind her eyes from turning into tears. Opening her eyes and glancing around the back room of Decadent Dips, she steadied her breathing. Salty liquid spilled, dripping from her lashes, then streaming slowly down her cheeks. She swiped away the droplets before they fell from her chin.

These tears weren't falling because of what she'd lost by walking away in a moment of panic, but for what she hoped to gain with a week of clarity. A week of searching her soul for the things that were really important to her. For what in life really mattered.

Taking a deep breath, she loaded the last of the chocolate body-sauce bottles into a box, then picked it up and headed out the door. She had a contract to fulfill after all, and these needed to be delivered before tonight. Before Isaac's bachelor party.

After putting the box in the trunk, she got in her car, turned on the ignition, and glanced at her watch. Jayla wet her lips as she debated where to take it. She'd called his cell phone, but gotten only voice mail. Left a message he hadn't returned.

She'd only been back to his place a couple of times, and he'd always been driving, but she knew the way. But going to his home, where they'd made love, felt a little too vulnerable to her. A little too tempting. All clothes had to stay on until she'd said what needed to be said.

Putting her foot to the gas, she eased into traffic and settled in for the drive out to the stadium. In the early afternoon, she hoped to find him there and deliver the box of bottled chocolate sauce to his office, where getting naked wouldn't be an option.

Thanks to traffic, the drive took over an hour from Coronado Island, and after three o'clock, she could only hope that on a Friday afternoon on the eve of his sister's wedding, he'd still be there to accept the body sauce.

And her apology.

With the box carried against her hip, she located his office. The door was partially open. Swallowing down the tightness in her throat, she attempted to slow the wild beat of her heart.

She was just about to knock when she heard a woman's voice.

Her own.

It was the voice message she'd left earlier, telling him she was on the way. Just a few brief moments, just a few short words. That he replayed. And replayed again.

Jayla's heart skittered to a stop, and her trembling lips turned into a slight smile. The message was clear, her words unslurred. There could be only one reason he'd listen to the voice mail over and over again.

He was listening to her voice.

As she'd done with the messages he'd left since they met that remained on her answering machine and in the digital files of her cell phone's memory.

When her voice began again, Jayla pushed the door open with her hip, her gaze finding Nathan's behind his desk. He snapped his phone shut and stood.

"Jayl—"

"Don't, Nathan." She put up a hand to stop his flow of words. Then with her foot, she closed the door. Crossing the room, she put the box of bottled chocolate sauce on his desk, her gaze unwavering on his.

With only the wooden desk separating them, she could smell his spicy cologne, see the tick of his pulse beneath the tanned skin on his neck, feel the heat coming off his body. Enough that being near him melted the last bit of ice from a heart she'd long ago put into deep freeze.

She wet her lips, her eyes traveling across his wide shoulders, down a chest she'd nibbled sauce from, to a bulge in his slacks that made her panties wet. His erection throbbed, and caused warmth to spread on her cheeks.

She met his questioning brown eyes. And she smiled. "Hi, Nathan."

He groaned, his pulse throbbing at his temples. His stare warm and welcoming rather than angry.

"Here's the sauce. You'll need these tonight." *I need you tonight.* Now. Tomorrow. Always.

Something hot and wet slid down her cheek, but she cleared it away with her fingertips, and sniffled. Squaring her shoulders, she lifted her chin, a shaking breath seeping from her lips.

"Nathan, I'm *gambling* here." Another tear sneaked past her defenses. "I'm making a bet, and anteing up by placing my heart on the table."

He grinned. "The odds are in your favor."

Something fluttered in her stomach—relief, awareness of how close happiness was. Desire. "Really?"

"Really, Jayla. There's only one way for you to lose this bet."

She studied Nathan's brown eyes, the way they brightened when he smiled, but smoldered with lust.

"How? How would I lose?"

Nathan wanted nothing more than to reach for her, but he held back. "You'll only lose if you fold your hand." His heart thumped hard in his chest. He understood how deeply these analogies affected her, with what her creep of an ex-husband had done to her. He understood the sacrifice on her part for her to come here and make such a gamble.

"Tell me why you left my sister's shower without saying a word."

Her lids closed and her lashes cast shadows against her cheeks. He watched as she took a strangled breath, a tremor moving through her body. Her small hands were balled at her sides, but he could see the determination in her stance. When her eyes opened, they were clear green, reflective of an inner strength.

"I left because I was afraid. Your sister and Lexi, they were talking about life—love, marriage, weddings, babies. Things I'd spent years convincing myself I didn't want or need." She gulped. "I was standing there listening, watching you across the room, and it hit me. *I was a liar.*"

She reached across the narrow desk and touched his chest, trailed fingertips downward to where turmoil twisted behind his navel. Her touch was light, but he felt every single stroke and it sent blood rushing from his head down to his dick. He wanted to crush her against him, but saw words lingering on her lips and knew she had more to say.

"I lied. I lied to you. And I lied to myself. I told myself that a simple life where I only cared about my business was something I could live with, something that could make me happy."

She scoffed, added a sassy roll of her eyes. "And I believed it, too, until you walked into the back room with all that blow-drying-berry charm. I told myself loving you would make me vulnerable. *A lie.* It made me strong."

She stepped closer, the movement wafting into the air the sweetness of her shampoo and a hint of chocolate. Her fingers grazed lower over the waistband of his slacks. A little lower and she'd feel his rocked-up flesh that pushed against his boxers. Her lips formed an O, then spread into a tentative grin.

Even now, with her lush lips tipped upward, the smile didn't reach her eyes, didn't dispel the worry and fear that radiated in the depths of her green stare.

But he could, by telling her how he felt.

"Jayla Bird." He rounded the desk, coming to stand where

he could touch her creamy skin, kiss her delicious lips, love her the way he wanted to. "My ante is on the table, too."

His hand slid behind her neck, used only slight force to slant her face toward his. And he kissed her. Gently at first, a mere brushing of lips, then a little more firmly. A little deeper. He smoothed his tongue across her mouth, damn near had his knees go when she opened for him. But he didn't linger or his hard-on would make him forget the rest of what he wanted to say to her.

"But, Jayla, I don't play the odds or make bets." He kissed her again, pressing his mouth to hers. Her delicate hands closed over his and she stepped closer into his embrace. "I'm not a gambler, Jayla."

Though it meant leaving the warmth of her body, the press of her nipples on his chest, the lushness of her curves, he dropped to his knee before her and removed the pink velvet box from his pocket.

"No gambling." He opened the box, revealing the pink champagne diamond. "I like a sure thing."

She gasped. Her expressive gaze went watery. "Nathan—" She broke off, a sob escaping. "When did you get that? How could you've known I'd be here today?"

"I didn't. I was coming to get you and not accepting no as an answer. Marry me. Say yes, or you'll force me to do things. . . ." His gaze shifted around his office, landing on the box she'd brought. "Smother you in chocolate."

Jayla giggled. "Yes, but the only thing getting dipped in chocolate is you." And she reached for a bottle before joining him on the floor.

THE CHERRY ON TOP

OF ALL THESE TREATS

". . . Happy birthday to you," Jayla sang, perched on the arm of Nathan's chair. She tore her eyes away from his niece, who sat in her high chair clapping chubby hands as everyone sang to her, and turned her gorgeous green gaze on him.

"I love you," she whispered, then removed the beanie cap off their son's tiny head and smoothed her delicate fingers through his soft golden curls.

She lifted their infant into her arms, his plump cheeks settling against her breast. She stood and turned to Nathan. Bending close, she spoke with her lips pressed to his ear. "I'm riding you hard tonight."

As she turned away, he swatted her ass, causing her to giggle, but their exchange went unobserved in the chaos around them. Jackson was across the room bouncing his youngest daughter on his shoulders, while his four-year-old insisted on helping serve the cake.

Lexi was there, helping the little girl with the plates, her stomach heavy again. Already on number three. Nathan grinned, his gaze shifting to his wife. Jayla was humming to their son, swaying her hips as she soothed him into sleep. The littlest things she did had him rock hard and aching.

Taking a deep breath, he stood and went to help his sister. A camera was slung around her neck, and she paused to snap shots between cleaning icing from her daughter's face. Then she pointed the lens on her husband, who carried a mountain of Barbie-paper-wrapped gifts.

Nathan backed away from the scene, leaning against the wall as his friends and family moved around the room. Air hissed between his teeth as he reined in emotion. Rolling his shoulders, he saw Jayla across the room, her attention fixed on him, her eyes questioning.

She was the perfect woman, mother. The perfect lover. Her small body knew how to please, from tight and wet, to lips that suckled chocolate from his cock, to breasts that were made to lick, to a heart that gave as well as it received.

Exhaling slowly, Nathan nodded at his wife. She smiled, kissed their son's head, then went back to singing.

From candied kisses, to sugared hearts, to warm melting chocolate, the world's best sex wasn't equal to the sweetness of love.

About the Author

Renee Luke believes in mixing the bitter with the sweet, as long as it's all dipped in chocolate. She dreams up her stories amidst the beauty of the Sacramento Valley, with her hero husband and four children, sharing the candied kisses, sweet hugs, and salty tears that add flavor to life. It's Renee's belief that there's nothing better than good books, great friends, and that real strength is the ability to break a candy bar into four pieces and only eat one. For more sugary treats and sensual romance, visit her on the Web at www.ReneeLuke.com.